PIGEON
PIE
and
Other Tasty Tales

Gordon
Henderson

Published in the United Kingdom
TAUP UK
Sheerness
Kent

enquiries@taup.co.uk

Menu

DEDICATION

This book is dedicated to my boyhood hero, Len Deighton, whose work inspired me to write my first short story when I was a teenager. The flush of my youth has dimmed, but my admiration for Deighton's genius remains as bright as ever.

Pigeon Pie

It was New Year's Eve and Pamela decided the cemetery was a fitting place in which to watch the old year prepare to die.

The badly neglected cemetery was drab and dreary in the gathering gloom of a mid-afternoon fast being turned into evening by a brooding and hostile sky that was trying to decide what to do with the unshed snow it carried.

A stiff wind swept crisp, brown leaves across dirty pathways and deposited them in rustling piles against chipped, grey tombstones. The leaves would remain there until the spring, when guilt-ridden relatives would clear a few of them away, whilst the remainder would simply rot, disintegrate and be eaten by the carpet of tangled weeds that spread across much of the cemetery; ever thicker each year.

But even in this sea of neglect, this ocean of decay, there was one island of colour to brighten the depressing scene. It lay beneath a tall, diseased elm tree; a new grave, recently filled, dressed in an overcoat of fresh wreaths.

Pamela stood alone at the graveside, head bowed, her thoughts confused as she tried to make sense of the jumble of questions that filled her head.

In truth, there was only one thing about the whole affair of which Pamela could be certain: Aunt Lettie was dead. Big, fat Aunt Lettie. Aunt Lettie the mouth. Aunt Lettie, who could nag, moan, argue, whine and gossip for hours on end with no noticeable pause for breath, had gone to join old Uncle Albert - unless, of course, he saw her coming first!

Above Pamela's head a solitary crow called out from the lower boughs of the crippled elm tree. It was a strange, haunting, almost human cry. The young girl looked up into the tangle of twisted, leafless boughs and shook her head.

Surrounded by the funereal silence, the oppressive gloom of the darkening skies and the graves of dead memories, Pamela found the cemetery had taken on an eerie aura that distorted the crow's cry out of all recognition, producing a sound that chilled her soul.

It was a cry that was not a cry. A sound that was many sounds, and yet was no sound. Almost human, and yet terribly inhuman. A croak, yet not a croak. A caw, yet not a caw. A scream, yet not a scream. A laugh, yet not… or, was it?

Pamela stared up into the tree until she spotted the bird, reassuring herself at the sight of its un-phantom like shiny feathers. A gust of wind pulled open the front of her coat, wormed its way inside and cuddled up against the warmth of her body. She shivered.

Poor old Aunt Lettie.

Poor old Uncle Albert!

Pamela stayed behind at the graveside after all the other mourners had scurried away to the warmth of their cars. Somehow she felt obliged, after all, she had been the only member of the family at Aunt Lettie's bedside on the night that the old girl passed away and it was there she learned Aunt Lettie's dreadful secret.

The young girl looked down at the garlanded grave and remembered again the semi-coherent tale her Aunt had related. Was the strange story true, or, was it simply the drug-induced ramblings of a dying old woman? Was the seemingly impossible, possible? Would she ever learn the truth?

Pamela shivered again as she mulled over what she knew of Aunt Lettie and Uncle Albert's life and death, together.

Aunt Lettie and Uncle Albert were married for over forty years. Long, long years of feuding; years of endless squabbles; niggling disagreements and full-scale matrimonial battles; years during which, through thick and thin, good times and bad, they hated each other with a passion that was as all consuming as it was blindingly obvious.

It was a complete mystery to everyone in the family why they ever married in the first place and only the Almighty knows how they managed to stay together so long without either one of them resorting to murder.

One possible explanation, Pamela decided, could have been the environment in which they lived for the majority of their marriage.

She was convinced that their home surroundings, and way of life, played an important part in postponing that final, fateful day of reckoning.

Aunt Lettie and Uncle Albert lived, as did most of their friends and relatives, in a little two-up, two-down terraced house in the East End of London. In this close knit community they both found, in their own particular way, a safety valve that released the daily tensions, dislikes and frustrations that slowly dragged their uncompromising relationship steadily and relentlessly towards the brink of disaster.

Aunt Lettie had her friends and neighbours - kindred spirits most of them - with whom she could rant and rave about the irritating habits of her "impossible old man". Lettie was able to let off the steam that otherwise, on more than one occasion, would have resulted in a very messy murder.

As Pamela stood beside her Aunt's grave a vivid picture of Lettie, in all her glory and in full flow, conjured itself into her mind's eye: Aunt Lettie, standing outside her paint-flecked front door, a cigarette dangling from her mouth; her permanently curlered hair half hidden under a tartan head-scarf. Her podgy arms were crossed and the massive bosom, which lay beneath the grease stained apron, quivered indignantly as she exchanged gossip and gripes from morning until night.

And what of Uncle Albert, with his cloth cap, diminutive frame, scaly bald head, rusty creaking laugh and sly, heavy lidded wink? Well, Albert had his pigeon loft, his pub and Leyton Orient Football Club to help draw off the bad blood from his system. He spent all his spare time in one or other of these sanctuaries, lambasting his wife to either his mates or his beloved racing pigeons!

So it was by such means that Aunt Lettie and Uncle Albert managed to get through married life without resorting to anything other than verbal violence. Then the local authority took a decisive hand in their fate.

Their home was one of the last in the neighbourhood to be demolished in the council's crusade for 'better homes', but demolished it finally was. Aunt Lettie and Uncle Albert, their prejudices, irritating habits, continual feuds and latent murderous intent, were uprooted from the house in which they lived for forty years, and were crammed into a wallpapered box on the eighth floor of a high-rise block of flats.

The council might just as well have packed the flat with unstable dynamite. Indeed, little did the sincere, grey man from the Housing Department know it, but when he handed over the shiny brass front door key to Uncle Albert, he as good as lit the fuse of an explosion that had waited patiently many years for the right time and place to happen.

Not that it was Uncle Albert who felt the mounting pressure; life in the tiny flat was at least bearable for him. He still managed to get out to the pub most nights, the "O's" still played at home every other Saturday and, although he had been forced to sell most of his pigeons, he was able to keep a handful of his favourite birds, Albert's most prized possessions, housed in a small loft on the flat's balcony.

Aunt Lettie was not so fortunate; her chief escape from the stresses and strains of a disastrous marriage disappeared along with her friends and neighbours. She was deprived of the sympathetic ears that had been the only real outlet for her husband induced anger.

She still saw her friends from time to time when she visited the shops, but the few snatched minutes of whining complaint were no substitute for the day-long, garden-fence, sessions to which her system had become accustomed. Like an addict deprived of drugs, Aunt Lettie soon began to experience withdrawal symptoms.

Slowly, but surely, as the long, lonely days dragged on, the tension mounted inside Lettie. Each of Albert's aggravating little habits cut at the delicate thread of her sanity; his perpetual sniffing, his mumbled insults, his heavy-lidded winks, and his way of chuckling for no apparent reason – a creaking, cackling, dry and mirthless laugh. Then, of course, there were Albert's pigeon's.

When they lived in their old house, Aunt Lettie had been able to ignore the pigeons. Stuck away, as they were, in their loft at the bottom of the garden, she had barely noticed them. Of course, she often complained about them, but that had been on a matter of principle. The pigeons themselves had not annoyed her; it was Albert's passion for them that grated.

But now it was impossible to ignore the bloody birds. Their

continual cooing filled the flat, following her wherever she went, until she could not rid her head of the sound. She came to detest the pigeons almost as much as she did their doting owner.

Finally, all the resentment, frustration, anger and hatred that festered inside Aunt Lettie for so long, grew too much for her to control. What little self-restraint she possessed deserted her completely. She decided the time had arrived to progress from the slings and arrows of verbal battle to a declaration of all-out physical war.

Everything appeared normal when Albert came home that night. His routine, unchanged for so many years, was the same. He slammed his way indoors, sniffed, laid his cap on the kitchen table, sniffed, scratched his scaly, bald head, sniffed, sat down at the table and sniffed yet again.

Albert stared down at the meal Lettie placed in front of him, sniffed, sucked his teeth and gave a theatrical grimace of disgust. He took a long draught from the bottle of beer that stood, ready opened, at his elbow, sniffed one more time for luck and then proceeded to polish off his dinner in less than three minutes.

When he was finished, Albert belched loudly, winked at the clock, sniffed hard and chuckled as he raised the beer bottle to his lips for a final long swig. That was when the routine was broken. Lettie spoke.

'Ow was it then?' A strange smile twisting her nicotine stained upper lip.

Albert looked down at his spotless plate. With a sniff and a shrug he grunted an inaudible answer.

'Good was it?' Lettie persisted. 'Eh? The meat pie? Good was it?' Her smile widened as she spoke.

Unaccustomed to seeing his wife in such fine spirits, and unsure where this was leading, Albert sniffed several times before replying.

'It was alright, I suppose,' he admitted grudgingly, still very much on the defensive. He stood up and belched again, then, with his cap set firmly back on his head, he made his way out onto the balcony.

'Tender was it? Eh?' Lettie called after him. There was no immediate reply and Lettie waited expectantly, listening to her husband muttering to himself on the balcony. When eventually Albert reappeared he wore a frown.

'Did you let me birds aht again?' He accused. Lettie grinned and shook her head, struggling to contain the laughter that bubbled up inside her.

'Well, the door's open and they ain't there, so, where the bleedin' 'ell are they then?' Albert grumbled.

Lettie could hold back the laughter no longer. Tears welled in her eyes as she gurgled insanely, trying to talk and laugh at the same time.

'Tender was they?' She taunted Albert. 'Eh? Tender was they?'

Albert clutched his stomach as the awful truth sank home. 'Oh! Gawd!' He wailed. 'You didn't? You wouldn't 'ave?' His pale face grew paler as Lettie's laughter answered his question. Albert was gripped by an uncontrollable rage. 'You filthy old 'ag!' He screamed.

As fury welled up inside him Albert's face lost its chalky whiteness and took on a hue of deep, thunderous purple. He raised his fist and made as if to strike his tormentor, but it was an act of violence he never completed.

Albert staggered and clutched at the table for support. With a clatter the beer bottle fell to the floor spilling its frothy dregs onto the tiles. Neither of them noticed. Albert screamed again as he felt an invisible hand squeeze his heart in a deadly, vice like grip. He struggled to suck air into lungs that for fifty years had been abused by forty cigarettes a day. It was an effort under normal circumstances, that day Albert had no chance.

Lettie's gleeful madness increased as she witnessed Albert's battle against the massive heart attack that gripped him. Her continuing laughter filled the old man's ears and intensified his anger.

'You old 'ag,' he managed to croak as he realised that his time was nearly up. 'I'll be back,' he vowed. 'Just you wait and see. I'll be back!' He tried to stand upright, for one last attack on his laughing wife, but the effort was too much for his failing heart, and came too late to have any effect. 'I'll s-s-s-see you d-d-d-dead,' he gasped. 'I swear it! I'll b-b-b-be back. Do you 'ear? I'll d-d-d-dance on your grave yet, you old cow!'

He paused as he slumped to his knees. 'Do you 'ear?' He repeated in a whisper. 'On your grave. You...' Searching for a suitably nasty name with which to express his feelings for his wife, Albert sniffed a couple of times and then dropped dead on the kitchen floor.

Nobody found out what led to Uncle Albert's sudden heart attack until Aunt Lettie made her death bed confession to Pamela.

'The bastard come back, Pammy,' Aunt Lettie told her niece with a wheezy laugh, 'e said 'e would come back and 'e bleedin' well did. The bastard said 'e would dance on my grave.' She paused. 'Sniff, sniff, 'e went, Pammy, and then 'e was gorn. But 'e come back alright. Just like 'e said 'e would.'

Aunt Lettie paused again, conserving her strength. 'Cor! You should 'ave seen 'im go, Pammy. Fair brung tears to my eyes, it did, 'ad to laugh.' The dying woman shook her head gently as she remembered. 'But I never, ever imagined that the old git really would come back'

Aunt Lettie lapsed into silence and for a moment Pamela thought she had gone, but soon the monologue continued.

'E tried to disguise 'imself, 'e did. When 'e come back, that is. But I knew it was 'im alright. Ha! No mistaking that bloomin' cackle of 'is, or 'is wink.'

Aunt Lettie shook her head again, but this time she grimaced in pain at the movement. 'Nah,' she went on. 'It was 'im alright, Pammy. 'E just stood there on the balcony, as bold as bloody brass. Wink bloody wink, 'e went. All the bloody time. But I got 'im, Pammy. The devil! Didn't I just! Pammy? Are you still there, girlie? Eh?'

Pamela squeezed the old lady's hand to show that she was with her.

'That's good. Listen, luvvie. Remember that old sword what your great granddad brung back from the Sarf African War?'

Pamela squeezed her Aunt's hand again to confirm that she did remember.

'Well, I 'it 'im wiv that.' Lettie chuckled. 'Chopped 'is bleedin' leg orf, I did. Chopped it right orf!'

There was another silence, longer this time. 'Oh, 'e come back alright. Come back to get me, same as 'e said 'e would,' another pause, 'ad to larf, I did. 'ad to bloody well larf. The way 'e 'eld 'is bloody stomach when 'e found aht 'e'd eaten 'is precious pidgins, fair green 'e was, Pammy.' Aunt Lettie sighed. ''ad to larf.' Yet another pause.

'But, 'e come back, didn't 'e, girlie? Like 'e said 'e would, but I got the bastard! Oh-oh! Then, just when I was abaht to finish the bugger orf, 'e upped and flew away, 'e just flew away, Pammy, and I missed 'im.

'Tell you want, girlie. You should 'ave 'eard 'im cackling as I fell over the edge of the bloody balcony. Gawd! I 'eard 'im cackling all the way dahn!'

Aunt Lettie laughed again before rambling on in similar vein for several more minutes. Finally she gripped Pamela's hand tightly and pulled her closer. Her words were faint now, she was going fast.

'But, I got 'im first. Didn't I, girlie? Eh? 'e might 'ave done fer me, but I got the bastard first. Eh? Pammy? Eh?'

But Pamela never had a chance to answer her aunt because, satisfied she had won her final battle with Uncle Albert, Lettie passed away happily.

Another gust of wind blew across the cemetery and Pamela shivered again. She looked up at the crow and stared at it long and hard; seeing it properly for the first time.

The crow just sat there in the tree and stared right back at the young woman, then it winked at her; a sly, heavy lidded, knowing wink. Letting out another of its human like cries the bird rose into the air and glided down to land on the wreath bedecked grave.

Pamela watched mesmerised for several long seconds, her mind grappling with what she now knew to be the impossible truth. Eventually, she turned on her heel and walked quickly from the cemetery, whilst the crow continued its one legged dance amongst the wreaths that covered Aunt Lettie's grave.

Bloodline

Sunday 29th July 1962

Music blared out from the small transistor radio that was perched on an upturned metal milk crate, in front of which a boy took guard with a cricket bat, as at the same time he sang along with Chubby Checker, whose voice was made to sound tinny by the plastic radio's tiny speaker:-

'Come on let's twist again like we did last summer.
Yeah, let's twist again like we did last year.
Do you remember when things were really hummin'
Yeah, let's twist again, twistin' time is here...'

'Come on Becky,' the boy interrupted his singing long enough to say. 'Don't hold back this time. Bowl me a really fast ball.'

He tapped his bat on the ground and grinned at the girl as he resumed his singing.

'Yeah round 'n around 'n up 'n down we go again.
Oh baby make me know you love me so then.
Come on let's twist again like we did last summer.
Yeah, let's twist again, twistin' time is here.'

Rebecca Driver stood at the other end of the makeshift cricket strip they had trodden into the lush oblong of lawn that ran along the side of the administration block of Boxham Power Station; whose huge smoke blackened building, with tall twin chimneys, dominated the skyline on the north side of the small coastal town in which they lived. Behind her a sprinkler sprayed water across the width of the lawn in a lazy arc.

The admin block consisted of offices and the works canteen, from the outside door of which they had borrowed the milk crate. On any other day of the week the youngsters would have been quickly shooed off the lawn, but none of the clerical staff worked on a Sunday. There were a number of maintenance staff on site, including Becky's dad, but they turned a blind eye to the use of one of the few remaining green spaces in the grimy, smog filled industrial town.

Now Becky stood with her hands on her hips and tried to scowl at her friend, but it didn't quite work; her frosty expression was betrayed by her sparkling, vivid blue eyes, and the way in which the ghost of a good natured smile tugged at the corners of her pouting mouth.

'Don't you dare patronise me, Ted,' she yelled at him. 'Just because I'm a girl doesn't mean that I can't bowl as fast as a boy.'

'Prove it!' "Ted" Dexter, nicknamed Ted after the captain of the England eleven in the 4th Test against Pakistan that was taking place at Trent Bridge, squinted against the glare of the sun and prepared for the leather rocket that he knew would soon be heading his way. Wryly, like the game in Nottingham, this one would probably end in a draw. His friend was no mean bowler and he knew he had dented her pride to such an extent that she would now try to take his head off with the ball.

Becky turned her back on Ted and took a dozen measured steps away from the bowling crease. She was a tall girl, with a thin, lithe body and short cropped hair. Dressed in brown baseball boots, dark blue denim jeans and a white T-shirt, she could have passed as a boy, except that at 15 years of age her bra-less chest was beginning to show a shapely swell that was the product of the genes inherited from her mother, who was a fashion model before three children added too many pounds to her waistline.

Ted loved Becky with a passion; not only was she was clever, funny and very pretty, but she was the only girl in Boxham who played cricket and understood the rules of the game. He tapped his bat on the ground again and narrowed his eyes still further as the air in front of him shimmered in a heat haze that he knew would make sighting the ball difficult.

The girl turned and started her run towards the bowling crease where, with a rapid cartwheel of her right arm she bowled a fast ball down the strip that bounced once, then reared up viciously towards his head.

At first Ted lost sight of the ball as it flew through the hot summer air, but he picked up its flight at the last moment. He moved deftly to his left, pirouetted on his heel and swung his cricket bat to make contact with the ball when it was shoulder height. The ball shot like a bullet back over Becky's head, landed just in front of the sprinkler before bouncing through the spray of water and across a wide expanse of tarmac towards the long metal bicycle shed that stood on the far side of the yard.

The girl was off like a shot after the ball, running into the water spray with a squeal and a pantomime act of arm waving and foot stamping, then she darted out the other side and resumed her chase. She almost reached the ball, when she gave out another squeal, this time in frustration as the ball disappeared through a gap in a broken metal grate that covered a manhole.

Later Ted would agonise over the fact that had Becky not wasted several precious seconds messing about in the shower of water, she might have caught the ball before it disappeared underground, and the chain of events would never have been triggered that was destined to lead to such tragedy.

The girl knelt down and shook her head as she heard the hard ball clatter noisily against a metal ladder that was attached to the inside of the dark shaft. She tried to lift the grate but it was too heavy, so she waved for Ted to join her and soon he was standing by her side, cricket bat still clutched in his hand.

'Give me a hand, Ted.'

'Do you think we should, Becks?' Ted stared down at the girl's wet T-shirt, against which her hard nipples pressed darkly. Hurriedly he tore his eyes away, but not before he felt a flush of emotion he found both exciting and disturbing.

'Oh, don't be a scaredy-cat. You want to get your ball back, don't you?'

And of course Ted did want his ball back. He knelt at her side and together they prised the grate open and let it fall back with a clatter against the side of the bike shed. Without more ado Becky put a foot on the top rung of the ladder and Ted noticed that her bootlace was undone. He pointed this out to his friend, but she brushed his warning aside

'It'll be OK,' she said impatiently. 'Come on, let's go find the

11

ball!'

'Do you think we should, Becks?' Ted asked again, looking nervously over his shoulder to see if anybody had heard the noise, but the girl had already disappeared into the darkness below.

'Becky, are you OK?' He called down into the black hole.

There was no answer at first and then the girl called up at him: 'The ball is down here somewhere, but it's very dark. Hang on there is a light on the ceiling, I'll see if I can find the switch.'

'Do you want a hand?' He asked.

'Do you have a hole in your bum?'

'There's no need to be crude, Rebecca!' Ted laughed, which made him feel better. 'OK, I'm on my way.'

He started carefully down the ladder, still with bat in hand, and was about halfway when he heard a click and immediately the shaft became noticeably less dark.

'I found the light, Ted,' the girl called out.

'Well done, Becks,' Ted replied as he reached the bottom of the ladder and found himself in a large chamber.

'Here's the ball!'

The girl picked it up and walked towards Ted, whose eyes were again drawn to the front of her wet T-shirt. She stood close to her friend with the ball in one hand.

'Don't be shy,' she said in a soft voice. 'You can touch as well as look.' She took Ted's free hand and pressed it against her breast.

Ted felt himself grow hot with need as he felt Becky's hard nipple against the palm of his hand. He squeezed gently and the girl let out a little gasp of pleasure. Leaning forward she planted a lingering kiss on his lips, which increased his need. But his hopes were dashed when Becky pulled away and ran towards what looked like a second tunnel on the other side of the chamber. She turned round and with a grin tossed the ball through the air to Ted. He caught the ball and slipped it into his trouser pocket with one deft movement.

'Let's play hide-and-seek!' Becky said with a giggle, as she darted into the tunnel. 'Count to a hundred and then come find me.'

Ted's stomach churned with a mixture of emotions. He felt uneasy and had a premonition that something terrible was going to happen and a part of him wanted none of it. But another part of him was excited at the promise offered by Becky's kiss and he wanted to find her and touch her again. Need eventually won over caution.

He started counting as he heard her footsteps running up the tunnel.

'One-two-three-four...' but before he even reached ten he heard a door swing open, followed by what sounded like a roll of thunder. He stopped counting. 'Becky, are you okay?'

There was no reply and Ted's earlier sense of unease returned, but now it was stronger. He headed towards the entrance to the tunnel and peered into it. In the distance he saw an open door, but beyond that only the blackness of what he took to be a third tunnel.

Ted walked slowly up the tunnel, his heart pounding wildly, conscious of a humming sound coming from the tunnel beyond the door. The hum grew louder as he got closer.

When Ted reached the door he saw the air in the doorway was shimmering like the heat haze in the yard above. He almost turned back, but he heard light footsteps in the tunnel on the other side of the doorway and then Becky called: 'Keep counting, Ted. No cheating!'

But Ted had given up counting. All he wanted was to find his friend as quickly as possible and get out of this place. He pushed his cricket bat into what he came to think of as the shimmer and was fascinated to see most of its blade disappear until all he could see was the handle and shoulder of the bat.

Ted pulled the bat back out of the shimmer and the blade reappeared. He tapped it against the cement floor of the tunnel and it gave a solid wooden clunk. It seemed no worse for wear. Reassured, he closed his eyes and stepped through the doorway.

As Ted's foot hit the floor on the far side of the doorway, and his body completed its journey through the shimmer from light to darkness, the hum grew into a whine. There was a flash of lightning and then a deafening clap of thunder exploded about his body. He felt his head spin and he collapsed to the ground overcome by nausea. At first he thought he was going to cover the floor of the tunnel with his lunch, but he managed to control his insides. Slowly the feeling of sickness passed to be replaced with a wave of faintness against which he struggled to retain consciousness, but it was a losing battle.

Somewhere, perhaps in another part of the tunnel system, perhaps even in his imagination, Ted heard the patter of running feet moving out of earshot, followed by a distant clap of thunder similar to the one he had just experienced. *That was another shimmer*, Ted thought as he finally allowed himself to be taken by the darkness of unconsciousness.

Sunday 29th July 2007

David sat in an easy chair in his lounge; the latest Stephen King novel on his lap, a whisky glass on the small table at his side, and Miles Davis quietly trumpeting *So What* from the music centre in the corner of the room. But he was neither drinking nor reading; instead he stared out of his ground floor apartment window across the park at the deepening gloom of a summer's evening that was fast becoming night. The window was open but this did nothing to make the air in the apartment any less hot and humid. There was a storm on its way.

Suddenly a flash of lightning lit up the jagged silhouette of the half demolished power station that stood on the northern outskirts of Boxham and a couple of seconds later a clap of thunder rolled across the park between his apartment and the rocky shoreline where the power station had been built eighty years before. The storm was close; indeed, the first spots of rain were beginning to patter against his lounge window.

He balanced his book carefully on the arm of his chair, rose slowly to his feet, turned on the light, closed the window and drew the curtains before returning to his chair. He picked up his book and started to read, but had barely finished a page before his eye lids dropped.

David woke when the clock on his mantelpiece struck midnight. His book had fallen from his lap and now lay closed on the floor at his feet. Something was tapping against his window and at first he thought it was rain, then realised the sound was too constant and rhythmic.

He stood up, stretched with a yawn and picked up his book. He flicked through until he found the page near the back he had been reading when he fell asleep and laid the open book spine uppermost on the seat of his chair.

The book was about mobile phone users who turn into killers. It was a good yarn and with only a few more pages left to read he decided he would try to finish it before going to bed, but first he would check out the still persistent tapping on the window.

He had no way of knowing that this decision would ensure that by the time he got round to reading the rest of the novel he would no longer be the same man.

David drew back the curtains and stared out at the pale face of a young girl. She was pretty, with short hair that had been plastered against her head by the heavy rain that was still falling. She stared at him with vivid blue eyes that were hypnotic in their intensity. She did not speak.

He left the window, went to open the front door and waved the girl over. 'Would you like to come in out of the rain?' He asked.

The girl did not reply, but accepted his invitation and stepped through the door into his apartment. She wore dark blue denim jeans and a white T-shirt, through which he could see her small, but shapely breasts, and the dark nipples which poked seductively against the wet cotton material. On her left foot she wore a muddy brown baseball boot, whilst her other foot was bare.

'Come with me,' the man said, leading her through to his lounge where he settled her into a spare armchair while he went to the bathroom. When he returned he was carrying a large bath towel, which he handed to her. 'Where's your other shoe?' He asked.

She shrugged and wrapped the towel round her thin body. She was shivering, despite the humidity. 'I lost it in the world between then and now,' she said in a vacant, almost dazed voice that made the man think that she was either high on drugs, or, suffering withdrawal symptoms.

David moved the book from his chair and sat down opposite her. There was something familiar about the girl, but his mind either could not, or, would not make the connection that might have dragged her identity out of his past. Suddenly he felt nervous and sensed that identifying his unexpected visitor was somehow

15

important. But he shrugged aside his feeling of unease and instead asked: 'Have you been taking something?'

'Taking something? I don't know what you mean.'

'Coke? Grass?'

'Coca-Cola?'

'No, cocaine.'

She looked at him blankly. 'I don't know what you mean,' she repeated.

At first he thought she was deliberately being evasive, but then realised she was deadly serious. The young girl had no idea what cocaine was. 'It doesn't matter,' he said. 'What's your name?'

At first the girl did not reply, instead she simply stared across at him, her eyes still puzzled. 'Why would I eat grass?' She asked.

The man laughed as he realised that she genuinely had no idea what he had been talking about.

'Grass is another name for a drug called cannabis. People don't eat it they smoke it.' He leaned forward and held out his hand. 'My name is David, what's yours?'

She took his hand, but looked at him in vacant silence for a while before answering: 'It was Rebecca, but I think my friends called me Becky, or, Becks.'

David frowned as the name rang yet another bell in his mind, but still the final connection escaped him. 'Was? Have you changed your name?'

She shook her head. 'No, but *I* have changed.'

This answer made no sense to David, but he did not pursue the point, instead he asked: 'Do you live in Boxham?'

The girl shook her head. 'I used to, but not anymore. Now I live back there.' She pointed out of the window, north in the direction of the power station.

'Have you far to go?'

'Oh, yes. Very far.'

'Well, you can't go home tonight. Would you like to stay the night? You can have my bed and I will sleep on the couch over there.'

Rebecca stared at David with her hypnotic eyes. 'Yes, I will stay the night with you,' she replied, 'but, we will share the bed.'

It was his turn to shake his head as he said: 'I'm not sure that would be wise.' But his refusal was half hearted as he felt himself falling under the girl's spell.

She stood up, threw the towel to the floor and held out her hand. 'Come,' she said.

'This really is not a good idea,' he said weakly, but got to his feet mesmerised by her piercing blue eyes.

'Come,' she repeated.

And so David took Rebecca's hand and let her lead him to the bedroom. Although he knew what he was doing was dangerous, he could not help himself and he watched in silence as the girl removed her clothes and slipped into bed from where she beckoned for him to follow suit. Despite his deep reservations David stripped off and soon he was nestling her thin body in his arms.

They lay like that for a few minutes, with the man telling himself that he would do no more than cuddle Rebecca and keep her warm, but his good intentions were ruined when she pulled herself free and rolled on top of him. Despite his best of intentions, David quickly became aroused.

Rebecca crouched over him, staring deep into his eyes as she lowered herself onto him, barely flinching as her hymen was broken. She began to move up and down, slowly at first, but then faster and faster, until her body glistened with perspiration. The last thing David remembered, before nothingness engulfed him, was feeling the warmth of their juices mixing together at the same time as he was gripped by a sublime ecstasy as the young girl lowered her mouth to his neck, bit into it with sharp fangs and began to suck.

When David woke up he found Rebecca was clinging to him tightly in her sleep. He looked at her young face and felt a deep sense of unease as he tried to remember the events of the previous night, but found he could recall little beyond the point when the girl bit into his neck and he was plunged into a debauchery of exquisite pain and raw passion.

He unwound himself from the girl's arms and slipped out of bed to visit the toilet, where he discovered blood on the inside of his groin. He frowned, guessing what this meant. He looked in the bathroom mirror and discovered blood round his mouth and bite marks on his neck. He closed his eyes and wondered what he had done. He felt sick and determined that it would not happen again.

But the girl was awake when he returned to the bedroom and opened her arms to him. She was naked.

'How old are you?' He asked.

'Does it matter?'

'Listen, Rebecca. I am sixty years old and last night I think I made love to my first virgin. What I need to know is; was it an under aged virgin?'

'Does it matter?' She repeated.

'It might do. I could go to prison if you are under sixteen.'

He frowned and tried to take his eyes of her firm young breasts, one of which bore vivid red bite marks. He closed his eyes to rid himself of the sight. 'How old *are* you?'

She smiled, 'Open your eyes, look into mine and tell me you really want to know.'

David did just that; he looked into her eyes and knew the answer straight away. Once again he was lost, and this time there was no turning back. Their body fluids had mixed together and they were now as one. He let his darker side take over and fell upon her. They joined together in an orgy of thrusting, panting, biting and blood-sucking, until finally, late into the afternoon, satiated, they clung together in sleep. Their fate was sealed.

When David woke up several hours later he felt refreshed and rejuvenated. Rebecca was already up and stood by the window fully dressed, except that she still wore a single baseball boot. The curtains were open and David could see the moon was high in the star filled sky.

She turned to him. 'Come,' she said. 'It's time to go.'

David slipped out of bed without argument and slipped on a pair of slacks, a Ralph Lauren polo shirt and a pair of loafers. 'Yes, it's time to go,' he agreed. 'Take me where you will.'

Without further ado, she led him out into the night.

They made their way across the park, skirted round the boundary fence of the derelict power station, with its large notices proclaiming that the site was dangerous, and onto the top of the high concrete seawall that acted as part of the town's flood defences. The

18

wall was about twenty foot tall and they had to make their way down a long flight of steps to reach a cement walkway at the base of the wall that bordered the sea.

Once on the walkway they headed east for about a quarter of a mile until they came to a large rusty pipe that projected from the wall. The pipe was about eight foot in diameter and David knew that it was an outlet that at one time had pumped polluted water into the sea in those days when protecting of the environment was secondary to the production of energy. The skeleton of the derelict coal fired power station above their heads showed that times and attitudes had changed.

Suddenly Rebecca jumped up onto the bottom rim of the pipe and disappeared inside it. David was taken by surprise and hesitated before following the girl, by which time she had been swallowed up by the darkness beyond.

He walked slowly along the pipe, his eyes adjusting to the dark, and up ahead to his right he saw a steel gantry, from which hung the mangled and loose front safety rail and entry gate. He heard a door open and a loud bang, like thunder, reverberated down the pipe towards him.

David made his way towards the gantry and pulled himself up onto its rusty platform. In front of him he found an open door in which the air was shimmering like a mirage on desert sand and was humming like a swarm of angry bees. He felt a sense of déjà vu. He had seen such a phenomenon before, but he could not remember where and when. Instinctively he knew that the shimmer was not harmful and he stepped straight through it into the tunnel beyond.

As David passed through the door there was another roll of thunder and he was almost overcome by a bout of dizziness. Momentarily his mind went blank. He closed his eyes to clear his head and pinched the bridge of his nose as he tried to work out where he was and why he was there. He remembered sitting down to read the remaining pages of Stephen King's latest book, but after that there was nothing.

David noticed a baseball boot lying on the ground just inside the door. He picked the boot up and sniffed it delicately, as if it were a fine wine. Immediately, he was gripped by a need that he could not explain. He closed his eyes again. *I need the taste of warm blood in my mouth.* He thought, without knowing why. *I need to feed.* He dropped the boot back on the floor and headed down the tunnel until he passed through another door into a chamber. Suddenly he heard a voice.

'Keep counting, Ted. No cheating!' It was a girl's voice.

Her voice, David thought, but had no idea who she was. He heard feet running and suddenly a young girl hurtled through a door on the opposite side of the chamber. She let out a loud squeal of alarm as she ran straight into his arms.

He gripped the girl's arms tightly and she began to struggle. He pushed her away until she was arm's length from him. She glared up at him angrily, but as he met her vivid blue eyes with his own she stopped struggling almost immediately. Her eyes closed, she began to tremble and her body began to glow with a strange light that grew in intensity until it was so bright David was forced to shut his own eyes. The dizzy feeling he experienced when he came through the door leading from the pipe into the tunnel returned and he began to tremble. When he opened his eyes he realised his body was giving out the same ghostly light that surrounded the girl. He noticed that the girl had only one shoe on her feet. That was when he remembered who she was. Rebecca!

David released the girl's arms and smiled at her. She did not pull away, instead she smiled dreamily back at him. Leaning towards him she turned her head and offered her neck.

As David's sharp fangs pierced Rebecca's throat she sighed with contentment and then began to whimper as her master drank his fill.

Sunday 29th July 1962

When Ted regained consciousness he opened his eyes to a blackness that was not quite total, but slowly his eyes adjusted to the dark. He was lying in a tunnel that formed a T-junction with the one he had just come from and was very similar in height and width, but much longer.

This tunnel too had bulkhead lights, but they were dead and lifeless. What little light there was in the tunnel came from the yellow strip of brightness that shone from the crack round the metal door behind him through which he had just come.

He used the door handle to pull himself upright and stood with his head pressed against the cold metal as he tried to clear his scrambled senses. Then he stiffened and stared at the door with a puzzled frown on his face. The door was closed.

How can that be? He thought. It had definitely been open when he stepped through the shimmer.

Ted looked over his right shoulder and stared down the tunnel. Despite the darkness, he saw a hint of a light in the distance. He closed his eyes as he felt nausea sweep over him, making his head spin, but they snapped open again almost immediately when he heard a noise, quiet, but distinct. It was a high pitched yelp of alarm. He recognised the voice immediately. It was Becky.

Ted pushed himself away from the door and started to make his way down the tunnel, swaying like a drunk; using his hand to steady himself. The wall was damp and covered in slimy lichen; and the air was foul and rank. It reminded Ted of the inside of the wartime Anderson bomb shelter that stood at the bottom of his grandfather's garden.

Slowly Ted's queasiness eased and he regained both his composure and his balance. With only a little more help from the wall he managed to reach the end of the tunnel without falling over. Later he would come to wish that he had stayed in a heap on the floor.

At the end of the tunnel Ted discovered a partly opened door. A ghostly white light seeped through the gap and when he opened the door fully he found himself looking into a chamber similar to the one he and Becky had first entered.

His eyes were immediately drawn to the source of the light; on the other side of the chamber, standing next to yet another tunnel entrance, were two figures surrounded by an unworldly, ethereal glow. He gasped in horror and felt sick to the pit of his stomach.

It was not the sight of the man towering over Becky that sickened him; nor was it the sound as the man sucked greedily on the young girl's neck; nor was it the puppy like whimpers panting from her mouth; nor even was it the distant, vacant look in his friend's eyes. No, what affected Ted most was the look of sheer ecstasy on her face.

'No, Becky!' He cried, in disgust and anger.

The man raised his head and studied the boy with eyes that were red and hateful. His face was as white as a sheet and a pronounced scar ran vividly down his forehead and across the bridge of his nose. From the corner of his mouth ran a thin rivulet of blood.

Ted had seen enough Hammer Horror movies to know that he was looking at a vampire, although the apparition in front of him was no gothic clad Peter Cushing. He, or, it, was dressed in blue denim jeans and a short sleeved shirt with the number five displayed on its right arm and the motif of a man on horseback above its left breast. Ted had never seen a top like it before, but, when he was a few years older, he would recognise it as a Ralph Lauren polo shirt and own one himself.

'No!' He shouted again, louder this time. He rushed across the chamber, his fists clenched and his arms flailing as he launched an attack on the monster.

But the vampire simply laughed and picked the boy up with one hand and tossed him across to the other side of the chamber, where he slammed face first into the jagged edge of a rusty metal cabinet, before recoiling and hitting the back of his head against the concrete wall with such a force that he was knocked senseless.

When Ted recovered, his forehead burned and his vision was blurred by the blood that dripped into his eyes. He wiped a sleeve across his face and looked across the chamber, but found it difficult to focus properly; it was like looking through a red-tinged, frosted-glass window. But slowly his vision cleared and he saw the vampire staring at him with a mixture of hatred and contempt.

The creature shook its head slowly and its top lip curled away from teeth that were still red with Becky's blood. Still staring into the boy's eyes it ripped open its shirt, took the girl's head between its hands and pulled it towards its bare chest.

'Don't do it, Becks.' Ted wailed. 'For God's sake, no!' But if the girl heard him, she chose to ignore his pleas. She bit into the vampire's chest and started to suck its evil and contaminated blood. She was lost.

The vampire raised a hand and pointed a long finger at Ted over the girl's head. 'Leave well alone, boy.' It hissed in a voice that was as cold as the grave. 'Don't meddle in things you do not understand.' It bent down and took the girl, still suckling like a baby, in its arms as if she were a doll.

That was when Ted noticed for the first time that one of Becky's baseball boots was missing. He tried to get to his feet, but only reached his knees. 'I'll kill you...' he managed, before he collapsed back in a heap on the cold floor. 'I swear I'll kill you,' he mumbled again as the vampire carried Becky towards the door through which Ted had entered the chamber.

The vampire stopped and looked down at the boy. For a moment Ted saw an expression on its face that could almost have passed as sadness. 'It is indeed your destiny to rid me of this torture, boy,' the vampire said in a gentle voice. 'But this is neither the time, nor, the place.' With those words the unholy creature disappeared into the dark tunnel beyond the door, still carrying the limp figure of Becky in its arms.

Ted felt himself slip back into unconsciousness, but not before wondering at the vampire's choice of words. Was killing it really his destiny?

Sunday 29th July 1962

Somehow Ted Dexter managed to find his way out of the chamber and stumble back along the tunnel to the door that led to the first chamber. There was no sign of Becky or of the vampire that had carried her away.

He touched the handle and immediately the door swung open to reveal the humming shimmer. A shaft of light shone from the tunnel beyond like a torch and Ted could see his cricket bat lying in front of the door where he had dropped it. He picked up the bat and without hesitation stepped through the door, with another clap of thunder reverberating about his ears.

A short while later Ted climbed into the sunshine and staggered across the yard to the administration block, where he collapsed on the ground, his face a mass of blood and his mind almost paralysed with shock and anguish. That is where a maintenance man found him half an hour later, dazed and semi-conscious.

The transistor radio was still pumping out tinny music, but Chubby Checker had given way to Pat Boone, singing "Speedy Gonzales".

Monday 30th July 1962

Because Ted Dexter spent most of Sunday evening in the Accident and Emergency department of the nearest hospital, which was twenty miles away from Boxham, the police did not get to interview him about the disappearance of Rebecca Driver until the following day. This delay gave Ted time to think through his ordeal and decide what he was going to say to the police and what he was going to do.

By Monday morning Ted was feeling slightly better; despite having his face heavily bandaged to cover the twenty stitches used to sew his forehead together, and despite having a throbbing headache that lingered until lunch time.

In the afternoon Ted's parents took him to Boxham Police Station where they left him to be interviewed by two policemen who introduced themselves as Inspector Hughes and Sergeant Powell.

The boy made a short statement, during which he told the policemen about the game of cricket he had played with Becky; how the ball had dropped through the broken metal grate; how he had helped her lift the manhole cover and how they had gone down the ladder to find the ball. He explained how the girl had run away and how, when he went to find her, he had collided with a cabinet and knocked himself unconscious. Ted did not mention Becky's wet T-shirt, or what had happened between him and her in the chamber. And numbed by the horror of his experience he did not tell them about the vampire that had eventually carried her away.

When he was making his statement the Inspector's shrewd gaze made Ted feel uncomfortable and at one point he felt the heat of a guilty flush on his cheeks and was pleased the bandage partially masked his face. But the policeman accepted his statement without comment and asked him if he would mind going to the power station to show them exactly where the previous afternoon's events had taken place. Ted agreed readily; anything to remove himself from the man's searching gaze.

'Are you feeling well enough to go below?' Inspector Hughes asked when they arrived at the bicycle shed, where the still open manhole had been cordoned off.

Ted nodded.

Hughes turned to his sergeant, 'You go first,' he said. 'The boy can follow you.'

When they reached the bottom of the ladder Ted showed them where the cricket ball had landed.

'Who found the ball?' The inspector asked.

'Becky,' Ted said. 'She threw it to me and then ran down that tunnel.'

He pointed across the chamber.

'Did you follow her?'

'Not straight away. Becky wanted to play hide-and-seek and made me count to a hundred.'

'A bit old for hide-and-seek, aren't you, lad?' Sergeant Powell raised an eyebrow.

Ted shrugged, but did not answer.

'But you followed her eventually?' Inspector Hughes asked.

The boy nodded.

'OK. Show us where you went.'

Ted led the policemen across the chamber and down the tunnel towards the door. Even from that distance the boy could see that the door was open. He could hear no humming sound and there was no shimmer in the doorway. He was not surprised to find that when they walked through the door there was no thunder or lightning and they found themselves in another tunnel that was as dry and light as the one from which they had just emerged.

Ted decided he had been right not to include in his statement anything about the vampire, or, what it had done to Becky. Without the evidence of the shimmer the policemen would simply think he was lying and wonder why.

The little group walked in single file up the tunnel and into the second chamber. It was empty except for a tall metal cabinet that stood against the wall to the right of the tunnel entrance. On the floor in front of the cabinet were a number of dark red spots, which the sergeant went to examine.

'It's blood,' Powell said, 'and look here...' he pointed to the sharp edge of the door, 'there's more blood on the door.'

'That's where I collided with the cabinet when I ran into the chamber looking for Becky,' Ted lied. 'Then I fell against the wall and knocked myself out.' He pointed at the wall alongside the cabinet.

'It makes sense, guv,' Sergeant Powell said as he bent to examine a stain on the wall, 'look, there's more blood here.'

'What happened when you came to?' Inspector Hughes asked the boy.

'I shouted out for Becky, but she didn't reply.'

'Did you see which way she went?'

Ted shook his head. 'No, but I think she must have gone down there.'

He pointed towards the tunnel on the opposite side of the wall, directly in front of which, twenty four hours before, a vampire had ravished his best friend.

'Did you go down that tunnel?'

Ted shook his head again. 'I didn't feel very well,' he replied truthfully.

'Okay. Let's have a look,' Hughes said and led the way into the tunnel, at the end of which was yet another door. It was closed.

Sergeant Powell stopped in front of the door and picked something up from the floor. 'Look at this, guv,' he said. It was a baseball boot.

'That looks like Becky's boot,' Ted said.

The policemen exchange glances, before Inspector Hughes opened the door and led the way through. They found themselves on a narrow gantry set into the side of a huge pipe, down which they could see water swirling towards an opening a couple of hundred feet to their left.

At the front of the gantry was positioned a small gate and when the inspector pushed it with his hand it immediately swung open above the rushing water. Again the two policemen looked at each other.

'Please take the boy back up top,' the Inspector said. 'Hand him over to his parents and then get onto the station and tell them that I want a diver here as quickly as possible.'

Thursday 2nd August 1962

Becky Driver's disappearance led to a full scale search of the area round Boxham Power Station, but the young girl was not found. Eventually the police concluded that she had fallen into the station's outlet pipe and been swept into the sea where she had drowned. However, her body was never washed ashore and the case remained open for many years.

Only Ted Dexter knew the truth. He also knew what had to be done.

He started by visiting his dad's garden workshop and used his lathe to sharpen the ends of two stumps to points that were so sharp they broke the skin of his finger when he tested them. He stowed the stumps in a large khaki canvas satchel he found under the bench on which the lathe was mounted.

Over the next couple of days he added to the satchel a mallet and torch he borrowed from his dad's workshop and a large decorative cross he bought from the local Woolworths store and to which he had attached a loop of cord. Finally he cut out from a hardboard sheet two oblong pieces, each measuring about twelve inches by eight inches, onto which he wrote a message, using a black felt tip pen. Satisfied, he put these in the satchel also, before storing it in the potting shed at the bottom of his garden.

By the Thursday after Becky disappeared his preparations were complete and he went to bed tired, but satisfied he was prepared for what he had to do the next day. He wondered briefly whether the shimmer would return to the door that led from his world to that of the vampire; but, as he closed his eyes, instinct told him that the shimmer would be back in time for him to use it.

That night Ted's sleep was troubled.

Dreams are often jumbled, surreal and sometimes frightening enough to wake you up. That is when they become nightmares. Ted's dream was a nightmare, so vivid it was almost real.

He was in the underground chamber with Becky and she was kissing him, however, unlike his experience in real life, in his dream there were no lights in the chamber and it was cold, damp and frightening.

Of course, Ted knew that Becky would pull away from him, and she did. That is the nature of dreams; they are often based on recollections and fact. Ted heard Becky's words as clearly as when they had first been spoken: "You can touch as well as look." At the same time he felt her soft breast beneath his hand and a longing in his groin. But just as he plucked up the courage to squeeze and caress her body, the girl pulled away from him and ran down the tunnel, leaving him hot and frustrated. But he was not to be denied; he chased her and caught her as she ran into the second chamber.

Becky slipped giggling to the floor, pulling him on top of her as she fell. They lay like that for what seemed an age; still and staring into each other's eyes. Then Ted slipped his hand underneath her T-shirt. She smiled encouragingly at him. He kissed her and felt the heat of her body as she arched it up against his own. He groaned. He wanted her so much.

Ted opened his eyes and stared into Becky's face. She stared back at him, her incredible blue eyes betraying her own wanting. Her lips were swollen with passion and as he watched she spread them wide to show a jagged fang on either side of her mouth. He stiffened and tried to pull away, but Becky had him in a grip of steel as she pulled his neck downwards.

Ted struggled and used his hands to lever himself away from those terrible teeth. He heard Becky hiss in frustration and he felt sick and angry. He grabbed Becky's throat and started to squeeze. Harder and harder he squeezed, keeping up the pressure on her windpipe until eventually her eyes glazed over and she went limp.

Ted sobbed in his sleep at what he had done.

In his dream he picked up Becky's limp body, which was as light as a feather, and carried her out of the chamber and back down the tunnel, but instead of stopping at the shimmer door he carried straight on until he reached the door to yet another chamber.

Ted saw himself push open the door of the chamber and walk in, except, now he realised that it was not him carrying the girl, but the man-vampire who he had seen on the day Becky disappeared.

This chamber was much smaller than the one from which he had just come and had the feel and look of a crypt about it. At the far side of the chamber there was an altar-like structure made of stone, at each end of which stood a tall black candle, and positioned in the middle was an upside down cross. Standing against both the right hand and left hand walls were low, oblong slabs of granite.

The thing that had taken Becky walked the few paces from the door to one of the slabs and carefully laid the girl on its hard smooth surface. It turned and stared straight back at the door, as if knowing that Ted was watching him in his dream. It moved menacingly towards him, its eyes red and hateful...

That's when the boy woke up whimpering and in a cold sweat.

Ted turned on the light. It was gone midnight and Thursday the 2nd of August had with little fanfare become Friday the 3rd. He slipped out of bed and checked to make sure that both his bedroom door and window was locked and there was nobody hiding either in his wardrobe, or, under his bed. Suddenly he felt ashamed of himself; he was being stupid. He reminded himself that he was 15 years of age and almost a man. But when he jumped back in the bed he pulled the covers over his head. Even *almost men* can be scared of the bogeyman.

Despite his fear Ted was soon asleep again and his nightmare resumed...

The vampire walked silently up the tunnel until it came to the door that led to the power station's water outlet pipe. The door was open and there was a shimmer clearly visible. The vampire stepped through the doorway. There was no lightning and no thunder, the creature simply disappeared. Ted was not surprised. He was beyond surprise.

Ted was not worried about losing sight of the vampire, because he knew where it was heading. He had no idea how he knew, but he knew. He stepped through the shimmer and found himself in a different world from the one in which he had been born and the one from which he had just come.

He knew he was in the power station's outlet pipe, but it was totally different to the one he had visited with the police only a few days before. For a start, the pipe was badly rusted, as was the gantry on which he now stood, and there was no water running through it. He should have been surprised, but he wasn't; strange things happen in dreams.

Still carrying his cricket bat, Ted jumped down into the pipe and headed along it until he reached the opening from which at one time it had discharged contaminated water into the sea. He clambered down onto the cement path and walked along the base of the seawall until he reached a set of steps. He ran quickly up the steps and was confronted by the decaying hulk of the deserted power station. He trotted round the boundary fence until he reached a park that was vaguely familiar. It was a hot day and on the other side of the park he could see a woman sitting on a bench reading a book.

Ted's forehead ached and when he raised a finger to it he discovered that his stitches had disappeared and his face was covered in blood. He walked across the park towards the bench. At first he thought it was Becky sitting there in the sun, but then he realised the woman was far too old. He walked past the woman, but she did not look up as he made his way through the park gate onto the pavement beyond.

He stared across the road at the apartment block opposite and saw a blind twitch in the window of the ground floor flat. He nodded his head and smiled. The blood on his face turned the smile into a ghastly grimace.

Friday 3rd August 2012

David stands in his darkened lounge. He eases aside one of the slats of the heavy window blind to reveal the sun drenched park across the road. On the other side of the park railings there is a gravel pathway. Set on grass beside the path is a wooden bench, on which sits a young woman reading a book. She is beautiful, with short dark hair and long tanned legs, made to look longer by the thigh high skirt she is wearing. But the thing that catches David's eye most is the sweep of her long neck and once again he feels a deep hunger gnawing at his insides. But he knows he must wait until night before he can feed.

David is sickened by the need that has shaped his life for the past five years. He is disgusted at what he has become; a leech on his fellow man. He would pray to God for release from his torment, but he no longer has a God. He is past redemption. He is one of the living dead.

The girl reminds him of Becky, who had so willingly helped him down the slippery slope to where he now finds himself. Or was it the other way round? *Becky, my love, I will come to you soon,* he swore to himself. *I promise.*

His eyes are drawn away from the girl by a movement in the corner of his eye. He sees a boy strolling across the park towards the girl, who does not look up. It's as if the boy is invisible.

The boy exits the park through the gate and stands on the pavement opposite David's apartment. He stares across at David's window. The boy is carrying a cricket bat in one hand and he has a deep gash on his forehead from which pours blood that covers half his face.

David raises a hand to his own face and with a frown feels his own scar. He closes his eyes, but when he reopens them the boy has not moved.

David releases the blind and as he moves the boy's face twists into a bloody distortion of a smile and he nods his head in a silent message. The man walks over to the old trunk that stands against the wall of his lounge and raises the lid. After rummaging around inside the trunk he takes from it a black and white framed photograph showing a boy and girl on a cricket outfield. Two handed the boy is holding a cricket bat on which he is balancing a cricket ball and the girl is applauding him. They are both smiling happily.

David puts the photograph back into the trunk and removes a cricket stump, which he carries over to the window. He pulls up the blind and flinches as the sunlight streams into the room and burns into his pale skin. He steps back from the window and into the shadows, but not before the boy sees him and beckons him with his forefinger. He holds the stump up into the shaft of light like a sword so that the boy can see clearly that the sharp tip of the stump has been stained almost black.

Satisfied, David pulls down the blind again and returns the stump to the trunk. He picks up the photograph and gently kisses the girl's image. A tear trickles down his face and drops onto the glass of the frame. He sets the photograph on top of the bookcase and closes the trunk.

David pulls up the hood of his tracksuit, puts on a pair of sunglasses, and, despite the heat of the day, a pair of gloves. Fully protected from the sun's rays he opens the front door and steps out into daylight for the first time in five years.

The boy has disappeared, but David knows where he will find him.

Friday 3rd August 1962

Ted would have preferred to visit the power station during the morning; the nights were drawing in and he did not want to leave it too late in the day. He knew it would be risky being in the lair of the vampire when the sun went down. But annoyingly his mother insisted that he join her on a visit to his older married sister and he could not refuse without raising her suspicions.

After a boring day, during which on a number of occasions Ted had to disguise his frustration at the interminable small talk, they eventually arrived back home at just after five o'clock. He had almost four hours before sunset, but dark clouds were building up in the south, threatening to bring an earlier end to the day.

Ted recovered the canvas satchel from the potting shed and headed for the power station. When he arrived he slipped through the gate without being seen and made for the bicycle shed, where he quickly pulled open the grate and climbed down the ladder, carefully closing the manhole cover behind him.

When Ted reached the bottom of the ladder he found the lights were on in the chamber and tunnel, but he took the torch out of his satchel anyway; he guessed he would need the torch soon enough and he was right. When he reached the door at the end of the tunnel the shimmer was back and the tunnel beyond was pitch black.

Ted viewed the shimmer nervously. He almost turned back, but he steeled himself and reaching into the satchel he took the cross and looped the cord over his head. As the cross made contact with his chest a feeling of power surged through him; stilling his fear and strengthening his resolve. He slung the satchel across his shoulder and without further hesitation stepped through the door; leaving behind his safe world of small talk and big sisters and entering the parallel world of horror that lay beyond.

Ted's entry into the Vampire's lair was once again accompanied by thunder and lightning, but although he was momentarily stunned by the effects of the shimmer, on this occasions the shock and nausea passed more quickly than it had before. Ted convinced himself this was because of the cross round his neck and it made him feel even better. He stood up and headed down the corridor that lay to his right, as he had in his dream.

The crypt was exactly where Ted thought it would be and as he entered the dark chamber he removed the cross from his neck and held it in front of him with his right hand, whilst holding the torch in his left. He shone the torch towards the side wall and saw Becky lying on the slab of granite. Her eyes were closed, but her chest rose and fell in a slow steady rhythm.

Ted swept the torch across to the other side of the chamber to the second slab where another figure lay. It was the man-vampire and it looked as if it was sleeping. Ted ignored the creature, instead he moved to the slab where the girl lay and slipped the satchel from his shoulder. He looped the cross back round his neck before removing from the satchel a cricket stump and the mallet. He laid the torch between her feet so that it lit up the length of her body.

Like the vampire, Becky looked as if she was sleeping and Ted began to hope that he might not have to go through with his plan. Taking the stump in his left hand and the mallet in his right, he used the latter to gently shake the girl.

Becky's eyes sprang open, but she did not move, instead she saw the cross round his neck and parted her lips and hissed at him like a snake. That was when his hopes were dashed. He realised he was too late to save his friend. She was no longer of his world.

Ted placed the point of stump above the thing that had been Becky and paused, hoping that she (he couldn't think of her as an "it") would struggle and make it easy for him, but the girl simply closed her eyes again and went back to sleep. Ted raised the mallet and drove the cricket stump deep into her heart. That was when his friend screamed with such anguish that it tore apart his own heart.

'Noooo!' Ted wailed at the ceiling as tears began to run down his cheeks. 'What have I done?' He leaned down on the stump and sobbed for what seemed ages, before he remembered that his job was not yet complete.

He pulled the stump from Becky's lifeless body with a horrible squelching sound that almost made him vomit and a gush of blood that sprayed his hand and left a dark trail across her white T-shirt. He put the stump on the floor and took one of the hardboard oblong pieces from his satchel and laid it on Becky's chest. The message on the board read:

Becky Driver

I love you xx

RIP

Ted picked up the torch and moved over to the other side of the crypt. He placed the torch and mallet between the feet of the vampire, then went back and picked up the stump from the floor. He stood over the vampire. Its eyes were open and stared steadily up at him. Ted almost turned and fled, but he grasped the cross again and regained his composure.

'Do it,' the vampire said in a soft, sad voice. 'Now is the time and this is the place.'

Ted snatched up the mallet, positioned the tip of the bloody stump against the thing's chest and smashed it with a power born of rage and hatred.

The vampire let out a scream as loud as that of Becky, but it was one less of anguish and more of joyful release.

The boy hammered down on the stump again and again and again.

With each strike of the mallet, blood spurted out of the wound and splashed up onto his hand to join that of Becky. Ted seemed not to notice the blood, but he did. Very much so.

Eventually Ted's rage abated and he dropped the mallet onto the floor and wrenched the stump from the vampire's body. He took the second piece of hardboard from his satchel and laid it across the monster's chest. It read:

> Ted Dexter
> I hate you.
> May you rot in hell!

Ted stared down at his hand and slowly he raised it to his lips. Delicately and deliberately he licked the blood of both vampires. With that action the bloodline between love and hate, young and old, and past and future was complete. His destiny was sealed.

Monday 6th August 2012

David "Ted" Dexter was found dead in his darkened apartment by his cleaner. He was impaled on a cricket stump that had been fixed upright into a hole drilled in the wooden floor. The sharpened tip of the stump had penetrated the man's body from front to back, piercing his heart on the way. There was blood everywhere.

The police found no evidence of an intruder and the subsequent inquest returned a verdict of death by suicide, the coroner basing his judgement partly on David Dexter's long history of mental illness.

However, the police did find one item of evidence in the apartment, although it did not relate directly to the suicide. Hidden in a secret compartment at the bottom of a trunk was a diary for the year 1962.

An entry in the diary led the police to an underground chamber in the derelict power station, where they discovered the desiccated remains of a young girl dressed in blue jeans, a white T-shirt and a single brown baseball boot.

The case file for the missing Rebecca Driver was finally closed.

Night The Music Died

The Surf Ballroom was hot and clammy and heavy with the body odour of a thousand youngsters for whom the American Dream was still alive. The atmosphere was electric with an excitement that lingered long after the end of the show.

The singer was sweating as he stepped from the stage. His head throbbed from an overdose of adrenaline and the effects of two hours of loud music, but he ignored the headache. As always the tumultuous applause and adulation that had accompanied his performance more than compensated for any temporary discomfort.

He dashed to his dressing room; there was a plane waiting for him on the runway of the local airport and if they were going to take off tonight the plane would have to leave within the hour.

The man packed away his guitar and removed his spectacles. With a hurried farewell to the boys from the band, he headed for the backdoor and clambered into the back seat of the Chevrolet that stood in the Surf Ballroom's small rear yard, its engine already ticking over. Soon they were heading for the airport.

It was an atrocious night; the rain lashed down, hammering against the roof of the car like so many handfuls of shingle thrown by a naughty boy. There were few other vehicles on the road and they made good time to the airport.

The small, twin-engine plane stood on the apron, amid the worsening storm, its propeller blades slicing through the torrent, smashing the cascading water into billowing clouds of fine spray. The singer wrapped himself more tightly into his trench-coat and made a dash for the plane in which his two companions already waited.

'The weather is closing in fast,' the pilot said as his last passenger eased into the seat beside him, 'are you sure you want to carry on?'

The younger man looked out of the cockpit towards the rain

lashed buildings, but it was almost pitch black outside and all he could see was his own pale face reflected in the Perspex window. In the seats behind him he could see his two flying companions, they were already asleep. He thought of Maria and the child she carried. 'Can we make it?'

The pilot shrugged. 'I can fly this baby anywhere. Whatever the goddam weather conditions; I saw shit much worse than this in Korea.' The pilot 0paused and looked at the young singer. 'Listen, bud, I ain't worried, but you're the boss. If you say we go, we go. If you say we stay, we stay.'

The singer was twenty-two years old, he was desperate to get home to his wife and his youth blinded him to any danger they might face. Like many of his age, he believed he would live forever. Perhaps he was right.

'We go,' he said without hesitation. He offered the pilot one of the wide, toothy grins for which he was famous and then closed his eyes. He felt the plane vibrate as the pilot powered up to maximum thrust for take-off, then they were airborne and he was on his way to her at last. He settled more comfortably into his seat and soon he was in a deep sleep.

The singer awoke with a start to find the plane pitching and rolling like a row-boat in a maelstrom. He looked out of the cockpit window and saw they were caught up in an electric storm of awesome intensity; jagged bolts of lightning knifed into the night and a gale force wind buffeted the plane as if it were made of balsa wood.

The little plane put up a tremendous fight; it bucked against the dreadful winds, refusing to be buffeted into submission, but slowly the battle was lost. The elements were simply too powerful.

The young man watched helplessly as the plane was sucked into a black, swirling whirlpool of cloud and his mouth moved in a silent prayer. Faster and faster they fell until, finally, as the little plane spun out of control, he passed out.

When consciousness returned to the singer the plane had miraculously pulled out of its spin. A bright ray of light sliced a gap in the black clouds beneath them. Immediately the aircraft dropped through the gap and glided gently down towards the rolling expanse of soya-bean fields below.

As they drew nearer to the earth, he saw that a circular section of the field had been flattened. He frowned, wondering who, or what, had carved such a symmetrical design from the tightly planted soya-bean crop, then he saw a number of people standing on the edge of the field and the riddle was solved. There were four of them; tall, brooding figures dressed in black hooded capes and carrying long-handled scythes.

Momentarily, the young man was frightened; then a stray finger of wind tugged loose the cape of one figure. The hood dropped to reveal the most beautiful face on which he had ever set eyes. Immediately his fear disappeared, to be replaced by a desperate longing. He quickly unfastened his seat belt, swung open the cockpit door and stepped out into tranquillity.

The storm still raged on; howling winds battered the dark Iowan landscape and lightning forked down regularly to alert the citizens of Clear Lake that a roll of thunder was on its way. But the storm bypassed the soya-bean field and as he jumped to the ground he was enveloped in a blanket of serenity that isolated him from the destructive elements that lashed the surrounding countryside.

The woman smiled and held out her arms. The cape fell fully from her shoulders to reveal a white ankle length dress that shimmered with an almost celestial glow. The singer ran to her, but stopped just short of those welcoming arms. For the first time he realised how tall she was. He had to crane his neck in order to gaze into her angelic face.

She smiled again and the light of love shone from her eyes. 'Come,' she said.

So he went to her and as he moved into her arms tears of happiness ran down his cheeks. She lifted his chin gently and he felt her sweet breath on his face as she bent towards him. He closed his eyes as she kissed him and he felt the breath being sucked from his body, whilst at the same time he was gripped by an ecstasy of such intensity that all remaining sense of reality left him. That's when he passed out again.

The singer awoke but he could not open his eyes. He was blind, but he did not care. He was in a state of semi-consciousness, suspended in a comfortingly warm void. He was safe and content and he just knew that somewhere out there the woman was watching over him. He slept.

When he awoke again he was hungry. He found himself trapped in a strange dream world in which, although he could not see, he felt safe and totally at peace with himself. He turned slowly and reached out with his hands to investigate his surroundings. He moved awkwardly in the weightless atmosphere, pushing forward in a gentle roll until he was able to kick against the soft yielding wall. Slowly it dawned on the singer that he was trapped in a huge, liquid filled sac.

As he investigated further he made two other puzzling discoveries; the first was that he was connected to the sac by a thick pipe and the second was that he was no longer hungry. He considered this for a few moments and came to the conclusion that he was on some kind of life support machine and he was being fed intravenously. This realisation scared the hell out of him at first. Jesus Christ! What else was being pumped into his body? But his fear quickly subsided as the gentle rhythmic throb of the sac dulled his senses and tranquillised him. He slept.

Once again the singer's sleep was disturbed, but this time his awakening was infinitely more frightening than before. The once cosy and secure sac in which he slept started to vibrate and its walls slowly began to close in on him. The sac squeezed against his body and as the singer tried to call out in alarm his mouth was blocked and the cry was killed before it had time to form. His body was wracked with convulsions and he felt a clamp tighten round his head. He screamed silently and thrust his head upwards in an attempt to escape the pain of the murderous clamp. Suddenly, he pushed his head loose and the clamp slid slowly down the length of his body. The pain was first transferred to his shoulders, then to his chest, his stomach and, finally, his buttocks. But at last he was able to struggle free and he lay for a few seconds recovering.

Then somebody switched off his life support machine and with it the flow of food and air that had sustained him for so long. He found himself slowly suffocating and he knew that before long he would be dead. He felt a sharp blow across his buttocks and he let out an instinctive yell of protest. Suddenly his throat was clear and warm, clean air flowed into his lungs. He cried out again, but this time in triumph. He was alive!

The woman once again towered over him and soon he was safe in her arms. He felt her lips on his forehead and the longing returned. He groped for her breast until at last he managed to pull that deliciously hard nipple into his mouth. He tasted her warmth and was satiated. He slept.

When the singer awoke he was confused. He could see, but he did not understand the messages being relayed to his brain by his eyes. What the hell was happening? What had happened?

He was lying on a bathroom floor. He was naked. One wall of the bathroom had been decorated in mirror tiles and as he caught sight of himself he screamed in disbelief. He was staring into the face of a baby. He felt himself being lifted.

'There, there my little darling,' the woman's gentle voice crooned. 'You are such a lovely little girl.'

Little girl? The singer started to whimper.

'But I'm not a girl,' he tried to explain. 'I'm a man. My name is Buddy Holly.'

But the only sound that escaped his mouth was the angry cry of a baby.

'Are you hungry? Do you want this?' The woman pulled his head towards her breast and instinctively he sucked. With the woman's milk came peace. He slept.

And so the baby who had been Buddy Holly slept and drank and slept again. Slowly memories of his past life became more and more blurred until finally they were forgotten completely.

The little girl stood on the stage. She was four years old and she played the violin like an angel. The clear, perfect notes that filled the music academy brought tears to the woman's eyes and she had trouble completing the application form that lay on her lap. Finally she blinked away her tears and entered her daughter's date of birth: February 3rd 1959.

'We are doing the right thing, aren't we, Ben?' She asked anxiously, 'You don't think she's too young to be enrolled in the Academy?'

Her husband shook his head, 'It's the best thing we can do for her. You heard what Professor O'Brien said; Holly is a musical genius.' He smiled, 'You know what, honey? There are two things I have never been able to work out.'

'What are they?'

'You never told me why you chose the name Holly.'

'It just came to me. When I was pregnant I felt the baby kick and at the same time the name Holly popped into my mind.' She smiled at her husband. 'The name stuck.'

'It's a good name,' he said as he took his wife's hand.

'What was the other thing?' She asked.

The man's smile broadened into a grin. 'If Holly is a musical genius, honey. I don't know where she got her talent. Certainly not from us; we are both tone deaf.'

Elize

It was one of those wild and vengeful nights on which the sea launches a periodic attack on the rugged cliffs of Cornwall. Encouraged by the howling battle cry of its ally the wind; the sea rose in mighty waves to smash to white foamed oblivion against a stout granite defence that had withstood such assaults for countless centuries.

And yet, even on a night when the forces of nature waged open civil war, there was one haven of relative serenity on that storm ravaged battlefield; Trebethan Cove.

Formed by a natural tuck in the rock face, the cove's narrow strip of rock studded sand was sheltered from the frightful elements beating against the northern coastline of Cornwall by the tall brown cliffs that surrounded it.

The waters of the cove were as flat and calm as the fringe of sand against which it lapped, belying the treacherous currents that lay just beneath the surface. Below the gently rippling waves the sea swirled and tugged at the fine sand of the beach, seducing and enticing it through the narrow mouth of the cove into the wider sea where the storm could attack it with impunity.

Trebethan Cove was deserted, with no sign of Man except for the same bric-a-brac of his existence that is washed ashore the world over. A dirty plastic drinking cup here, an empty soft drink can there, a torn carrier bag in the middle of the beach and, at the base of the cliff where the long footpath zigzagged down to join the sand, a crumpled raincoat.

Robert was not immediately concerned when the police contacted him and reported that his brother was missing. Jimmy regularly dropped out of circulation and during such periods nobody would see hide nor hair of him for days on end. But, like the proverbial bad penny, he always turned up eventually.

Jimmy had spent the winter doing casual work in Cornwall, or, so he claimed, although Robert insisted on calling his brother's activity: "bumming around"! Jimmy had drifted along the coast from one small village to another, telephoning home when the urge took him, or, when he needed an urgent loan.

The police told Robert that his brother was last seen in the small seaside hamlet of Trebethan, where he boarded with a Mrs Tregowan. It appeared that he had not actually found any casual work in the village, out of season there was little enough work for the locals, and he seemed to have spent most of each day wandering along the rugged coastline, taking photographs and writing poetry.

Then, one gale lashed Monday, Jimmy got up in the middle of the night, walked out of Mrs Tregowan's neat little cottage, and was never seen again.

The landlady did not notify the police of Jimmy's disappearance until Thursday. As she explained, there had been no reason to suspect there was a problem before then. Jimmy had paid in advance, all his belongings were still in his room and his bed was slept in on Monday night. It was only after two nights without sight or sound of Jimmy that Mrs Tregowan called the police. Eventually, during her interview with the police, the landlady half remembered hearing the front door open and close in the early hours of Tuesday morning.

The police carried out a cursory search of the area, but since he was not a minor and no crime had apparently taken place, they did not over extend themselves. The police came to the conclusion that Jimmy had taken a night-time walk, slipped from the treacherous cliff-top and been swept out to sea.

They could offer no explanation why Jimmy might have ventured out of the house in the middle of a storm-lashed night. Although, in private, the local bobby had his own theory: 'Probably high on something,' he ventured to the landlord of The Galleon as he supped his evening pint. 'These city folk are into that sort of thing, you know. Why else would he walk along the cliffs on such an atrocious night unless he was out of his head on drugs.' The policeman looked knowingly at the landlord and then added: 'Dolly tells me that the lad was a poet.'

So, in absence of the any evidence, the police simply added Jimmy's name to the long list of missing people already on their files and then contacted his next of kin; Robert.

There was not much going on in the office at that time, and any outstanding work could be handled easily by his partner, so Robert decided to drive down to Cornwall. He was still not particularly worried about Jimmy, assuming there was a logical and straightforward explanation for his brother's disappearance.

No, if the truth be told, Robert was using his missing brother as an excuse to get out of London and take a much needed break. Cornwall in the spring was as good as anything, he decided. He left London early the next morning and by mid-afternoon he was driving into Trebethan surprised at how tiny it actually was. It was a pretty place and he could understand his brother's attraction toward it; it suited him too.

Dolly Tregowan was a plump, homely woman who insisted that Robert use up the outstanding days paid for in advance by his brother before accepting any further payment.

Jimmy's effects were still in his bedroom, stacked in neat piles on the sturdy oak dressing table. There were clothes, photographic equipment and an exercise book full of poetry. Robert read through the poems, although he was not sure why. Perhaps he half hoped there might a clue to his brother's whereabouts among the neatly, hand written pages.

After he had ploughed through the entire book he returned to one particular poem that seemed out of keeping with the rest. He read it again:

For Elize
Her eyes, so black, are full
Of a passion born of youth.
Her lips, though nectar tasting
Are as cold as the sea so blue.

She is beautiful, this woman-child,
More radiant than the sun,
With the body of a goddess,
We must be joined as one.

I yearn to receive her shy, young touch
And her kisses on my face.
I want to hold her close to me
And caress her without haste.

To know her body, as I know my own,
Would make my life so free.
If only the feelings I have for her
Were returned, in kind, to me.

Words are not enough to tell
Of the desire in my heart for her.
How I would love her, if I could
With a love that's strong and sure.

On the face of it an ordinary poem, a not very good ordinary poem at that; just one more effort from the pen of a not particularly talented amateur poet. However, when compared with the other poems in the exercise book, it took on a greater significance. All Jimmy's other works were full of angry verses and abrasive words that condemned the endless abuses inflicted on our environment as perceived by an idealistic young man. Poems full of barbs fired at the heart of a corrupt and unjust society.

Yet, amongst all the bitterness, there was "For Elize"; a poem of tenderness and love. Who had inspired such passion? Was Jimmy with her now? If not, did she know where he was? How could Robert find this mystery girl? Did she even exist?

On the dressing table lay several packets containing photographs. Robert flicked through them, hoping he might find a picture of the girl. He drew a blank; all the photographs were of animals, or birds, or the local landscape. Then Jimmy's digital camera caught Robert's eye. He picked it up and switched it on and accessed the photo memory store.

As he scrolled through the photos a frown creased his forehead. He had convinced himself that he would find a picture of the mystery girl amongst the photographs and that somehow he would be able to use this to find her, and perhaps Jimmy, but there was nothing.

He was deeply disappointed and at the same time puzzled. The photographs were all of the same subject; a large rock, set on a strand of beach, viewed from different angles and taken in varying degrees of light. Robert scrolled through the photos again, looking for some clue that he might have missed. He shook his head. Why on earth would Jimmy have taken so many photos of the same rock?

'How odd,' Robert muttered to himself. 'Odd, and bugger all help!'

He shrugged and decided that he needed a drink.

The Galleon was Trebethan's only public house. It was a cosy, one bar affair with a low wood-beamed ceiling and a seafaring atmosphere heightened by numerous nautical relics that hung from the blackened beams.

The focal point of the pub was a massive wooden replica of an ancient sailing vessel that was positioned above the bar. It was magnificent; with gleaming hull, starched white sails and a burnished mermaid at its bows.

'Beautiful,' Robert remarked to the landlord as he ordered his drink.

'Aye. That's a replica of the Golden Mermaid,' the man explained with a friendly smile as he pulled a pint of best bitter.

The landlord was a big, jovial man with a huge handlebar moustache and a stomach that flopped over the waistband of his trousers. Robert invited the man to join him and he accepted with alacrity.

'Did you build it?' Robert asked.

'Good heavens, no, sir. She's been hanging there for donkeys' years. There's some says that she were built not long after the original Mermaid went down with all hands, and that was at the end of the Eighteenth Century.'

They talked for several more minutes about the Mermaid. The landlord told Robert how the ship had been sunk off Trebethan Cove whilst smuggling in brandy from France. He went on to explain that all on board were lost, including several men from the village. Then Robert asked the landlord if he remembered Jimmy.

'Oh, aye, nice lad he was. Quiet like. Intense, I guess you'd say.

Don't get many young 'uns round these parts this time of the year. Plenty when the season starts, mind, but not this early.'

'Any idea where Jimmy might be? Did he mention anything about leaving Trebethan?'

The landlord shook his head.

'Are there any young ladies in the area who Jimmy might have taken up with?'

'Not as I know of, sir.'

'Are you sure?'

'I told you, sir,' the man said patiently, 'we don't get many young 'uns round these parts this early in the year.'

'I don't necessarily mean visitors,' Robert persisted. 'Are there no young girls in the village?'

'No, sir!' the landlord said emphatically. 'Look, sir, Trebethan is what you might call a dying village, if you get my drift. All the young 'uns, including my own daughter, have long since left. Gone off to Bristol, or, Plymouth. There's nobody left in the village under the age of fifty.' The man paused and drank deeply, and expertly, from his beer glass. 'I know this isn't a very nice thought, sir,' the landlord went on, 'but have you considered the possibility that your brother might have drowned? Trebethan Cove is notorious, you know. It's deceiving, see? It looks calm enough, even when there's a storm raging, but the undercurrents hereabouts are damn treacherous. A swimmer can be pulled out to sea within minutes. Just can't help themselves. There's been many a lad lost off Trebethan Cove over the years.' The man nodded sagely. 'Many a lad,' he repeated.

Robert dismissed this possibility out of hand. It was absurd. He knew his brother better than that. 'Jimmy go swimming in the middle of the night? In a storm? I don't believe it! He might have given the impression sometimes that he was irresponsible, but, in his own way, he was quite sensible.'

The landlord nodded his agreement, but his smile carried its own unspoken message. 'I've heard it all before!' It said.

After Robert left the pub, he spent an hour or so wandering round the village, asking questions to which he received the same dispiritingly negative answers. Finally, frustrated by his lack of progress, Robert made his way along the cliff top to Trebethan Cove.

It was a pleasant, peaceful walk. The early spring sun was warm on his face and what little breeze there was barely stirred the misshapen trees that had been permanently bowed by the gale force winds that regularly ravaged the cliff top.

Robert stood and looked down at the cove, a hundred feet below. The beach, and adjacent sea, was almost entirely enclosed by the curve of the high cliffs, with the mouth of the cove no more than a dozen feet wide.

Vivid images were conjured up in Robert's mind of sailors, from ships like the Golden Mermaid, ferrying contraband into the sanctuary of the tiny, secluded cove, there to be met by willing villagers from Trebethan, who quickly spirited the smuggled goods away to secret caverns, far from the prying eyes of the excise men.

Suddenly, Robert started out of his daydream. His heart beat faster as he saw somebody on the beach. A woman. No! A girl! Could this possibly be the girl from Jimmy's poem? Robert made his way down the zig-zag cliff path as quickly as the uneven surface would allow and soon he was on the beach.

The girl sat on a rock and stared through the mouth of the cove towards the endless expanse of ocean beyond. Robert stopped in his tracks, struck by the strange familiarity of the scene. He experienced a deep sense of déjà-vu, but this sensation soon passed as his attention focused on the girl and he found his emotions stirred in a way he had never thought possible.

She was dressed in those old fashioned clothes that some modern girls affect to wear. A long, ankle length skirt, worn over stocking-less legs, a white linen, off-the-shoulder blouse and a crocheted scarf, tied in a knot at her bosom, that hung in a triangle down her back. The girl wore no shoes and, as she sat there on the rock, swinging her legs back and forth with an absent-minded nonchalance, her toes dragged slowly through the soft sand.

As Robert approached the rock the girl stood up and turned to face him. He stared at her, spellbound by her beauty. She had raven coloured hair that hung loose and free down to the base of her spine. Her face was pale with flawless skin and features as exquisite as a porcelain figurine.

Her full, generous mouth was set in an enigmatically sad smile that was mirrored in eyes so dark they looked like shiny black orbs floating in a pure white sea. She stood with the setting sun behind her and Robert could see the firm, shapely curve of her body through the cheap cotton clothes she wore. In that instant he knew this was the "goddess" of which Jimmy had written.

'Thee came then?'

Her quiet lilting words were like music to Robert's ears. He tried to speak but found that his throat was constricted and his lungs were suddenly empty of air. He nodded instead.

'Us did know thee would come t'find 'e.'

'Jimmy?' Robert eventually managed to blurt out.

The girl smiled her sad little smile and nodded.

'How do you know who I am?' Robert stammered, still overwhelmed by her loveliness.

'Jim did speak of thee oft,' she replied. 'Us did know straight away as who thee were.'

'Where is he?' Robert asked.

She moaned softly then said: ''E be gone, so 'e be.'

'Gone? Where?'

She pointed through the mouth of the cove towards the sea.

''E be gone,' she repeated. 'Us did try t'save 'e, but us be too late. Always too late.'

Robert sat down on the rock and lowered his head. So, it looked as if Jimmy was dead; dragged out to sea by the murderous currents as had been rumoured. He shook his head and looked up at the girl. He studied her carefully as she stared motionless out over the water. She seemed oddly disorientated and her movements and speech were painfully slow, as if every gesture and sentence was an effort.

At first he suspected that she was under the influence of some drug, but then he saw the bright intelligence in her clear eyes and decided her behaviour was more the result of deep grief. It was a grief they both shared and the man suddenly felt a burning desire to comfort this strange and lovely girl.

'Where do you come from?' He asked quietly. As he spoke he drew her to sit on the rock beside him. The girl pointed and for the first time he noticed the small wooden dinghy that lay at the water's edge. The girl obviously lived further up the coast and probably rowed to the cove each day to take advantage of the shelter and privacy it offered.

'Us must go,' she said, jumping to her feet.

'No!' Robert cried. He could not bear to see her go. Not yet. He wanted her to stay at his side; to be close to him.

'Us must go,' she repeated. The light was fading fast.

'At least let me take you home.'

'Nay. T'aint time yet. But worry thee not, when time be right us'll come.'

'Where do you live? Can I see you again? When can we meet?' Then in desperation he pleaded: 'I want to help you.'

At first the girl did not reply, instead she continued to stare out through the entrance of the cove, apparently oblivious of his words. She was as far away as the red ball of sun that even now sank slowly into the Atlantic Ocean.

'I must go,' she said eventually as she turned back to Robert with tears in her eyes. 'Will thee really 'elp us?'

'Of course.'

She smiled briefly at his words, then turned and ran quickly to the dinghy. Before Robert could join her and offer assistance she had expertly pushed the boat into the water, jumped in and was gone. With well measured strokes she rowed out of the cove and was soon lost in the gathering gloom.

'What's your name? When can we meet?' Robert called after her, but she either did not hear him, or chose to ignore his questions.

That night Robert read Jimmy's poem again and again, savouring the words as if they were kisses from the girl's mouth. 'Her eyes, so black, are full, of a passion born of youth, beautiful, this beach child, body of a goddess, long to receive her shy young touch, want to hold her close, love that's strong and true,' he read aloud.

So mesmerised was Robert by the mysterious girl's beauty that his own sense of loss was forgotten. It was as if his grief at Jimmy's death had been anaesthetised by her very presence at his side earlier that day. Now, the more he thought about the girl, the less he remembered of his brother until eventually his mind was empty of all but the loveliness of her face, the unspoken promise of her soft young body and a determination to make her his own.

Each day Robert found her sitting on the same rock, staring moodily out to sea. She told him her name was Elize, but revealed little else about herself. She remained an enigma. He tried to coax more out of her, but she simply ignored him, losing herself in a world to which, so she appeared to have convinced herself that her lover would return at any time.

So Robert gave up trying to strike up a conversation with the mysterious girl, instead he was content to simply sit with her and watch her, which she didn't seem to mind. He feasted on her beauty and waited; hoping his patience would eventually be rewarded and that she would emerge from her cocoon of mourning and grow to want him as much as he so desperately wanted her.

The only time that Elize showed any sign of animation was when Robert repeated his offer of help; she clasped his hand tightly and made him promise to keep his word. She told him the time would come when she needed him and urged him to be ready. When he agreed, as he always did, she would kiss him full on the lips with a passion that stayed with him through the night.

Each evening Robert asked Elize if he could escort her home and each evening he received the same quiet refusal.

'Nay, taint time yet,' the girl always insisted, 'but don't thee worry. When time be ready, I'll come fer thee. Wait a while, I beg. Jus' wait.'

And so Robert waited, until one day the weather changed for the worse. The wind howled in from the sea, bringing in its train a cold driving rain that battered the village and kept indoors all but the most foolhardy. But Robert was enticed out, driven on by the new found love that consumed him. As usual he visited Trebethan Cove, fighting his way through the solid curtain of water, hardly able to stand in the face of the raging gale.

But, of course, Elize was not there. Robert was not surprised, but such was the agony of his loneliness, he stayed on anyway, hoping beyond hope she would suddenly turn up. Finally, the squelching discomfort of his position made him accept the inevitable; Elize was not coming.

For the rest of the day Robert moped about in his bedroom, his depression deepening in direct proportion to the increase in volume with which the wind screamed through the chimneys of the village and the more heavily the rain hammered against his window.

If only he knew where Elize lived; he so much wanted to be with her. He sensed somehow that today would have been the right day. Today perhaps, she would have been ready for him. Today might have been the beginning of something special between them. But it was not to be. He had no way of contacting her. It was useless.

And so the long, terribly lonely hours passed and as day turned to night the pelting rain slowly subsided to little more than a heavy drizzle. However, the wind seemed to draw extra energy from the dwindling power of its erstwhile ally and the angry howl became almost deafening in its intensity.

At first Robert did not hear her call; barely a half whisper, lost in the cacophony of sound that tormented the sleep of the villagers. When finally he recognised the voice calling his name he dismissed it as a figment of his imagination. But the voice persisted.

Robert dashed to the window, his heart beating wildly. Elize stood in the street outside, the wind tugging at her skirt, pressing the soft wet material against her lithe young legs in a way that excited him.

'Come thee!' She called. 'Tis time. Us need's thee. Hurry, man, hurry!'

Robert, who was already fully dressed, grabbed his raincoat and ran to join Elize in the wind lashed street below. Without allowing him time to put on his raincoat, and ignoring his questions, the girl grabbed Robert's hand and tugged at him follow.

'Come thee! Hurry! Hurry! Time be runnin' short.' Her words were urgent and tinged with desperation.

Robert followed without question. He did not know what catastrophe had provoked such panic in his "goddess", but he did know he would go to the ends of the earth, if needs be, to help her.

Down the cobbled street they ran, with Elize pulling and Robert blindly following, still clutching his useless raincoat in his hand. Along the gale lashed cliff top they raced, first to Trebethan Cove and then down the tortuous zig-zag path to the beach. Robert continually stumbled on the treacherous, rain sodden surface as they descended until finally, right at the bottom of the path, he slipped, dropping his raincoat. Taking both his hands, one in each of hers, Elize pulled the dazed man to his feet.

'Come! Come!' She urged him as she led him quickly to the dinghy. Robert hesitated, viewing the tiny craft with deep apprehension. The water in the cove was flat and still as a mill-pond, but Robert could see that the ocean outside was broiling like a witches cauldron.

'Come! Come!' Elize shouted. 'Quickly, man. Thee promised t'elp un when I did need thee. Please! Thee promised!' She tugged at his hand urgently. ''Tis time! Hurry!'

Robert got into the dinghy and they cast off. Robert rowed. It was easy at first, but it became hard, back breaking work once they were out of the shelter of the cove and he was battling against the full force of the savage wind whipped sea.

It was a nightmare. A nightmare that Robert could do nothing to stop. He wanted so badly to call a halt, to turn round and return to the safety of Trebethan Cove, but he could not do it. It was as if he was bound to the oars by invisible chains.

Pull, out, forward, dip; pull, out, forward, dip; pull, out, forward, dip.

Behind him in the bows he could hear Elize shouting, but his tired and befuddled mind could make little sense of her words.

'Wait! Wait!' Her voice rose to a scream as it fought against the howl of the wind. 'Hold on! This time I do save thee, my darlin'. Hold on, I do 'ave another 'elper.'

Elize turned and screeched at Robert: 'Hurry, man! Hurry! Harder, harder! Row harder! 'Tis time! 'Tis time! Hurry!'

And Robert hurried, oh, how he hurried. Every sinew of his body strained until he ached with exertion. His heart beat louder and louder by the minute, swelling inside him, throbbing in his ears. Oh, God! It must explode soon. But still he hurried.

With a great effort Robert managed to twist his head and look behind him at the girl. He gasped; shock and fear froze his brain. Elize stood in the bows, legs apart, arms outstretched, urging him on whilst at the same time staring ahead into the night and screaming the same message: 'We be comin', m'dear, m'darlin'. I do save thee this time, Jeremiah. Wait on un.'

But it was not this vision of Elize that chilled Robert's blood colder than the heaving ocean through which they battled, it was the huge black shape that towered above the dinghy.

It was a ship. A ship that glowed strangely in the night. A ship whose deck was lined with open mouth sailors screaming to be saved from the gates of Hell. A ship, with broken masts and torn sails. A ship that last sailed those seas, long ago, in days when smugglers plied their trade along this part of the Cornish coast. A ship with a burnished gold mermaid figurehead at its bows.

'Too late, fool! Thee be too slow! Damn thee!' Elize cursed as she turned to Robert, her face contorted in rage and frustration. 'Fool! Fool! Too slow!'

She shook her fist at the man and then returned her attention to the sinking ship.

'Oh, Jeremiah! I be sorry, my love. I did try, darlin'. I did try. Don' thee worry. I do keep tryin' 'til I do save thee. I promise thee.'

That's when Robert screamed as his sanity slipped away and was still screaming when the vortex created by the sinking galleon sucked the dinghy and it occupants to the bottom of the cold, dark ocean.

It was one of those wild and vengeful nights on which the sea launches a periodic attack on the rugged cliffs of Cornwall. Encouraged by the howling battle cry of its ally the wind; the sea rose in mighty waves to smash to white foamed oblivion against a stout granite defence that had withstood such assaults for countless centuries.

And yet, even on a night when the forces of nature waged open civil war, there was one haven of relative serenity on that storm ravaged battlefield; Trebethan Cove.

Formed by a natural tuck in the rock face, the cove's narrow strip of rock studded sand was sheltered from the frightful elements beating against the northern coastline of Cornwall by the tall brown cliffs that surrounded it.

The waters of the cove were as flat and calm as the fringe of sand against which it lapped, belying the treacherous currents that lay just beneath the surface. Below the gently rippling waves the sea swirled and tugged at the fine sand of the beach, seducing and enticing it through the narrow mouth of the cove into the wider sea where the storm could attack it with impunity.

Trebethan Cove was deserted, with no sign of man except for the same bric-a-brac of his existence that is washed ashore the world over. A dirty plastic drinking cup here, an empty soft drink can there, a torn carrier bag in the middle of the beach and, at the base of the cliff where the long footpath zigzagged down to join the sand, a crumpled raincoat.

The Talking Goose

eil, stranger! Would ye nay tarry a while wi'me, fer I sense we are well met this day? Mayhap it doth please ye t' pull up yon chair and hear the tale I would tell. I warrant 'tis a tale like none other ye've heard, for 'tis of lust, intrigue, death and magic I would speak.

'The tale is set many moons ago in Lundia, a land far away t'the north, ruled at the time by King Boris the Brave, although, I warrant 'twas Boris's wife, Queen Gloria, who were the real power in the land. Let me set the scene, if ye will.'

Life was simple in the Royal Court of Lundia; when Queen Gloria spoke, King Boris listened; when Gloria asked, Boris gave; when Gloria ordered, Boris obeyed; what Gloria wanted, Boris delivered.

So it was that Queen Gloria influenced all the important decisions taken in Lundia; appointments to the Grand Chamber of State and to the High Chancery; setting the annual national budget; determining the level of taxes; determining foreign policy and even setting the date of public holidays, one of which Gloria insisted fell on her birthday.

And it was Queen Gloria who took all the small decisions herself, such as who should be invited to the frequent grand dinners, which entertainers should perform for their guests and even what her husband should wear.

King Boris the Brave hated being under the thumb of his wife and often daydreamed of being rid of her, but a day dream is just a day dream. The truth was that despite his name, the origin of which had been lost in the mists of time, although it was rumoured amongst those who drank in the local inn that he was given the appendage because he didn't cry when as a baby he was dropped onto the hard stone nursery floor by his wet nurse. Boris was not brave at all, in fact he was petrified of the consequences should he have their marriage annulled.

Gloria was well liked by her subjects, many of whom remembered with affection the pretty farmer's daughter who had caught the eye of the young King when she was just sixteen years of age and who had become their Queen the following year.

It's all very well those dolts idolising my wife, Boris thought, *but they don't have to suffer the lash of her tongue every day. By all the gods in Heaven, didn't he have reason enough to have his marriage annulled? Had his wife not failed to provide him with the son and heir he so desperately wanted?*

In fact, Gloria had failed to give birth to an heir, full stop; she was as barren as the icy wasteland that buttressed the western boundary of his kingdom and to which Boris would dearly love to banish his wife.

It was hardly surprising that in recent years their marriage had become loveless and sexless. To compensate for this emotional loss Gloria had taken comfort in a succession of worthy causes, the success of which endeared her even more to the good citizens of Lundia.

King Boris couldn't be bothered with worthy causes, which bored him to distraction, instead he comforted himself in the arms of a string of nubile, and very discreet, maidens from the far northern territories of his kingdom, an area that was renowned for producing statuesque blondes, the most recent of whom, a sweet young twenty-something called Marietta, had so bewitched him that he lay awake at night scheming about how he could see more of her. He was particularly put out because, despite all his energetic efforts, the young girl had refused stubbornly to share his bed.

Boris was confident that given time he could break down the girl's resistance, however, the problem was that the northern territories were hundreds of miles away and particularly difficult to reach in the fast approaching winter. Boris dared not risk the potentially hazardous journey once the October snows came and yet he was impatient for more time with Marietta. The solution came to him quite by chance in the shape of the Annual Michaelmas Fair.

Every year, once the harvest was safely stored away, farmers, tinkers and tradesmen would travel in from every part of Lundia for a huge two day fair that took place in the grounds of King Boris's castle in the country's capital of Auksberg.

There were scores of stalls, performers, wizards, fortune tellers and sweet pastry sellers, but one of the biggest attractions at the fair, just ahead of the bearded lady in popularity, was the talking goose.

Of course, everyone knew that the goose didn't really talk; this was obvious even to the hundreds of common folk who streamed to the fair to hand over ten santis for entry into the small tent in which the goose performed. They might be peasants, but they were not stupid peasants; they recognised a trick when they saw one. They knew that the goose's owner, Josef Volkman, a native of the northern territories, was not only an expert animal trainer, but was also a highly accomplished ventriloquist. But trick or not, the talking goose was still fantastic entertainment.

But King Boris knew the truth about Josef Volkman and his talking goose, because Mr Volkman just happened to be Marietta's father and she had revealed her father's secret on one un-chaperoned meeting, during which she consumed enough mead to be indiscreet, but without it affecting her ability to successfully fight off the attempt by Boris to seduce her.

Boris knew also that Marietta would be making the long trip to Auksberg with her father, as she had every year since her mother died. He realised this was a golden opportunity and laid his plans accordingly.

'I see in yer eye the look of a doubter, my friend, but I would ye hear the rest of me tale before making up yer mind, if it doth please ye so. 'Twas on Friday o'the last week o'September, in the twenty first year o'the reign of King Boris the Brave, tha' the good folken of Auksberg awoke t'the sights, sound and smells o'the Lundia Annual Michaelmas Fair. Let this humble story-teller set the scene fer ye.'

Bright indeed were the bunting and banners that flapped gently in the early autumn breeze; a group of musicians, dressed in colourful court dress, played patriotic tunes from a platform that had been erected against the castle wall, next to the drawbridge; fragrant smoke rose from wood fired stoves on which chestnuts were roasted, pies were baked and sausages were grilled.

It had rained heavily the previous day and the grounds of the castle were churned into a sea of mud by a thousand trampling feet, but nobody seemed to mind the slippery conditions, because any discomfort was counter balanced by a clear blue sky in which the sun was warm enough to remind people that although the short autumn was just round the corner, summer had not entirely deserted Lundia.

Certainly the mud did not dampen the enthusiasm of the young children who shouted excitedly as they chased each other through the canvas awnings of the maze of tents and stalls that were set out in a circle stretching from the moat in the south to the guardhouse that stood next to the entrance to the King's quarters.

Somewhere deep in the middle of the maze of stalls stood a small green canvas tent on the front of which was pinned a large sign that read:

Greta The Amazing Talking Goose!

The Lundia Annual Michaelmas Fair opened as the eight o'clock bell rang out from the chapel and a queue was already forming outside Greta's tent by five minutes after the hour had struck. The queue lengthened and shortened throughout the day, but never disappeared entirely. Such was the goose's popularity.

Of course, King Boris and Queen Gloria did not have to bother themselves with waiting in the queue to see Greta; such is the privilege of being head of an absolute monarchy. Instead, the tall figure of the Lord High Chancellor, Andris Vykrintas, pushed a passage for the royal couple through the knot of impatient citizens, eliciting not a few whispered grumbles as they strode majestically into the shadowy tent towards the gilt chair on which sat Josef Volkman's most profitable source of income.

Boris had seen Greta before, but this was his wife's first visit and her immediate reaction was one of disappointment. The goose was; well a goose. Okay, so the bird was sitting on a frayed satin cushion on a chair from which the tarnished gold gilt was peeling, but there was little doubt that Greta was still a bird, whose off-white feathers were showing obvious signs of moulting. It didn't help that

59

the goose looked up at Queen Gloria and made a noise that was somewhere between a squawk and a snort.

'Is that it?' Gloria asked scornfully. 'Is that all it does?'

'What did you expect?' Boris asked.

'I thought it would talk, not hoot at me.'

'It? Who is "It"?' The goose asked in an irritable voice. 'Hear me well, duchess. Mayhaps "It" might speak if thee was less rude.'

Gloria looked at the goose, astounded. 'Whaaat?'

'I be not an "it", I be a "she",' the goose repeated. 'And I'll happily talk t'thee, but only if thee treats me with respect. Do thee kenna, duchess?'

'I am not a duchess,' Gloria protested huffily. 'I am Queen Gloria of Lundia.'

'Oooooh! Excuse me for opening me beak,' the goose said, although, in fact, its beak neither opened nor closed; the words simply appeared to bubble up from deep within its long neck. 'I listen well t'thee, with thy posh voice and thy fancy ways, and I be overwhelmed wi' shame at meself, so I be.'

As Greta spoke, King Boris looked intently at Volkman and saw the man's lips move very slightly. He narrowed his eyes and smiled to himself. He had to admit that Josef was clever, very clever.

Gloria did not even glance at the goose's keeper; her full attention was concentrated on his bird. She blushed as its sarcastic words hit home. Despite her position and imperious nature, at heart she was a decent person who was proud of her humble background.

'I pray thy pardon, mistress, if it doth please ye so,' she said briefly in almost a whisper, using the country dialect of her youth. 'I fear I let me pride lead me t' forget the lessons in civility learned at the knee of me pa.'

The goose bobbed its head gently. 'I offer thee me pardon gladly, duchess, 'cos pardons cost naught,' the goose said, seemingly mollified by Gloria's contrition, then added: 'However, I canst nay pray thy pardon in return, duchess fer I kenna naught about civility, 'cos sadly I nay remember me pa nor his knee fer I fear he saw the inside of a hot oven long afore me beak broke the shell of me ma's egg.'

'Ask ye nay my pardon,' Queen Gloria replied, genuinely

touched by the goose's words. 'Ye may call me duchess, if it doth please ye so.'

'Thee are right kind, duchess, and thee may call me Greta. Are we well met then, thee and me, and shall we be friends?'

Gloria's face lit up with pleasure, transforming her previously somewhat dour features to a vision of beauty. Boris did not notice this change in his wife, but Andris Vykrintas did and smiled to himself. He studied the Queen discreetly from beneath his hooded intelligent eyes.

She was taller than many of the women who came from the southern border territories of Lundia, indeed she was almost as tall as her husband (who, truth to tell, was not the tallest bean pole in the bundle), although from the point of view of Vykrintas, she was pleasingly shorter than him. He liked that in a woman. However, Gloria's dark hair, olive skin, deep brown eyes and sensuous lips were typical of the looks of the sunnier climate enjoyed by children born in the region of her birth. This was not the first time that the Lord High Chancellor had admired from afar the Queen's beauty and the way her regal bearing emphasised the swell of her generous and shapely bosom.

'Aye, we are well met and I'd be right proud t'call ye my friend,' Gloria said.

'If it doth please thee so.' The bird dipped its head again, as if in tribute. 'So, let me tell thy fortune.'

It was well known throughout the kingdom that one of the highlights of Greta's performance was when she read the fortune of those who were rich enough, or stupid enough, the more cynical of Boris' subjects reckoned, to part with the two silver pieces that Josef Volkman now demanded be placed on the battered Tarot cards that were stacked neatly on the table in front of the chair on which the goose sat.

Queen Gloria was keen to witness this amazing act; she nudged her husband with a sharp elbow and indicated with her head that he should do the goose owner's bidding. With a sigh King Boris opened his pouch and took out two shiny 100 santis pieces and laid them on top of the Tarot cards.

Quick as a flash the goose picked up the coins with its beak and tossed them to its owner with a twist of its long neck. Volkman caught both coins in mid air and in the same deft movement slipped them into the pocket of his tunic. The small crowd that clustered round the Royal couple burst into applause at this show of dexterity.

'Shuffle the cards, if it doth please thee so, duchess,' Greta said, nudging the pack a couple of inches towards Gloria.

That trick with the cards alone was worth the 10 santis entrance fee paid by those of my folken who entered this place, King Boris decided, as he watched his wife skilfully shuffle the large Tarot cards. Gloria put the cards back on the table in an untidy pile that the goose nudged into a neat pile with its beak.

'Turn o'er the top card and place it on the table afore thee,' Greta said.

Queen Gloria reached towards the pack of cards, but stopped as a sudden chill of foreboding froze the muscles in her arm before her fingers could touch the top Tarot card.

But unlike her husband, Gloria had courage and determination; she quickly shrugged aside her misgivings and forced herself to pick up the top card before laying it gently on the table in front of her, face up, to reveal the picture of a knight sitting on a horse carrying a scythe. There was a sharp intake of breath from the spectators who were watching the bizarre vignette with wide eyes.

The visor of the knight's helmet was raised to reveal the head of a skeleton and across the top of the card was printed: **XIII DEATH**.

Gloria looked up at the goose; suddenly her face was almost as white as the horse on which the knight sat.

'Be nay alarmed, duchess,' Greta said in a soft voice. 'There's more t'death card than thee might suppose. Aye, 'tis true the thirteenth card canst bring bad luck, and aye, it canst mean the ending o'life, or, a relationship, but hear me well, the death card canst mean just as well the beginning o' both. So, turn o'er another two cards, if it doth please thee so, and let thee and me see wha' events lay ahead fer thee.'

Without hesitation, and with a steady hand that belied the turmoil in both her head and her heart, Gloria turned over another two cards. The first showed a woman wearing a crown sitting on a chair, the words at the top of the card read: **III THE EMPRESS**.

The second showed four crossed wooden staffs; written at the top of the card was the number **IV** and at the bottom the word **WANDS**.

The goose stared down intently at the cards. 'Aaaah!' It mused eventually. 'I see fertility. I see a change in thy life. I see a long, dark corridor leading t'bedroom decked in crimson silk. I see tiny feet and hear the tinkle o'childish laughter.' Greta looked up at the Queen. 'There be a babby on the way.'

Gloria clasped her hands to her breast. *Could this be?* She asked herself. *Is it possible that our long wait will soon be over?* So taken was she with the notion of bearing a child and providing Boris with the heir that he so desperately wanted, she quite forgot she and her husband had not shared a bed for over five years.

But Boris had not forgotten; he studiously stared down at his fingernails, so as not to betray his true feelings, nor, give any hint of his plans for the future. 'God's teeth!' He declared. 'That's a rum prediction and no mistake.'

He looked up finally and smiled kindly at his wife, although any warmth in his smile failed to reach his piercing blue eyes. Despite not being particularly tall, Boris was an imposing figure who had been considered handsome in his early years. He had a sturdy frame, but some of his muscle, built up by a still burning passion for field sports, was beginning to turn to fat as he approached his forty-third birthday. He had a ruddy complexion, with hair and a bushy beard of a reddish tinge that betrayed his Nordic ancestry.

'Come my dear,' Boris said. 'I fear it is time to leave the future and concentrate on the present. We have many other fair attractions to visit this day.'

'But I would that the goose tells me more,' Gloria protested, reverting to the language of the court.

'Nay, duchess. Two silver pieces gets thee but a three card reading,' the bird explained. Its beak opened slightly wider and for a moment Gloria could have sworn that it was laughing at her.

'Then we shall pay you another two pieces of silver, won't we Boris?'

'Another day, madam, another day.' Boris took his wife's arm and eased her towards the exit. 'I promise we shall have the goose and its master visit the castle soon and you will have your fortune read in private and to your heart's content, although there is much I would tell you of both man and beast.'

'How soon?'

Boris turned to his Lord High Chancellor. 'The Michaelmas Fair finishes on the morrow. Make arrangements for the goose keeper to bring the bird to the throne room on the Sabbath, immediately after morning service. I would discuss with him purchase of the goose.'

Andris Vykrintas bobbed his head in a brief bow. 'If it pleases your highness.'

'Does it please you?' Boris asked his wife.

'Yes, my husband.' Gloria squeezed Boris's arm and unashamedly fluttered her eyelashes at him. She could not remember when she had felt happier. 'Perhaps there is something in what the goose predicted,' she whispered in his ear: 'Perhaps, tonight we should... you know...'

Boris did indeed know and immediately decided that tonight, and mayhap tomorrow, he would get drunk such that he would be capable of nothing other than snoring should he manage to stagger down the staircase to his wife's bed chamber.

He knew Gloria would be upset and very angry if he failed to visit her chamber, but that was a price worth paying to avoid her bed. More importantly, her anger would stoke up the resentment that was such an important part of his plan.

'Well, stranger, wha' thinks ye o'me tale thus far? D'ye kenna yet the twisted path it be taking? Ye say, naught, but methinks ye'd hear if King Boris gauged well the depth o'his Queen's anger. Then I'll nay tease ye further; ye should know tha' Boris had the truth o'it. Gloria was right angry, but in tha' way at least her reaction was surely predictable; but the chain of events tha' led from her anger was less so, fer it were t'have far reaching consequences fer the good folken of Lundia. But, I get ahead of myself, fer first I must tell ye o'certain other things.'

King Boris the Brave's ploy worked and he made it through to Sunday without visiting his wife's bed, although he did have a thumping headache and a mouth that tasted like an elk's arse;

however, even these side effects of his mead soaked binge had disappeared by noon when the Lord High Chancellor entered the throne room followed by Josef Volkman, who in turn had his goose waddling along behind him.

Andris Vykrintas took his place behind a long table positioned against the side wall, on which were stacked a number of large books. He glanced over at the Queen, who sat on a throne next to her husband. Gloria sensed the High Chancellor's eyes on her and turned her head slightly to enable her to look directly into his eyes. She felt a flutter of excitement in her stomach and nodded imperceptibly before quickly returning her attention to the goose and its keeper.

Boris did not notice the exchange of glances between Gloria and Vykrintas, but if he had, it would never have occurred to him that it was anything other than natural pleasantness; he certainly would never have guessed that when he had failed to turn up the previous evening, his angry wife had sought out the Lord High Commissioner to let off steam.

Andris Vykrintas had been a willing listener and Gloria had opened up to him in a way she had never done with anyone else before. Her anger had turned to tears of self pity and Andris had comforted Gloria, showing her the tenderness for which she had long craved. One thing led to another and for the first time in her life Gloria shared the bed of a man other than her husband. It had been a new, exciting and deeply satisfying experience.

Now, as King Boris smiled down at Volkman from the top of the steps on which his throne was perched. Queen Gloria, who sat next to her husband on an identical throne, felt a warm glow of fulfilment and expectation. She had been pleased also by a promise from Boris to buy the goose, although typically he tried to pour cold water on her enthusiasm by claiming that the goose did not really talk and that it was all a ventriloquist's trick. Gloria had refused to believe him and insisted Boris bought the goose anyway.

'So, my friend, how much must I pay to take ownership of your fine goose?' Boris asked without preamble.

Volkman shook his head sadly. 'I pray thy pardon, sire, but 'tis nay as easy as tha'. Greta would nay survive without me here t'look after her.'

'Surely we can come to some arrangement, good fellow; how much for your services?'

'Naught would gi'me more pleasure than t'serve thee so, sire, but sadly I've many other beasts t'look after and winter draws nigh, if thee kenna.'

'Then I shall look after her.' Gloria said in a voice that broached no argument.

Volkman looked thoughtfully at the Queen. 'Well, 'tis true me goose seems taken wi'thee, but Greta be right sensitive and pines something terrible when she be adrift from them she knows best.'

'Is there nobody else who could take your place and comfort the bird until it became more used to my wife?' Boris asked.

Volkman shrugged and rubbed his chin.

The Lord High Chancellor stood up with a rustle of his heavy fur lined cloak and coughed discreetly.

'What about your daughter?' He asked. 'Did she not accompany you to the fair?' His questions were delivered more as statements, reminding them that his network of spies kept him well informed of everything that took place in the kingdom. Queen Gloria immediately latched on to this information.

'Is it true?' She asked the farmer eagerly. 'Is your daughter really here in Auksberg?'

Volkman nodded his head. 'Aye, 'tis true me dotter be with me and even now she prepares the horses fer our journey north.'

'But that is perfect!' Gloria said. 'The girl can help me look after the goose until we have bonded properly?'

'Well, 'tis as likely as nay tha' Greta would take t'thee better wi'me dotter fer company, so she would,' Volkman agreed. 'But I be nay sure Marietta would agree t'stay in Auksberg. Fer a start, where'd she live? I'd nay see a dotter o'mine stay in the Blue Boar. It be nay seemly, if thee kenna me meaning?'

'That is not a problem,' Gloria said. 'She can stay here in the castle. We have more than enough bed chambers, including one close to the King's own stable, where the goose could be housed. Is that not the truth of it Lord High Chancellor?'

Andris Vykrintas nodded his agreement, the expression on his face inscrutable.

'Will you not at least ask her?' Gloria urged the farmer.

'Aye, majesty. I'll ask her, if it doth please thee so, but I make naught promises about the direction of her answer.'

'Then you shall ask her this very minute,' Gloria insisted, leaping from her throne. 'I will come with you and tell her all about the lovely chamber that will be hers. It has the most glorious drapes and linens and I know that she will love it.' She tugged Volkman's arm and pulled him towards the door. 'Come, come, let us go.'

So excited was Gloria, as she dragged the farmer from the throne room, that she failed to notice the knowing look the farmer exchanged with King Boris.

'Aye, as ye'll see, my friend, the plot doth thicken and there be intrigue in the air. I'd ye kenna the truth o'it, 'cos much blood is t'be spilled afore me tale be ended. Ye'd kenna also 'twas our noble King Boris who did set the tragedy in motion when, in a manner o'speaking, it be he who unlatched the paddock gate and let his prize cow escape.

'For, unbeknown t'Boris, his Queen had dipped her toe in the waters of adultery and had found the sensation right pleasing. Gloria decided t'visit more of the Sea of Desire and was nay disappointed wi' wha' she found there. However, her joy at tasting again the fruits o'womanhood was muted somewhat by her problem wi' the goose.'

'How many times must I tell you? The goose cannot talk. Can you not understand this simple fact; Volkman is nothing other than a very clever ventriloquist? That is the truth of the matter.' Boris looked down at his wife and saw that she was not convinced. 'Look, whatever you might choose to believe, a goose is just a goose and geese do not talk!' The King's voice had an edge to it now as he became increasingly more exasperated.

He pointed to the bird that lay sleeping on a silk cushion positioned on the floor in front of the blazing fire that warmed up the robing room in which they sat. 'That thing has been with us for over two weeks now and has not uttered a word. All it does is eat, sleep and shit.' Boris stared down at the goose through narrowed eyes.

'Most of which seems to find its way onto my boots!'

'Eating makes Greta happy and she needs to be happy and content if we want her to talk.'

'So where is the girl? Was she not meant to keep the goose happy?'

'Marietta decided that Greta is so comfortable now in my company that it was time for me to start looking after her on my own.'

'Well, time for the goose is running out. If it's going to talk it had better do so by the end of the week, because if it remains silent a minute longer, it will find itself looking at the inside of our largest roasting pan.'

'Shush!' Gloria warned. 'She will hear you.'

'Shush yourself, woman,' Boris said jumping to his feet and heading for the door. 'I've had enough of this nonsense. I'm off hunting.' He opened the door and was about to step into the corridor beyond when he stopped and turned back towards his wife. 'But hear me well; that stupid bird has until this coming Sabbath to find its tongue, or, I will take great delight in personally ripping it out from its throat and using it as stuffing.'

With those final words of warning Boris slammed the door and stormed off in the direction of his stables. Gloria stared silently at the door and felt a tear roll down her cheek.

'Fret thee nay, duchess,' a voice said. 'Mayhap, 'twill nay be me saying goodbye t'this world.'

Gloria looked at the goose with a look of joy. 'Ye *canst* talk!' She exclaimed, lapsing into the dialect of her youth.

'Aye, that I can, when it pleases me so.'

'But ye've said naught for two weeks. Oh, how I wish it had pleased ye t'speak such just a short time ago when me husband were present.'

'Mayhap I still had naught to say, but I were listening and listening well. Doth thee kenna?'

'But yer eyes were closed. I thought ye were asleep.'

'Doth *thee* hear with thine eyes?'

'I take yer point! So ye heard everything that me husband said?'

'Of course.'

'So ye canst see why I be so upset.'

'Aye and I be right taken wi'thee fer thy concern.'

'Oh, Greta, what are we t'do?'

'Well, fer a start I'll read thy fortune again, if it doth please thee so.'

Gloria immediately felt her spirits rise. She nodded and said: 'I'll fetch the cards. They be in the drawer o'me dressing table. Wait here.'

'I be going on nay journeys, duchess.'

Soon Gloria was back and had placed a low table in front of the goose and laid the pack of cards on its weather beaten surface. She pulled her chair closer to the table and sat down, staring across expectantly at the goose.

'Thee kenna wha' t'do. Shuffle the pack, turn o'er the top card and lay it face up on the table.'

Gloria did as she was told and soon The Emperor lay on the table, although the picture was upside down with the name facing towards the goose. Gloria reached to turn the card round the other way but Greta tapped her hand gently with her beak.

'Nay, duchess, leave the card as 'tis.'

'How so?' The Queen asked.

''Tis right important fer a true reading. Ye should kenna the meaning of a reversed card be different t'upright card,' the bird explained. 'Now deal thee eight more cards and place them, one at a time, in the position I show thee. Doth thee kenna?'

Gloria nodded, turned over the next card and laid it where the goose indicated, directly above the first card. It was The Empress and was also reversed. The next card was the Five of Wands and went on the table above The Empress. This was followed by The Lovers and The Wheel of Fortune, both of which were laid in turn below The Emperor on the table. The final four cards were The Star, which was reversed and showed a picture of a full breasted naked woman, The Devil, The Queen of Swords and a card showing a man wrestling with a lion, which depicted Strength. The former two cards were laid on the table directly to the right of The Emperor and the latter two were positioned to its left.

The goose stared silently at the cards for what seemed an age before saying in a soft voice: 'This card represents thy husband.' She tapped The Emperor. 'Being reversed shows him t'be weak and untrustworthy.'

Queen Gloria nodded her agreement, but did not speak.

'Thee must be on thy guard fer plots agin thee,' the goose said before tapping The Empress. 'This card speaks of domestic upheaval and infertility.'

Gloria frowned. How could the goose know such things? This was indeed magic. 'And what of the next card?' She asked hurriedly, not wanting to dwell on such a delicate subject. 'What manner of card is this?' She pointed to a card that showed five crossed staffs.

'Why, 'tis but the Five of Wands and it speaks much o'the disagreement, strife and tension betwixt thy husband and thee I did touch on previous, but it shows naught the cause.' Greta paused before saying: 'Note thee well this next card 'cos 'tis The Lovers and hints at a new carnal adventure for thee, or, somebody close t'thee.'

Gloria blushed and insisted hurriedly: 'Well 'tis nay me!'

'Thee nay can say tha' fer sure, duchess, 'cos the morrow is a new day, but if 'tis true then it canst only mean...' The goose let the rest of her words dangle and instead moved on quickly to the next card that showed a wheel on which were perched three monkeys. 'Verily, 'tis The Wheel of Fortune,' she explained, 'and it shows me that somebody, be changing the path of thy life. Mayhap the next card shows who tha' might be.' The goose tapped The Star. 'It be somebody thee nay canst trust; somebody who wishes thee ill; somebody who plots agin thee.'

'Who is this person?'

Greta swayed her long neck to make her head move from side to side. 'On tha' matter the cards are silent, but wha' be clear is this card,' she tapped a card showing the horned figure of The Devil, accompanied by two naked maidens, 'shows thee carry the burden o'despair and hopelessness on thy shoulders.'

The goose looked at Gloria intently. 'But, Duchess, everything be nay lost. There be some fair signs fer thee. This card, fer instance, represents strength. It be as plain as the nose on thy face thee has courage and patience in abundance. Methinks, thee will need both in good measure in the days tha' lay afore thee, so thee will.'

'And the final card?'

'The Queen of Swords. Another fair card tha' shows thee canst defeat thy enemies, but thee must prepare thyself. Remember tha' dangerous days lie ahead fer thee; identify them who would'st do thee harm; and lay well thy plans t'defeat them. Doth thee kenna?'

Queen Gloria nodded slowly, but said nothing; instead she stared down at the Tarot cards with a thoughtful expression on her face. She needed to speak with Andris Vykrintas without delay. The goose said nothing either, it simply watched her with its mouth wide open in its silent, mocking laugh.

'Methinks, stranger, ye would I reveal t'ye wha' business King Boris was about whilst his Queen was in discourse wi'the goose. Ye need t'think lust. Lust has a right strange impact o'er the minds o'grown men; it leads them t'lose all reason in pursuit o'their carnal urges; they remember nay the lessons o'good sense learned a'the knee o'their pas; they let their loins rule their heads and them o'royal blood be nay immune. And so 'twas the King's pleasure t'visit the chamber of the goose keeper's dotter with lust large in his mind.'

'Well if I may not touch you at least let me look at you,' King Boris pleaded after his advances had been rebuffed by the tall blonde girl who stood in front of him.

Marietta giggled and pirouetted in the middle of her bed chamber, pulling out the sides of her dress, so that it rose high up her shin as she spun, revealing her frilly underskirt and shiny red shoes. As she giggled, her breasts moved enticingly beneath the clinging satin bodice of her dress.

'By all the gods in Heaven, my beauty,' Boris moaned in frustration, 'but you have a pert body and no mistake.'

'Why thankee, sire. But are ye not taken wi'the fair clothes I put on special for ye?'

'The clothes are as pert as you, but I would prefer they were hanging on any other body but yours right now.'

'Mayhap yer wife's?' Marietta grinned.

'You tease me wench! You know well what I mean.'

'But did yer wife nay loan me both dress and shoes 'cos I needed something nice t'wear? And was it nay she who said t'would nay be seemly fer me t'be living in such a grand chamber wearing naught but me farm clothes. Mayhap some day, sire, ye will teach me words in the manner o'the court, so I canst speak as fine as I dress?'

'I care not what you wear, my beauty, the less the better, I say. As for your mouth, I have other uses for it than to teach it new words. I would kiss you such that your body craves mine the way I crave you.'

Marietta giggled again. ''Tis words such as them tha' warn me I must take care when I be alone in yer company.'

'I am but flesh and bones, with desires like any other man.'

'Aye, and 'tis such desires tha' worry me greatly.'

'I could take you anyway,' Boris said; a hint of anger in his voice, 'right here and now, on the floor of your chamber. See the snake of desire is ready.' He pointed to his groin where a hard shape pushed out the front of his silk trousers.

''Tis true, me lord,' Marietta said softly, 'ye could take me at yer pleasure and do wi'me as ye will, for I'd nay fight ye.' She held her right hand in the air in silent testament: 'But I swear on the grave of me dear departed ma tha' me body would be nay more exciting for ye than a bag of me da's taters. Hear me well, sire.'

'I hear you very well, my beauty,' Boris replied, all the anger gone from his voice. 'But...'

'But naught, sire. I wager ye'd much prefer to have me willing and wanton when ye lay wi'me. Be tha' the truth o'it?' As she spoke Marietta moved close to the King, her bosom pressing gently against his chest. Without warning she kissed him on the mouth and at the same time dropped her hand to squeeze him firmly, but agonisingly briefly.

He groaned and tried to put his arms about her waist, but she easily shrugged him aside and stepped back quickly, moving out of his reach.

She grinned at him, her eyes sparkling with merriment. 'Sire, mayhap me touch will remind ye wha' pleasures await if ye be patient. Of course, that's if ye do still want me?'

'Ye gods, I want you, wench. I want you such that I will explode if I am denied you much longer.'

'Ye kenna wha'be needed, sire. Unless ye want me t'wipe yer innards from the walls of me chamber ye'd best do something about yer wife and do it right quick.'

'Now hear me well, my beauty. I swear before all the gods in heaven there is nothing that I want more, except to feel your sweet young body 'neath mine.' Boris smiled knowingly at the girl. 'Trust me well when I say that the time is close when I shall have both my wishes come true.'

'Is tha' the truth of it, me lord?'

'Yes it is.'

'And how will this come about?' Marietta asked, so Boris told her about his plan.

'And be me goose a willing party to yer plan?' She asked.

'Aye, a more than willing party.'

'And when will the deed be done?'

'That, my beauty, is something best left unsaid at this time; you need but know that I speak true. It is going to happen and I will be rid of my burden at last.'

'Then mayhap ye'll have yer pleasure with me earlier than ye think.'

Taking this as an invitation Boris reached for the girl, but she pushed him away again. 'Nay, sire, t'aint yet the time.'

'And so, my friend, the flame o'King Boris's lust was fanned and naught could stop our drama hurtling t'wards its tragic end. Would ye hear more o'Boris and his plan? Aye, methinks ye would and who am I t'deprive ye of yer entertainment? But, be warned, stranger, the pace moves rapidly. The next act sees Queen Gloria pleading with Greta to talk.'

'You must believe me, husband, she was talking.'

'Well, the damn bird is not talking now!'

'But Greta told my fortune, as she did at the fair,' Gloria insisted. 'And then we spoke of many things. I swear to you my husband that I am telling the truth.'

'I am sure you believe you are, woman, but I fear you were

either dreaming, or, had a sudden turn of the vapours. I will ask the apothecary to make you up a potion to still the turmoil in your mind.'

'I need no potion,' Queen Gloria insisted crossly. 'I had no vapours and I was not dreaming.'

'Then let me hear the goose talk.'

Gloria looked at Greta through eyes that narrowed dangerously. 'Listen, my friend, show him the truth of my words, or, it will be the worse for you.'

The goose stared back at Gloria from its silk cushion, but said nothing.

'Talk to me as you did before.' The Queen's voice was ice cold and menacing.

'It matters not if and when the bird talked to you, woman,' the King said. 'For you cannot deny it now is as silent as the rubbish pit into which its bone picked carcass will be thrown next week.'

'Hear him well,' Gloria hissed again, 'this is no idle threat he makes. You are at deadly risk if you remain silent.'

The goose looked from Gloria to Boris and back again. For one moment Gloria thought Greta was going to speak, but instead she closed her eyes and went to sleep.

'I'm sorry I were angry with ye yesterday,' Gloria said to the goose the next day when they were alone in her chamber, 'but I'm afeared for your safety. D'ye nay kenna that me husband will have ye killed if he has nay heard ye speak by the end of this week?'

'I understand right well, Duchess.'

'Then why did ye nay talk when asked?'

'Cos 'twould make nay difference to me fortune. D'ye nay kenna tha' thy husband's mind is set; talk, or, nay, come the Sabbath this goose is t'die.'

'But we cannot allow that to happen, Greta. We must do something!'

'Mayhap there be a way.'

'How so?' Gloria asked hopefully. So the goose told the Queen its plan.

For the next three days Boris insisted that Gloria bring the goose to the throne room each morning so that he could interrogate it. The Queen happily obliged, half hoping that Greta would change her mind and talk in front of Boris, thereby allowing her to avoid the dreadful deed that she had agreed to undertake. But the goose said nothing and on the following Saturday Boris sealed his own fate.

'Tomorrow is the Sabbath,' he said, 'and I have instructed cook to prepare a banquet, the centrepiece of which will be this plump goose that sits before us. What say you to that, wife?'

'As you will, husband,' Gloria said obediently, looking down so that Boris could not see the hatred and anger in her eyes. *So the die is cast,* she thought and began to lay her plans even as her husband strode from the throne room and headed towards the stables for his afternoon ride. She glanced across to where Andris Vykrintas sat at his book laden table writing on a velum sheet. Perhaps good might come of this after all. She thought, allowing herself a secret little smile.

Marietta was waiting for Boris when he visited her bed chamber that afternoon; as was his custom on returning from his hard daily ride. As usual he was drenched with sweat from his exertions and had the smell of the stables about his body. Marietta was put off by neither the sweat nor the smell; indeed as the days went by she found both them, and the King himself, increasingly alluring.

Each time Boris visited was the same; he tried to seduce Marietta and was left frustrated when she fought him off. But each day he won a little more ground, with the girl allowing him to take slightly more liberties and let their kisses become increasingly more passionate, to such an extent that by Saturday afternoon she let him explore beneath her skirts as far as her knee and fondle her breasts through the tight bodice of her dress as they kissed.

'Nay, sire, nay!' Marietta pushed Boris away from her. 'T'aint yet time.' But the warm feeling in her lower pelvic region hinted that her body was not listening to her voice. The truth was that she liked the taste of tobacco on the King's lips as he kissed her; she liked the roughness of his beard against her soft cheek; she liked the musky smell of his manhood; she liked the feeling of the silk bodice rubbing against her nipples as the King's calloused hands kneaded her breasts; and above all she liked the intoxicating sensation as he pressed his groin against hers.

'Then when?' Boris asked; his voice husky with unfulfilled lust.

'Soon, sire. I promise.'

'How soon?'

'Mayhap the morrow,' Marietta replied before thinking: *And mayhap earlier!* Once again she felt the heat grow between her legs as she looked down at the hard bulge in the front of the King's trousers.

'In that case tomorrow cannot come soon enough.'

'Certainly nay fer yer trousers, which likely will be ruined if we do naught 'bout taming yer snake of desire?' She giggled. *And me own desire.* She thought. *I can nay wait another hour t'satisfy me longings, let alone another day!*

'Night fell early tha' fateful Saturday, if ye kenna, as black rainclouds clouds spread 'cross the sky from the north, snuffing out wha' daylight were left. 'Midst the gloom tha' filled Auksberg Castle three bodies made their preparations fer later tha' eve.'

Marietta sneaked along a darkened corridor, her features hidden by the hood of the black cloak she wore. She reached a flight of stairs. Quickly, but silently, she went up the stairs until she found herself in another, narrower corridor that led directly to the Queen's chamber. She pressed her ear against the door but hearing nothing she pushed it open gently and with heart in mouth she slipped into the room. She needn't have worried; the chamber was deserted and as quiet as a graveyard. Queen Gloria was about her own business in another part of the castle.

Marietta carried in one hand a thin metal candlestick from which a tallow candle cast a giant, flickering shadow on the grey granite walls of the chamber. She knew where to head and quickly found what she was looking for in the far corner of the chamber. She pulled aside a heavy satin curtain to reveal a rail on which hung more dresses than any maid could expect to wear in a lifetime.

Slowly and delicately she brushed her hand across the store of dresses, feeling under her fingertips the fantastic fabrics with which they were made; satin, filoselle, lamé, velvet, lace, damask, chiffon and taffeta. She had never seen such luxury. This was a veritable treasure trove of clothes. Eventually, her eyes settled on a white damask shift dress. She smiled. It would be perfect for her needs; pure, simple and virginal. She slipped the dress from its hook and tucked it under her arm beneath her clock. She knew that in this dress she would be irresistible. She smiled to herself and thought: *I warrant any dress I wear t'King's chamber this night will remain nay long on me.* But on that she was wrong. Horribly wrong.

Marietta closed the curtains and tiptoed silently towards the door. She was about to reach for the handle when her eyes caught sight of a pair of red slippers thrown carelessly under the bench that stood against the far wall. She recognised them immediately. The Queen wore them often and the young girl had coveted them since first she had cast eyes on them. They were beautiful, with an intricate pattern of beads sewn into the shiny satin material from which they were made.

She cocked her ear and reassured by the silence in the corridor outside the room she ran quickly to the bench and snatched up the slippers. Their extravagance would highlight the simplicity of the dress. She wanted everything to be right because tonight she intended giving King Boris an evening to remember. She smiled as her stomach fluttered with excitement. She would have an evening to remember also and if the King's plan succeeded it would be the first of many such evenings.

At about the same time Marietta was rummaging through Gloria's dresses to find something suitable to wear, the Queen was sneaking into the castle's main kitchen. Although the cook and his assistants had already finished for the day, Gloria could see that preparations for the next day's banquet were well under way.

Despite the kitchen being deserted and dark, the air in the big room was heavy with delicious cooking smells: smoked ham and boiled bacon; the aromatic sweetness of the thick, dark honey that had been used to coat the haunch of roast venison; the sharp tang of vinegar in which mixed pickles were being soaked; pungent herbs from the castle kitchen garden, which were drying from a rack hanging from the ceiling; and underpinning all these smells was the sweet fragrance of the pine logs that had been used to heat the kitchen's ovens.

But no food was visible; it had all been stored away in the huge larder that filled most of the wall at the end of a long kitchen dominated by a heavy oak bench that stood in the middle of the floor.

Along the left hand wall stretched a huge cooking range, its wood fuelled stoves still hot to the touch. On opposite wall hung a long line of pans and other kitchen utensils, including knives of all sizes and descriptions. She smiled; it was for one of these that she was visiting the kitchen.

Gloria tested the blade of each tentatively with her finger. The goose's instructions had been explicit; the knife should be very sharp and of a size such that it could be concealed beneath her cloak.

She found a knife that was perfect for her needs; it was about six inches long, had a well worn handle and the blade had been honed so many times that parts of it were only as wide as her finger. The blade finished in a fine point and was razor sharp.

She smiled in satisfaction, secreted the knife in the inside pocket of her heavy black cloak, slipped back out of the kitchen and headed for her chamber to wait patiently for the Harvest Moon to show itself above the far horizon. That would be the time to strike.

At the precise moment that Gloria was smiling to herself in the kitchen, King Boris was smiling down at the goose, which was settled on a bed of hay in the stable.

'Are you sure it is as you say?'

'Aye, majesty, I warrant it so.' Greta replied. 'The Queen even now visits the kitchen t'select the weapon she's t'use t'end thy life.'

'And you told her what to do?'

'Aye, my lord, as ye instructed; I explained the type o'knife t'select; where t'hide it such that she nay be detected should she happen upon one o'thy servants. I told her t'wear soft shoes such tha' she be as quiet as a church mouse; how best t'stab thee if thee be abed and what t'do mayhap she were called on t'creep up on thee from behind.'

'Which of course will be the case.'

'Aye, but I could nay tell her tha'.'

'You say it true, my feathered friend. And when does she intend to strike?'

'This very eve, sire; when the Harvest Moon doth first show itself in the sky.'

'You have done well. Your master will be well rewarded.'

'He'll be right pleased, sire.'

'On the rising of the moon, you say?'

'Aye, if it doth please thee, majesty.'

'Then time is pressing and I must be away to prepare myself.'

'Stranger, I sense ye knows me strange tale approaches its climax and in tha' ye'd be right. The final act o' our little drama is well nigh. Plans are laid, the stage is set and the three principle characters are on a collision course tha' I warrant'll have disastrous consequences fer at least one o'the players.

'If we look right close we'll see the first actor on the scene is the youngest and the fairest by far, if it doth please ye. The dotter of Josef the goose keeper, makes her way silently along the long dark corridor tha' leads t'the King's chamber. The flickering light from the stubby beeswax candle atop the candlestick she carries throws shadows across the delicate features o'her face; half hidden as 'twas by the hood o'her robe.'

Marietta stopped at an arched window that was set into the wall halfway along the corridor. She peered out across the fields that circled the castle and saw that the clouds had drifted off towards the south, leaving behind a clear, star filled sky and rain soaked fields. The smallest sliver of moon rose slowly from the depths of the dark landscape.

Marietta smiled; she loved the moon and being a farmer's daughter the Harvest Moon was her favourite. Suddenly a gust of wind blew through the window and snuffed out the stub of candle.

The girl swore silently to herself; she carried no tinder box with which to relight the candle. She hesitated for a few seconds, weighing up whether or not to return to her chamber, but the Harvest Moon was already beginning to send a shaft of moonbeam through the window, so she decided that its insipid light would have to be enough for her to find her way along the corridor. She shrugged her shoulders, slipped the candlestick into the pocket of her robe and headed towards the king's chamber.

What Marietta did not know was that this was a decision she would not live long enough to regret.

King Boris peeked out from behind the curtain concealing the alcove in which he stood. With one hand he pulled open the curtain just far enough so that he could see through the crack with one eye, and with the other he grasped the handle of a long sword.

Boris froze as he heard the soft pad of footsteps approaching the alcove and felt his muscles tense as a shadow passed across his line of vision, but he relaxed somewhat when the footsteps went past the alcove without stopping. He pulled open the curtain a fraction more and saw the figure of a woman tip-toeing towards the chair that stood in front of the fireplace. In the chair sat what looked remarkably like a man, but was in fact nothing more than a cleverly disguised scarecrow. Boris was well satisfied with his handiwork.

The woman wore a dark cloak from beneath which could be seen the hem of white satin dress and a pair of red beaded slippers that he recognised immediately. Boris nodded in satisfaction. The slippers belonged to his wife and were made from the softest (and quietest) satin. It looked as if his plan was working, thanks to the goose.

Gently and noiselessly Boris swept aside the curtain and crept after his wife, who from her body language had no clue she was being followed.

The woman stopped behind the chair and took a knife from beneath her cloak. Boris moved in closer, hardly daring to breathe, and as he did he distinctly heard a giggle. The bitch! He raised the sword in anticipation.

When Gloria left the kitchen she returned immediately to her chamber, where she removed the wooden shutter from her window, drew up a chair, pulled her heavy robe about her and sat staring out into the night. She had thought she would be scared by the task she faced, but instead she felt remarkably composed.

She took the knife from her cloak pocket and laid it on her lap. She ran her finger along the cold metal blade and smiled as she settled down to wait for the moon to rise. It was not a pleasant smile. She closed her eyes and, despite the chill in the night air, she dozed.

When Gloria awoke the Harvest Moon was already starting its journey in the night sky. She sprang to her feet and ran towards the stairs that led to her husband's chamber.

Marietta gently pushed open the door and slipped into the King's chamber, which was lit by a blazing fire that crackled and sputtered from a fireplace set into the far wall. Sitting hunched in a heavy oak chair, slumbering in front of the fire, was the unmistakeable figure of the king. He wore a fur robe pulled up round his ears and a nightcap on his head.

She left the door ajar and tip-toed across the stone floor towards the King with a mischievous smile on her face. When she was within a pace of the sleeping man she took the candlestick from beneath her robe and clutched it in her right hand, with her other she covered her mouth to stifle a giggle.

The young girl reached out and gently poked the King's back with the candlestick. The stub of candle pushed into fur robe and left a wax mark on it, but there was no reaction from the King. She prodded him again, more sharply and this time he moved, falling slowly forward from the chair onto his face.

Marietta was so startled that it never once crossed her mind to question why the King would be wearing a fur coat and hat whilst sitting in front of such a hot fire; but then it is mistakes such as these that are the difference between life and death.

Boris watched as the woman he thought was his wife reached out and stabbed twice. The force of the second lunge caused the scarecrow to topple forward and as it did so the King struck. He swung the long sword in a wide arc and brought it down on the back of his wife's cloak at the base of the hood.

There was a loud thwack as the sword sliced through the heavy cloth of the cloak before connecting with flesh, bone and tendons as it severed his wife's neck with a gush of blood that flew quickly across the grey granite hearth in a fine spray.

The woman's head, detached from her body, popped from the hood by the force of the sword's blow fell with a thud on the floor next to the chair, where it lay amidst a mass of blood stained blonde hair looking up at Boris through sightless blue eyes.

The body stood upright for several seconds before finally realising it was missing a vital part; it dropped the candlestick and then collapsed in a heap on the opposite side of the chair to where the head had landed. Boris stared at Marietta's head in stunned disbelief and mounting horror. He dropped the sword with a clatter, picked up the head and cradled it lovingly in his arms.

And that's exactly how Gloria found him a few seconds later.

When Gloria found the door to her husband's chamber ajar, she hesitated briefly before slipping through the gap and padding quietly into the room. Boris was standing at the other end of the room, staring down at something cradled in his arms.

It was only when she was within touching distance of her husband that the Queen saw what he was holding and with mounting horror she saw the body lying on the floor on the other side of the chair.

Boris looked up at his wife with bemused eyes.

'She's dead,' he said in a voice that sounded as if he was trying to convince himself he was wrong. 'I don't understand; it was supposed to be you come to finish me off, not her.'

Gloria nodded, her brain whirling, she quickly took in the grisly scene and immediately worked out what had happened. She pulled the knife from within the pocket of her cloak.

'And so I have,' she said as she drove the knife deep into Boris's heart with a single thrust. The King let out a gasp before toppling over backwards, still clasping Marietta's head to his chest, pushing over the heavy chair as he fell.

Gloria bent over and took the head from her husband's dead embrace and positioned it close to the dead girl, then she pulled the knife from her husband's chest and after wiping its handle she put it in Marietta's hand.

As Gloria stood up she noticed the candlestick lying on the floor under the upturned chair. She pushed her husband's body from the chair and pulled the heavy chair to the side of the chamber where it usually stood; picked up the candlestick and stood it on the bedside table; stripped Boris's robe and hat from the scarecrow and stashed them away in the alcove in which the rest of her husband's clothes hung; finally she picked up the scarecrow and was about to throw it out of the window into the moat below when she stopped in mid action.

A puzzled frown creased her forehead as a thought struck her: her husband had prepared the decoy and had lain in wait for her, that was obvious from his last words, but how did he know she would be coming to his chamber tonight? But for the grace of God, and the unplanned catnap that had delayed her by a few minutes, she might well have been the one whose head was no longer attached to her body. Her eyes narrowed as she let the scarecrow drop to its watery grave.

Gloria decided that she would visit the kitchen once again, but first she must make sure that she was not implicated in the death of her husband. She looked around the room and decided that a cursory glance would lead anyone investigating what had taken place in the room to conclude that the girl had stabbed the King in the chest only for him to cut off her head before he died.

Of course, there might be those who would look at the evidence and decide otherwise, after all Lundia's judiciary contained many clever men, but, it was most unlikely that any of those clever men would ever have the opportunity to view the murder scene, because Gloria would make certain it was the Lord High Chancellor who personally investigated the circumstances of the King's death. There was no doubt in her mind to what conclusion her new lover would come. Andris Vykrintas was very ambitious and she was still Queen.

Gloria smiled and decided she would not be sleeping in her own bed again that night.

It was a chambermaid who found the two bodies when she went to the King's room to empty his chamber pot. When the hysterical girl was eventually stopped as she ran screaming across the castle's upper hall, it was to the Lord High Chancellor's office she was taken.

Whilst the chamber maid was discovering the gory murder scene in the King's chamber, Queen Gloria was entering the King's stables. She walked over to the stall in which the goose was bedded down and pushed open the stable door. Greta looked up and if a goose could look startled, then it was startled, but it soon recovered its composure.

'Heil, Duchess, be it time t'visit thy chamber for a chat?'

'Not today, my friend,' Gloria replied, abandoning the peasant dialect with which she often conversed with the goose. She stood in front of the goose with one hand on her hip and the other out of sight behind her back. 'Today our business will be conducted here in your chamber.'

The goose looked at the Queen nervously and stretched its long neck, which is exactly what Gloria wanted. In a single rapid motion she brought her hand from behind her back to reveal a meat cleaver. She swivelled on her left heel, twisted her right hip and with a graceful, but powerful movement of her arm she swung the cleaver in a deadly arc that sliced through the goose's neck.

Greta's head bounced against the stable wall and came to rest on the bed of hay. Its eyes stared up sightlessly at Gloria; its mouth open in the mocking laugh with which she had become so accustomed.

'Goodbye, my treacherous friend,' Gloria said. 'Your days of telling lies are over.'

Andris Vykrintas conducted a thorough investigation of the murder of King Boris the Brave. He interviewed all the witnesses in a quiet measured way, considering each in turn with his probing, intelligent eyes, whilst making copious notes as he did so; a practice that unsettled a number of those blameless souls who were questioned. He then locked himself away in his chambers for several days before presenting his judgement to the Privy Council.

The King had been murdered by the goose keeper's daughter, no doubt following the instructions of her father.

So proclaimed the Lord High Chancellor.

Josef Volkman was immediately arrested; tortured by having his eyes poked out and his tongue cut off; and, because he refused to answer the charge of treason made against him, was found guilty and condemned to death.

So proclaimed the Lord High Chancellor.

The farmer was accused, tortured, tried and executed by being hung, drawn and quartered, all within forty eight hours of the Privy Council being informed of the conspiracy in which he was surely involved. With the traitor's death, justice was delivered to the good folken of Lundia.

So proclaimed the Lord High Chancellor.

King Boris the Brave had lived up to his name and had died with honour, killing his evil assailant following a desperate struggle to save the life of his wife, who was the assassin's next intended victim, before being mortally wounded himself in the process.

So proclaimed the Lord High Chancellor.

Of course, with Josef Volkman's death, the last person who was party to the dead King's plan, and the involvement of the goose, was silenced, but the Lord High Chancellor made no proclamation about that.

The goose keeper's remains were taken to the four corners of the kingdom and hung from trees, as a warning to any other who might be tempted to take part in similar treacherous acts. Marietta was buried in an unmarked grave in a paupers' graveyard on the very outskirts of Auksberg. There were no mourners.

King Boris the Brave was buried in the crypt of Castle Auksberg and hundreds of dignitaries, drawn from all regions of the kingdom and beyond, attended the funeral service and the wake of thanksgiving that followed.

For the wake, Queen Gloria organised a sumptuous feast that was spread across three long tables positioned at one end of the Grand Hall and was accompanied by a hundred flagons of mead that stood on a fourth table against one of the Hall's side walls. The centrepiece of the food ladened tables was a huge goose complete with tongue and herb stuffing.

'Wha's tha' ye ask, stranger? Wha' became of Queen Gloria?

Aaaah! Well therein lies a right deep irony o'which I'll gladly tell ye, if it doth please ye so.

    'Three moons after the death o'her husband, our beloved Queen found herself wi' child. Naturally the Privy Council did assume the child were King Boris's final legacy t'the guid folken of Lundia. T'ensure the continuity of the monarchy the Queen's counsellors were keen t'see the babe born into a royal household tha' included both ma and a pa.

    'So, fer the sake o'the kingdom 'twas decided t'waive the conventional rules of mourning, which required a widow t'mourn fer a full year afore taking another husband. Permission were given fer Queen Gloria t'wed the Lord High Chancellor, who was installed immediately as Prince Regent and was universally praised fer his selflessness in offering hisself up as surrogate pa t'another man's babby.

    'Only three people knew the truth o'the wee'un's real pa and one o'them were slowly rotting away in the castle crypt.

    'The Queen were duly born a healthy son, who were followed a year later by a babby brother.

    'In total Gloria and Andris begat ten offspring, which, if naught else, proved tha' the absence o'an heir t'Boris during his lifetime was nay the fault o'Gloria, if ye kenna me meaning.'

The Feast of Bessie Brandon

Greg Martin laid the letter on his desk and sighed deeply. His life right now was a mess and the single sheet of paper, with just half a dozen platitude filled sentences was the final straw. He leaned back in his chair and closed his eyes as he recalled the disastrous chain of events that had ended in today's disappointment.

It started with the slow deterioration of his business; fuelled by a fall in orders as the world was gripped by yet another recession, which in turn led to a worsening cash-flow that was exacerbated by a sudden steep increase in bank interest rates.

This financial pressure, combined with an increased number of his customers who defaulted on their invoice payment dates because they faced a similar financial squeeze, forced Greg to spend more time than he would have wished debt collecting and devising cost cutting measures to keep the bank off his back, and less time on promoting his business, which neglect in turn led to a further fall in orders. He was soon caught in a depressing, soul destroying vicious circle.

At the same time his creditors were chasing him for settlement of his bills. Most recently it began with a polite computer generated reminder letter, followed a couple of weeks later by a phone call from a credit manager whose world weary voice developed a hard edge when told by his secretary that Mr Martin was out of the office.

The next stage, when the company's patience was finally exhausted, was a threatening letter from a solicitor and then, when this failed, there was a visit from a little man in a grey suit who, whilst full of apologies, insisted on repossessing the new computer system on which Greg's future expansion plans were based.

Greg did not argue, after many months of trying to delay the inevitable, his resistance was finally worn down, besides which, the little man was escorted by a somewhat larger companion whose suit was considerably tighter than his smaller companion's and bulged menacingly in all the right places.

To add to Greg's woes, his long suffering wife, Angie, finally came to the end of her tether. Fed up with the increasing frequency of his bouts of depression; his alarming and eccentric mood swings; the constant financial pressure; the endless bickering and his uncharacteristic irritability, she had taken off two weeks ago to destination unknown, leaving neither telephone number, nor, forwarding address, just a short, sad note of regret.

It said much for Greg's state of mind that he did nothing to try and track Angie down.

Now he received this letter; this final kick in the teeth. In one last desperate attempt to save his business Greg had put together an ambitious, and very expensive proposal for a Saudi Arabian contract that, if successful, would have been worth over £10 million in turnover to his company and, more importantly, with a profit margin that would have wiped out his debts and guaranteed the future of his business.

But it wasn't to be. The letter that lay on the desk in front of him confirmed the rumours circulating in the industry that the contract had been awarded to an American PR company. So all the time, effort and hard-won money he had invested in the proposal had been wasted. His gamble had been lost.

Greg opened his eyes, picked up the letter, screwed it into a ball and threw it into the waste basket. Absent-mindedly he rifled through the rest of his mail, a collection of brown envelopes that he didn't open because they looked suspiciously like bills and final demands; then he stopped as one particular envelope caught his eye. It was brown like the rest but what grabbed his attention was not that it was addressed to his wife, but that it was written in her neat hand writing. With a twinge of guilt Greg slit open the envelope and pulled out a letter.

He frowned as he read it. It offered Ms Angela Martin and partner a voucher (attached) an all expenses paid week at a hotel in Devon. Slowly Greg's face cleared as he remembered how several months before, when he had been in one of his congenial moods, he and Angie had entered a competition in which they had been asked to match particular types of holidays with place names. They had not won the competition, the first prize which was a safari holiday in Kenya, but they had been awarded one of ten consolation prizes. This was it.

'Come and spend a relaxing week at the exclusive Harrington Hall Hotel,' he read aloud, thinking that it would be a good way of putting off the inevitable call to his accountant setting in motion the wheels needed to put his company into administration. He reached for the telephone and booked a room for a week starting that very day. Being out of season the hotel was delighted to receive his call, which was only slightly muted when he explained about the free voucher that he would be using.

Finished, Greg tucked the voucher into his jacket pocket and with an extravagant flourish of his arm swept the remaining unopened brown envelopes into the wastepaper basket to join the balled up letter. He hurried out of his office and upstairs to his bedroom. Five minutes later he had thrown a few things into a bag, had locked up the house and was already manoeuvring his Mercedes through the Friday night rush-hour traffic towards the M3.

Harrington Hall is an imposing Tudor style manor house that has been the family home of the Montagues for many centuries. It is now run as a private hotel by the Hon. James Perry and his wife, Sara Montague-Perry, the last surviving member of a county dynasty that stretched back to the Pilgrim Fathers.

Situated on the very edge of Dartmoor, the Hall dominated the northern boundary of the tranquil village of Torcham and was as much a focal point of the rapidly growing community as the magnificent spire of St Peter's Church, which dominated the skyline on Torcham's southern border.

The village itself is a typically English village. Mentioned in the Domesday Book, Torcham has a beauty and character the like of which can be seen the length and breadth of the country, but, it has a particularly enchanting quality that can rarely be rivalled anywhere outside the West Country.

Architecturally Torcham is a confused jumble of building designs, periods, shapes and sizes; from large Tudor beamed detached houses, to tiny terraced cottages. Some of the buildings are arranged, somewhat haphazardly, around a large village green, however the majority, in the main built more recently to a modern design, nestle together to form a newer estate in the east of Torcham.

Greg gleaned all this information from the glossy coloured brochure he found on the heavy dressing table that stood in one corner of the large, but cosy bedroom to which he was shown late the previous evening. Now, as he pulled aside his bedroom curtain, he could see that the promotional leaflet was not exaggerating.

When Greg had arrived in Torcham it had been pitch black outside. This morning, with the early spring sunshine turning the overnight dew into a thousand diamond clusters, he could see the village in all its glory. It was indeed enchanting, almost magical in fact, and he felt his spirits begin to lift as he came under its spell.

From his bedroom window, high on the top floor of Harrington Hall, Greg looked out across the village green to the clock on St Peter's Church showing him that it was just after eight o'clock. He realised with a start that he had slept for almost nine hours; the most he had in the past few trying months during which his nights were beset with insomnia as his mind grappled with his mounting problems.

Already there was a lively bustle about the village. Greg could see small groups of people who, whilst tackling their tasks in an apparently disorganised way, were obviously working towards a common goal.

At one end of the green, nearest Harrington Hall, a handful of villagers were erecting a marquee. Around the edge of the green another group was busy hanging colourful lines of bunting from trees and lampposts. In front of the church two men unloaded from the back of a battered old van broken pieces of furniture, branches and other combustible bric-a-brac, which they handed to a line of young helpers who then lugged it towards the centre of the green where yet another group of people was busy constructing what was the largest bonfire Greg had ever seen.

There was a knock on his bedroom door and Greg remembered he had ordered breakfast in his room. 'Come in.'

The maid was young, with dark curly hair and Latin features

that at first sight seemed too heavy to be pretty, but once she smiled, showing her gleaming white teeth and letting her sparkling eyes speak volumes, her true beauty was revealed. Greg quickly established that her name was Sonya and she was from Madrid.

'I put it over there?' She asked in heavily accented, but confident English. She nodded towards the coffee table that stood against one wall.

'Thank you.' Greg watched as the girl arranged his breakfast on the table. 'Tell me, Sonya,' he went on as she completed her task. 'What's the big occasion?'

The maid frowned at him, 'Senor?'

Greg pointed out of the window.

'Ah! The Feast.'

'The feast?'

'Si, senor. The Feast of Bessie Brandon. It is tonight. We all invited. Every peoples in the village they go. Senor?'

She motioned for him to take his seat at the coffee table.

'Who, or, what, is Bessie Brandon?' He asked as he settled into the armchair and let Sonya spread a starched linen napkin across his lap.

The girl shook her head as she straightened.

'I not know, senor,' she replied with a shrug of her shoulders. 'I just know every peoples in the village they go to Feast.' She paused then asked: 'Perhaps you go, senor? Si?' Another of those wide smiles lit up her face.

'Si,' Greg agreed. 'If I can get a ticket.'

'No ticket for Feast.' Sonya assured him as she made her way to the door where she turned to face him. 'No ticket,' she repeated. 'No pay. Peoples just go.'

'That's even better!' Greg laughed before tucking into the best tasting breakfast he had eaten in months.

Greg was back in his bedroom after spending the day wandering round Torcham watching the villagers making preparations for the evening's festivities and revelling in the air of natural good humour with which the tasks were performed.

It was April 30th, too late for Easter visitors and too early for the summer tourist trade to get under way, so those few outsiders, like Greg, who were privileged to be part of what was obviously a special day for the village, found themselves treated like honoured guests.

Greg experienced none of the cautious reserve sometimes shown to outsiders in close communities and he found the villagers very approachable. He soon established that The Feast of Bessie Brandon was an annual event, held on the same date each year.

There was a bonfire, fireworks, Morris dancers, a puppet show and a goodly supply of food and drink. When Greg poked his head round the door of the marquee during the afternoon he saw trestle tables laden with an assortment of refreshments that bore witness to the variety and abundance of the spread that The Feast offered.

But of Bessie Brandon herself Greg was able to learn very little. Most of the villagers he spoke to knew only the barest details about her: she was the daughter of a leading member of the 17th Century Torcham community who was burnt at the stake as a witch.

One old man to whom Greg spoke did remember a story told to him by his grandfather and passed down from his grandfather, about how outraged villagers, convinced of Bessie's innocence, attempted to rescue her from the bonfire, but were too late to save her.

The story went on to tell how, despite their failure to rescue the young girl, the villagers' action was rewarded when Bessie Brandon returned to earth as an angel and blessed the village with a bumper harvest. So it was that every year, in the hope of encouraging another successful harvest, a spring feast was laid on in Bessie's honour. At the same time, an effigy of her was ceremoniously burnt on a bonfire as a celebration of her martyrdom. This was the centrepiece of The Feast of Bessie Brandon.

'Weren't much of an 'elp last year though,' the old man moaned. 'Damn awful 'arvest, so 'twere.' He sniffed loudly and winked at Greg. 'Still, The Feast be a bloody good excuse fer a booze up!'

Greg smiled to himself as he remembered the old man's words. *Good*, he thought as he stepped out of the shower, *I'm just in the mood for a drinking session.* He wrapped a towel round his waist and wandered over to the drinks cabinet. 'Might as well get started,' he said out loud as he poured himself a generous measure of whisky. Above the cabinet was a bookshelf; one of the books caught his eye.

It was a slim volume and entitled: "A Parish History of Torcham". He lifted the book down and flicked through until he found the index. There were several references to Bessie Brandon and Greg quickly turned to the first on. He began to read.

Bessie Brandon was born in 1632 to John Brandon, a wealthy landowner and farmer. As the youngest of nine children, her early years were uneventful and apart from the registration of her birth there is no mention of her in Torcham's parish records. This anonymity ended when Bessie was 14 years old.

By the mid 17th Century witch mania was sweeping England. Any community that suffered even the most minor mishap was moved to blame its misfortune on the presence of witches. Upper Fordham, an adjoining parish, was no exception and when several cows were stricken with colic the village elders sent for Matthew Hopkins.

Matthew Hopkins was an interesting individual. He was known to be a Puritan and a failed lawyer. In addition, it is highly likely that he was a pervert and sadist to boot. He was also the most notorious of all the English witchfinders.

In his self appointed role as Witchfinder General, Hopkins travelled the land, charging twenty shillings a visit, plus all board, lodgings and travelling expenses. He received this fee whether or not he found any witches in the vicinity. If he did unmask a witch then he demanded another twenty shillings. Being a witchfinder was a very profitable career.

It is not clear how, or why, Hopkins widened his net to take in Torcham. It is possible one or other of the good folk of Upper Fordham pointed him towards the unsuspecting village next door as a means of deflecting his attention from his own community. Why his eye fell on Bessie Brandon is perhaps easier to understand, by all accounts she was "a comely, delicate and tender maiden, with skin as soft as the petals of a rose", and the particular methods Hopkins used to obtain his confession can only lead us to assume that he appreciated such qualities in his victims. In short, he liked young, pretty girls.

The most vivid description of the methods used by the Witchfinder General is contained in The History of Torture by Daniel P. Mannix. It reads:

Hopkins' favourite method of detecting a witch was "swimming" the accused. The woman's hands and feet were tied crossways behind her, the big toe of the right foot being tied to the thumb of the left hand and vice versa. She was then carefully laid on a blanket spread out on a quiet body of water, like a mill pond. If she floated, she was a witch and Hopkins burnt her. If she drowned, she was innocent, and Hopkins was always the first to acknowledge that he'd made a mistake.

If the woman kept quiet, she usually floated. If she struggled she usually drowned and Hopkins lost his twenty shillings. So the witchfinder was forced to use other methods. The accused was taken to a convenient room, stripped naked and tied in a sitting position on a stool for twenty four hours without food or sleep. All witches had a familiar, a sort of pet demon, that visited them at least once a day, and the demon might take any shape. If any living creature, including a fly, was seen in the room during this period, it had to be the witch's familiar and her doom was sealed.

In case no flies showed up, Hopkins still wasn't beaten. Witches fed their familiars from a spot on the body from which the demon sucked a special fluid. This place was insensible to pain. So Hopkins stuck needles into the accused until she either confessed to being a witch or he found a numb spot. There are several such spots on the human anatomy and one of Hopkins' helpers, an old woman named Mary "Goody" Phillips, knew them all. However, in case Goody was off testing another witch, Hopkins could usually get a girl to confess by saying: 'I have tested you everywhere with this long needle except up the nipples of your greats. Do you confess or shall I try there?'

Most girls confessed.

The method of interrogation actually used by the Witchfinder General on Bessie Brandon is not recorded; however, that she was found guilty is in no doubt. The villagers of Upper Fordham got their scapegoat, Matthew Hopkins got his forty shillings and poor Bessie Brandon got the stake.

The execution took place in Torcham before a sullen and resentful audience. The Brandon family was highly thought of in the parish and Bessie seemed to have been particularly well loved. Remarkably, for a period in which fear of the supernatural tended to blind even the most rational of men, few villagers seemed to believe that the quiet young girl who made such a wonderful flower arrangements for St Peters' Church was guilty as charged. Even fewer believed Matthew Hopkins' theory that Bessie's regular excursions to Harrington Woods to collect wild flowers, were nothing more than an excuse to consort with animals and other creatures of the devil.

To a man the villagers refused to have anything to do with preparations for the execution and it was left to Hopkins and his assistants, with the help of several willing volunteers from Upper Fordham, to make the arrangements for what turned out to be a particularly harrowing event.

It was the usual custom to strangle victims before the flames actually reached them, however, because of an unexpected mishap Bessie was subjected to unmerciful agony. Parish records include the following description of what was to be the only known execution to take place in Torcham:

The maiden was fastened to the stake with a rope around her waist and under her arm. A second rope was placed about her tiny neck. The faggots, these being light brushwood mixed with straw, were piled around her and the executioner set his torch to the stack.

Bessie Brandon stood serene and calm as the faggots burst into flames. Although the maiden's head was bowed those who witnessed the dreadful spectacle could see her lips moving in constant prayer and were amazed at her bravery and composure. As the flames leapt higher the crowd urged the executioner to tighten the rope and to no longer delay the act of mercy.

Thereupon, the executioner tugged manfully on the rope but as he did, so the flames bit into the rope and it broke asunder at which a great gasp went up amongst the crowd. Soon the flames were licking at the young maid, who used her hands in a desperate attempt to push away the faggots. As the flames seared her exposed flesh she began a dreadful wailing and moaning.

This pathetic noise proved too much for the villagers to contemplate and led by the vicar, Father Percival Constance, the crowd surged forward as a single entity. Although beaten back often by the scorching heat of the fire, several villagers attempted to pull the blazing faggots away from Bessie's writhing body. Other villagers angrily manhandled aside all those of the maid's tormentors who tried to prevent the rescue, including the Witchfinder General, who finally retreated from the village with a chorus of curses and insults ringing about his ears.

Eventually the perseverance of the villagers was rewarded. Despite collecting many burns, the rescuers were able to cut Bessie from the stake and drag her from the terrible hell to which she had been so unjustly consigned.

But the villagers' collective valour was to no avail. Even as they laid her upon the cool grass of the village green the poor young innocent expired, but not before she proved her saintly qualities by opening one last time her burnt and blistered mouth. In a quiet and gentle voice she forgave her torturers and then offered a moving blessing to those who had delivered her from the threat of eternal damnation and given her the opportunity of a decent Christian burial.

Thus a legend was born and over subsequent years the bare recorded facts have been embroidered and elaborated by rumours, folklore and other unsubstantiated stories, until Bessie Brandon's place as a true martyr has been assured by an annual festival honouring not only Bessie's death, but also her alleged return to the village in angelic form. This, the earliest enhancement of the story, seems to have originated in the 18th Century, where the first written reference can be found in the diary of Sir Arthur Montague; one of many items of historic value that have been permanently loaned to Exeter museum by Sir Arthur's descendants.

Sir Arthur's diary recounts a story of how in the month following Bessie's death, Devon was hit by the worst frost in living memory. Many acres of crops were affected and local farmers were predicting the poorest harvest for many years. The villagers braced themselves for a lean winter and prayers were said in St Peter's asking for divine intervention in Torcham's hour of need.

It was the vicar who first received a visit from Bessie Brandon. Father Percival found her standing alongside the altar when he visited St Peter's to light the candles prior to evensong. She was dressed in the clothes in which she had been executed; a long black dress with a pure white starched bib and cuffs, and a white peaked bonnet. However, all signs of the burning had disappeared and her face wore the beatific smile of one who is finally at peace. A strange celestial glow shone about her, which spread out from deep within her body to light up the dark shadows of the church and bathe the priest in a pool of serenity.

Then Bessie spoke and Father Percival was no longer in any doubt; his mind was not playing tricks; he was in the presence of an angel. He fell to his knees in awe and praised God for letting him witness this miracle. The angel blessed the vicar and immediately he felt the scars he bore still from his own attempt to save Bessie from the fire melt away into nothingness. Father Percival closed his eyes in prayer whilst the angel went on to bless Torcham, its inhabitants and the crops on which they depended. When he opened his eyes Bessie Brandon had disappeared.

The priest was not the only person in the village to witness Bessie's return; all those others who had been injured whilst attempting to rescue her from the bonfire were witness to a vision in one form or another. By the following morning, not a single villager bore a scar from any of the injuries received as a result of the abortive attempt to prevent the young girl's execution and when they went out into the fields to begin the day's work, it was to be confronted by the sight of sturdy, healthy corn. That year's harvest turned out to be the best ever.

It was in the same year, a century later, in which Sir Arthur recorded the story of the angel's visitation, that the first Feast of Bessie Brandon was held...

There was a knock on Greg's bedroom door and a woman's voice asked: 'Senor, are you coming to The Feast?'

'What?' Startled, Greg automatically jumped to his feet and went to open the door, but stopped in his tracks when he realised that his towel was no longer round his waist and he was stark naked. 'Okay, Sonya. I won't be long, I just need to shave.' Hurriedly he slipped the still open book onto the coffee table and snatched up the towel from the floor. 'You go on without me,' he urged as he dashed back to the bathroom to get ready. 'Don't worry about me, I'll join you later.'

There was a carnival atmosphere about the village. Coloured bulbs were added to the bunting that was draped from the branches of the trees and lines of them were hung across the top of the high poles placed across the village green. The refreshment tent was bedecked with lights and two floodlights were positioned to train their bright yellow beams on St Peter's Church, emphasising the beauty of its steeple.

The village green itself was crowded with people, many of whom were in fancy dress. Greg lost count of the number of young girls dressed in the black and white garb he now knew was worn by Bessie Brandon, but the reason for the popularity of the costume was explained when he entered the refreshment tent; a poster affixed to an upturned pasting table announced a competition to find the Annual Feast Queen.

The competitors were assembling at one end of the marquee. With their sombre black dresses, white starched bibs and white bonnets, the contestants looked remarkably alike. Greg did not envy the judges their task of choosing the best dressed girl.

By the time Greg was enjoying his third cup of steaming punch, poured by a large, big bellied man dressed in a bright red waistcoat and black breeches, his round, cheerful face framed by massive sideburns the Feast Queen competition was under way. He watched as a steady procession of contestants made their way to the low platform erected to act as a small stage.

It was hot in the tent and the air was full of noisy excitement. After a while Greg closed his eyes feeling his head begin to swim. He felt beads of perspiration on his forehead. As he began to sway he swore under his breath:

My God! He thought. *That punch is damn powerful stuff. What the hell do they put in it?* Greg decided he had better get out into the fresh air as soon as possible otherwise he was in great danger of flaking out. He shouldered his way through the milling crowd towards the exit.

When Greg arrived outside, he leaned up against one the poles on which the bulbs were strung and took a deep breath. Behind him, in the tent, a cheer went up and a girl squealed. This was followed by several raucous laughs, then a chant went up: 'Burn the witch! Burn the bitch! Burn the witch! Burn the bitch!'

Suddenly the tent door burst open and several people ran out to join the crowds that thronged the village green, they were closely followed by a group of youths carrying a struggling girl whose long black dress had ridden up her legs to reveal a pair of long white bloomers. As they caught sight of the girl, some of those in the crowd took up the chant: 'Burn the witch! Burn the bitch', whilst others in the crowd took up a different chant of: 'No, no, no! Will ye not learn? No, no, no! She shall not burn!'

As the rival chants grew in volume a gap opened up in the solid wall of humanity and the girl was borne deep into the mass of revellers. Soon the little group was lost from sight in the darkness and Greg could only judge its progress by the ebb and flow of the chants. He was just about to push his way through the crowd to find out what was happening to the girl, when he heard a voice behind him.

'Senor! Senor!'

Greg turned to see Sonya heading his way. She was accompanied by a woman who, although stockier and older, bore an unmistakeable resemblance to the young maid.

'Senor, this is my sister Maria.' Sonya introduced the woman, who smiled nervously at Greg. 'She come from Madrid, like me.' The girl explained. Maria looked as if she had been crying. 'My sister, she is holiday here in England. She is holiday with her daughter.'

Maria moaned and dabbed her eyes with a handkerchief as a cloud of sadness passed across Sonya's face and the light of her smile went out.

'My niece, she has name Anna, but senor, Anna, she is missing.'

'Missing?' Greg tried to reassure her. 'Well she can't be far away, Sonya. After all, Torcham isn't very big.' He turned to Maria. 'Where did you last see your daughter?' He asked, but Maria simply shook her head.

'My sister, her English is just a little. You understand, senor?' Sonya said apologetically and then turning to her sister she spoke rapidly in Spanish. Maria replied with much shrugging and expressive flourishes of her hand. Sonya turned back to Greg.

'My sister she say there is many, many peoples here. So easy for a young girl to get lost. Si? She say Anna went to get a Coca-Cola.' Sonya motioned towards the refreshment tent. 'She never come back.'

'How old is your niece?' Greg asked, the worm of unease wriggling in his stomach. A loud cheer rent the air behind them. Glancing over his shoulder Greg saw that another spotlight had been turned on, this time trained on the huge bonfire that loomed darkly and menacingly above the heads of the jostling crowd. He turned back to the maid.

'She twelve, senor,' Sonya replied, 'but tall for her age.'
She indicated with her hand to show the girl's height. Taller than the maid.

'And how was she dressed?' Greg already guessed the answer.

'Like all the other girls, senor. Like Bessie Brandon.'

'Okay, Sonya, here's what we'll do,' Greg said calmly, trying to keep the growing unease from his voice. 'I'll help you find Anna. You and Maria go and check the refreshment tent again and I will go and look over there by the bonfire. Don't worry; I'm sure we'll find her.'

Sonya explained this to her sister as she led her off by the arm. Greg's head was still spinning from the affects of the punch, but without hesitation he dived into the crowd. Up ahead he heard a roar of excitement and a chorus of boisterous wolf whistles. He craned his neck and peered over the heads of those in front of him. What he saw made his blood run cold.

Of course Greg knew that his fear was totally irrational; such things simply did not happen in the 21st Century. But something deep inside him, some primeval sixth sense, told him it was indeed happening. There, in front of the baying crowd, a struggling figure dressed in black was being tied to a stake at the base of the bonfire. Branches and brushwood were being piled round the figure until all that could be seen was a starched, peaked white bonnet.

A tall man in a long black cloak stood beside the bonfire. In one hand he held a blazing torch, which slowly he raised until he was holding it aloft. There was a momentary, expectant hush and then another mighty roar from the crowd as the man threw the torch onto the bonfire, which, with a sharp explosion, burst into flames.

Greg fought his way frantically through the crowd, cursing and swearing as he pushed people aside. Now he could actually see the face of the girl beneath the white bonnet. Her eyes were closed and her face was calm and impassive as if she were sleeping - or drugged!

Slowly the girl's head lifted and her eyes fluttered open, at first blank and dreamy, but then alert, knowing and frightened. She stared straight at Greg and he felt waves of nausea engulf him, turning his stomach and weakening his legs.

And the flames were getting higher, their heat fanned Greg's face. Then the girl screamed in agony and blood curdling sound filled his ears and the same time that the sickening smell of singed flesh filled his nostrils, revulsion filled his stomach, fear filled his heart and anger filled his brain.

'You bastards!' Greg swore as he elbowed his way through a group of jeering youths. 'No!' He screamed as he finally broke free of the arms that were trying to hold him back. Around him several warning shouts went up, but he could hear nothing but the girl's dreadful wail.

Then Greg was at the bonfire frantically pulling aside the burning branches with his gloved hands. He could see the girl's twisted, tortured face through the swirling smoke and the orange and yellow flames that were already burning into the bottom half of her body. The youngster still stared beseechingly into his eyes and momentarily she smiled wanly as she recognised that he was trying to rescue her.

The girl was very young and pretty, with a round face framed by wisps of black hair that curled down below the brim of her white bonnet. The smile quickly disappeared and her eyes screwed shut as pain contorted her face and forced open her mouth in a long scream of agony.

Greg renewed his efforts; pushing and kicking aside the burning wood until he was able to reach deep into the guts of the fire where the girl was held. He didn't bother trying to untie her bonds; instead, he threw his arms about both girl and stake. With a huge effort, and with his eyes stinging and his head spinning him towards unconsciousness, he wrenched the stake loose. Then with the last of his strength, and just before he was overwhelmed by darkness, he stumbled out of the debris of the bonfire, hauling girl and stake free as he went.

'Where did he come from?'
'Dunno, 'e just appeared from nowhere.'
'Who is he?'
'Bloody outsider.'
'Talked to him today, seemed a nice fellow.'
'Staying at the Hall.'
'Came out the crowd like a madman.'
'Must've thought she was for real.'
'But I told 'im it were a dummy.'
'We should have stopped him.'
'But we had no idea what he was going to do.'
'What do you think?'
'Did e' see her?'
'Bessie?'
'Aye.'
'He was damn lucky.'
'Could have killed himself.'
'Is he okay?'
'Hardly a scratch on him.'
'Not a single burn.'
'Miraculous.'
'Aye 'e saw Bessie alright.'

Greg heard the jumble of voices as he slipped in and out of consciousness, they meant nothing to him. Then he felt the cool air on his face and he began to cough.

'Move back. Give him some air.'
'He's coming to.'

Greg looked up into the jolly face of the bartender from the refreshment tent. With a grunt he sat up and looked around. He was encircled by villagers who studied him with varying degrees of concern and curiosity. He coughed again and eased himself into a crouch. Several people stepped forward to help him to his feet. One of them was Sonya.

'Are you okay, senor?' She asked. That's when Greg remembered the nightmare in which he had so recently been a participant.

'Anna,' he croaked and looked about wildly. The circle of villagers parted and he saw the crumpled heap on the ground. Even in his distressed condition Greg could see that it was the charred remains of a not particularly well made dummy. 'But I saw...' he paused as he noticed Maria standing by the smouldering bonfire, at her side stood a young girl. He turned to Sonya. 'Anna?' He asked.

'Si, senor,' Sonya replied. 'She was in the tent. The peoples, they made her take part in the contest.' She smiled. 'Anna, she enjoy it.'

'Oh, God! I feel so embarrassed,' he said to the barman. 'I'm sorry if I've spoilt your fun. I was either hallucinating or drunk. It must have been your punch.'

'Don't worry yourself, sir,' the man said with a grin. 'It happens to us all occasionally.'

'Senor?' Sonya tugged at Greg's sleeve. 'Are you okay?'

He nodded.

'Come along, senor,' Sonya took his arm gently, 'I take you back to your room. Si?'

'Si!'

Greg sat slumped in an armchair in his bedroom. At his elbow was a large glass of whisky. Another generous measure, drunk in one sustained gulp, was already beginning to settle his nerves. As the whisky's warm glow began to spread through his body he began to feel better.

He picked up the history book, which still lay open on the coffee table and started to read where he left off... *It was in the same year, a century later, in which Sir Arthur recorded the story of the angel's visitation, that the first Feast of Bessie Brandon was held...*

The phone rang.

'Hello?' He said as he continued to read the book.

Legend has it that Bessie Brandon returns to Torcham on that night...

'Hello, Greg. It's Angie.'

'Angie?' Greg repeated weakly, this was all getting beyond him.

...and shows herself to a chosen few...

'Yes.'

...who are thereafter blessed with good fortune...

'Angie. Where are you?'

'Home,' his wife replied. 'Where I belong. I'm sorry, Greg. I shouldn't have...'

'It's okay, Angie,' he tried to interrupt her, but she ploughed on, whilst with half his mind he continued to read the book.

...Whilst there is no documentary evidence to support this legend, it is true that there have been several reported cases in Torcham...

'No! Let me finish. This is important to me. I shouldn't have walked out on you the way I did, Greg. You needed my support and I let you down. I'm truly sorry.'

...of the almost miraculous recovery from illness occurring on or about the 30th of April each year...

'I was a pig,' Greg said.

'I don't care. You had every right to behave the way you did. I knew you were going through a difficult time with business and everything and I didn't even try to understand.'

'But how did you know I was here?'

'I found the letter telling me I'd won a weekend for two, but the accompanying voucher had disappeared and I put two and two together.' Angie paused. 'Are you on your own, Greg?' She eventually asked quietly.

...for instance, a Mr Michael Sporson, who lived in Torcham...

'Of course I am.'

'Good. I just thought perhaps...'

'No. Angie. There's nobody else and there never has been.'

...and who won a fortune on the football pools back in the 1980s...

'I see you've a letter here from Saudi Arabia,' Angie said.

'Yeah, bad news.'

...has always maintained that he saw Bessie Brandon...

'How do you know? The envelope hasn't been opened. It was on the doormat when I let myself in.'

...although he did not realise it at the time. Mr Sporson maintains that he saw a young girl tied to a stake in the Feast bonfire...

At first Greg could not grasp what his wife was telling him, then excitement gripped him as he realised what this strange turn of events might mean.

'Open the letter, Angie,' he said in a husky voice.

...on the night prior to the Saturday on which his eight draws came up...

'Are you alright, Greg? You sound funny.'

'Open the letter, Angie,' he repeated.

...Mr Sporson, who now lives in Jersey, insists he was convinced there was a girl on the bonfire and tried to get to her, but was beaten back by the heat...

There was silence for a moment and then Angie said in a quiet voice: 'You've got the contract, darling.'

'No, Angie. *We've* got the contract.' Greg insisted, his voice measured and unemotional. Strangely the news had come as no real surprise and yet he was still amazed by his own calmness. 'We've won it?'

...Mr Sporson now believes that the girl he saw was Bessie Brandon.

'Yes! You... we've won the Saudi contract.'

'But what about the Yanks?'

'It says in the letter, and I quote: "the company originally selected for the contract has since gone into liquidation and is no longer able to provide the necessary guarantee of completion within the time scale set out in the tender document. We would therefore like to meet with you to finalise contractual details... blah, blah, blah!"' Angie laughed. 'So what do you say to that?'

Bessie Brandon stared up at Greg from the book. It was a black and white picture of an old painting, however, there was no mistaking that pretty young face; small and round with wisps of black hair that curled down below the brim of her white bonnet.

'I say thank you Bessie Brandon!' Greg raised his wine glass in a silent toast.

'Bessie who?' Angie asked, with a hint of suspicion in her voice.

'Never mind, Angie. Just get yourself down here straight away. We'll spend the rest of the week together and I will tell you all about her.'

The New Year's Resolution

Jeremy looked out of the window of the top floor of the high rise flat in which his beloved Grandma Pat lived and died. In the distance the London Eye stood stark against a sky that was as black as his mood. Jeremy smiled, but there was no warmth in dark shadowed eyes that brimmed with tears. It was a grim smile of resignation. He knew what had to be done; no longer a case of if, but when.

It was New Year's Day. A time when resolutions are made and subsequently broken: giving up smoking; doing more exercise; cutting out biscuits and cakes; restricting alcohol to weekends; being more positive. Like millions of other people Jeremy had made each of those resolutions at one or other First of January, but usually his determination wavered by mid month and disappeared completely by February.

This year would be different. This year Jeremy would not reach February, because he had resolved that before the end of January he would commit suicide. And this year he was determined to stick to his resolution.

As Jeremy stared out across the London skyline he mulled over the events of the disastrous year that had come to an end just a few hours before. Finally the tears came, rolling slowly down his cheeks and as if in sympathy the heavens opened up and rain lashed against the window in a drumbeat that echoed round the empty flat.

It was true; he had suffered a disastrous twelve months; one financial problem following another; a year filled with sadness and loss. So Jeremy decided he could take no more. He was at the end of his tether. Enough was enough. There was no prospect of an improvement in his fortunes and it was time to go the way of the old year.

Death called.

But for the time being his plan had been thwarted. Jeremy shook his head in frustration. He stared down at the hard concrete forecourt of the block of flats that lay far below him. Jumping from the window sill of Grandma Pat's flat, as he had planned, would bring about a quick, if somewhat messy end. But it was not to be; the window was sealed and unbreakable.

Jeremy sighed in resignation, turned away from the window and headed for the door. There was a scattering of envelopes on the hall carpet that looked suspiciously like bills. He picked them up and stuffed them in his pocket. He would deal with the mail later; he had more important things on his mind than sorting out Grandma Pat's gas and electricity bills. Then Jeremy smiled grimly to himself as he realised that the bills would probably be somebody else's problem, but he had no idea who.

There was nobody left to care what happened. He was Grandma Pat's last remaining relative and the only other person left to sort out her affairs would be her solicitor; "That nice Mr Wetly," as she had called him. The very same Mr Wetly who no doubt would ensure his own fee was paid before he distributed what was left of Grandma Pat's meagre estate amongst her creditors.

At least the old girl had a good send off, Jeremy thought. He had seen to that, using money he did not have to pay for the traditional funeral, including a hearse drawn by black horses with tall plumes on their heads, which he knew his grandma would have wanted. The funeral had cost five thousand pounds, but when you are already a couple of hundred grand in debt, what did it matter?

Soon it would be his turn. But who would organise his funeral? Who would care that he was dead? Who would even notice he had gone? Perhaps his secretary, Molly, would shed a tear; she would understand how he felt, because she had seen her own share of heartache when her husband ran off with a girl half his age, leaving Molly lonely and deeply in debt.

No, his secretary certainly would not be able to afford to pay for a funeral for him, nor was it likely she would want to sort out his financial affairs, and once he realised there was nothing left in Jeremy's bank account to cover his fee, not even Nice Mr Wetly would be willing to do that.

Jeremy opened the front door and took one final look round Grandma Pat's flat and remembered...

He remembered how she had always been there for him, through thick and thin and how she had raised him as her own child when his father was killed during the Falklands War and his mother ran off to Uganda with a tribal chief, who turned out to be just another itinerant conman who gave her nothing but the HIV virus from which she eventually died without ever returning to England.

He remembered how Grandma Pat had tutored him at home, bringing out a natural talent for finance and business that led to a bursary at Westminster School and degrees from Oxford and Harvard. It was she who had shown him how to track the rise and fall in shares, when to buy and when to sell.

He remembered how she was always pleased to see him when he found time to visit her tiny flat, which he did frequently, no matter how busy he was.

He remembered how pleased she was for him when he met Jane and how she made his wife-to-be so welcome and at ease when he first introduced them.

He remembered the look of pride on her face when the twins were born and the tears in her eyes when Jane and he told her they were calling the boy David, after Grandma Pat's husband, who had died before Jeremy was born, and the other twin Patricia.

He remembered how just two short years ago she had been there for him on the day the drunken Lithuanian lorry driver crashed into Jane's spotlessly clean Renault Clio, killing her and the twins instantly.

He remembered sitting with Grandma Pat on the sofa by the window of this very flat, on the day that he buried his family, and how he sobbed on her shoulder as she stroked his hair in the same way that she had done when, as a little boy, she told him his mother was never coming home.

He remembered the look in her eyes when she asked how he was doing and the way she pretended to believe him when he said business was good, when the truth was that since the death of Jane and the twins he had simply lost interest in share trading.

But worst of all was the memory of the day, only a couple of weeks before, when he turned up at Grandma Pat's flat to find the front door open and the burly form of a paramedic standing in the hallway and the feeling of utter despair when he discovered that the last remaining love in his life had been taken from him.

Grandma Pat was dead and now as Jeremy closed the front door of her flat for the last he was determined to join her. He leaned back against the cold wood and closed his eyes. He was certain that his grandma was in a far better place. He smiled as he pictured her sitting on a bench in a beautiful, heavenly garden, chatting amiably with Jane as the twins scampered playfully on the lawn in front of them.

The image stayed with Jeremy as he headed out into the rain soaked street. He spent the next couple of hours meandering down grey characterless streets, with no real idea where he was going, his mind mulling over how he had reached his present position.

His problems started when Jane died. Up until then his financial advice business had done well, supplemented by share trading successes, some shrewd, some lucky. Jane's death changed everything; his concentration suffered, which in turn affected his shrewdness. At the same time, as if in recognition of the loss of his wife, his luck changed. A couple of share deals went belly up, which not only set him back several hundred thousand pounds, but because he had advised his clients to buy and sell the same shares, he lost half of his client base almost overnight.

The problem was that he no longer cared; money meant nothing to him. Without Jane, life was not worth living. Eventually he sought an escape from his misery in a brandy bottle and soon he was on the slippery slope to ruin. The financial problems piled up and by the time he had started to pull himself together it was too late. All his money was gone and he was a couple of hundred thousand pounds in hock to his bank, an overdraft secured on the empty house in which he lived his lonely life, but which no doubt he would lose when the bank issued the inevitable foreclosure notice.

The only thing that kept him going during those long depressing months was the knowledge that he had Grandma Pat to whom he could always turn for spiritual, if not financial, help. Seeking the latter help was out of the question; not only because his grandma had no money, but because Jeremy's pride would not allow him to admit to her that he was a failure. But even that last reason to live was snatched from him when Grandma Pat died suddenly from a massive coronary, leaving him alone in a world in which he no longer felt a part.

So now Jeremy wandered the streets of London, thinking of the past and planning to ensure there was no future; not in this world anyway. He looked around and found himself walking along Westminster Bridge Road towards the River Thames. Despite his hat and coat he was soon soaked to the skin by the icy cold rain that continued to lash down from the dark clouds above.

Jeremy looked up, squinting as the rain beat against his face. Behind the Park Plaza Hotel the London Eye filled the darkening late afternoon sky and he noticed without much interest that despite being New Year's Day all of the capsules were occupied as they inched slowly round on their perpetual sightseeing tour.

Jeremy walked under the railway bridge in front of the Plaza Hotel and momentarily he was sheltered from the rain. Almost miraculously, when he emerged back into the open only a few seconds later, the rain had turned to snow and by the time he reached Westminster Bridge a blizzard swept across the Thames in a dense white curtain.

Jeremy trudged slowly across a deserted Westminster Bridge; head down in the face of the biting wind and the swirling snow, before stopping at the bridge's midpoint. He leaned over the green painted wrought iron parapet wall and stared down onto black surface of the river that lay over twenty feet below him. The sluggish water called to him with a gentle, tempting whisper that belied the treacherous current that tugged at the underside of the surface, creating small white caps.

To Jeremy's right Big Ben struck four and as if on cue flood lights lit up the bank on the west side of the river, turning the snow into a ghostly sheer veil through which the glorious architecture of the Houses of Parliament could just about be seen.

Jeremy pulled himself up onto the parapet wall and stood with his legs apart, balancing himself by holding on to the ornamental light column. The murmur from the river grew louder as if sensing that another life was about to be sacrificed to the demons that lay beneath its surface.

'Hello,' said a voice from behind him.

Jeremy looked over his shoulder as the shape of a man appeared as if from nowhere on the pavement behind him.

'Are you going to jump?'

Jeremy stared down silently at the stranger, who was short with a round jolly face. His head had a halo of white hair circling a bald head on which a thin layer of snow had settled. He had sharp blue eyes that stared knowingly back at Jeremy. He looked like a mischievous monk. He was leaning heavily on a walking stick.

'What's your name?' The man asked.

'Jeremy,' the younger man replied as he turned his back on the stranger and stared down into the water far below.

'Good to meet you, Jeremy, or, might that be Jerry?' The man said in voice that was as soft and cultured voice as an old fashioned news reader.

'Jeremy.'

'Fine, Jeremy it is then.' The man smiled up at him. 'My name is Clarence.'

Jeremy looked over his shoulder at the stranger and could not help smiling back. 'Clarence? Not Clarence Odbody; Angel Second Class?'

'No, just Clarence.' The man stared up strangely at Jeremy. 'Who is this Odbody?'

'It doesn't really matter,' Jeremy said. 'He's just a character from an old film that is shown on television every Christmas Eve without fail. You must have seen it.' He smiled again.

Clarence frowned and stared up into the sky as if seeking divine intervention. The snow settled on his eyelashes, but he didn't seem to mind. Suddenly he clapped his hands in delight. 'Of course! I remember now! *It's A Wonderful Life!*' He beamed happily. 'The film is about a banker called George Bailey, played by James Stewart, and an Angel called Clarence, but listen Jeremy, I'm no Angel Second Class.'

Jeremy laughed. 'Don't worry, I'm no banker!'

'So what are you doing up there?'

'It's a long story.'

Clarence pulled a packet of cigarettes from his pocket and

offered it to Jeremy, who shook his head. 'I shouldn't either,' Clarence said, 'but old habits die hard.' He put a cigarette into his mouth and lit it with the flame from a match that he sheltered from the wind with a cupped hand. He took a deep drag, closed his eyes in evident pleasure before blowing out a cloud of smoke that was quickly swallowed by the snow.

'I needed that,' he said. 'It's strictly non smoking where I'm currently living and it's been a long time since I had a cigarette.' He took another long drag. 'Listen, I'm chilled to the marrow, but I'm in no hurry to get back home, so why don't we pop to the Red Lion for a warming drink and a chat?'

Jeremy didn't move.

'Anyway, there is little point jumping at the moment because it's low tide and the worse that will happen is that you'll end up to your backside in mud.' He took a final suck on his cigarette and flicked his butt over the parapet into the water. 'Come on, I'll buy you a beer.'

Jeremy shook his head, but he smiled again and jumped down from the parapet. 'I'd sooner have a brandy.'

'Me too, my boy!' Clarence laughed as he took the younger man's arm and guided him towards the far bank, limping along with the help of his walking stick.

As they crossed the road and headed up Parliament Street towards the Red Lion, Jeremy realised that the snow had stopped. He looked up and saw the sky was clearing and a bright full moon emerged from behind what remained of the cloud to show the Man in the Moon smiling knowingly at him. As the sky cleared the temperature dropped another couple of degrees and the two men were pleased to reach the warmth of the pub.

Once inside the pub Clarence patted his pockets, one at a time, before admitting that he had no money with him. Jeremy laughed and bought them both a drink, insisting that his new companion should have a double brandy. Clarence did not argue and soon they had taken their drinks to a quiet table in the corner of the bar.

'Is it really low tide?' Jeremy asked as they sat down.

'I have absolutely no idea, my boy,' Clarence replied with a grin.

'And what about the depth of the water?'

'I must confess that might have been another teeny-weeny exaggeration on my part.' Clarence took a sip of brandy and rolled it delicately round in his mouth before swallowing it with an expression of contentment on his face. 'Do you know, my boy, that brandy is an even bigger pleasure than the cigarette?' He stared into the younger man's eyes. 'So tell me, what's so bad that you want to kill yourself? Do you want to talk about it?'

Jeremy told Clarence his story and when he had unburdened himself he did feel a little better; not enough to weaken his determination to stick to his New Year's resolution, but he did decide at least to put it off until the next day.

'You say you have nobody. No Family. No friends.' Clarence said.

Jeremy shook his head.

'You are wrong. Everybody has somebody, somewhere.'

The younger man was about to argue, but paused. Was he right? Was there nobody? What about Molly Martin? After all, hadn't they found solace in each other's company; sharing both their misery and their beds.

The problem was that although the sometimes drunken lovemaking sessions had provided them with a temporary respite from loneliness, they both realised the relationship was doing nothing to alleviate their underlying unhappiness and by mutual, unspoken agreement they returned to a purely platonic, professional relationship.

But occasionally the need for Molly's company, and her body, returned and he found it difficult to resist the temptation to restart their relationship and he sensed that she felt the same way about him. There was a bond. 'Perhaps there is somebody. Her name is Molly Martin and we did have a thing going.'

'There you are. Go home and contact her.'

'I don't think so; we decided to end our relationship and it was pretty final.'

'Listen, my son, there is nothing more final than suicide!'

Jeremy stood up. He didn't like the way the conversation was going; not one little bit. He was beginning to feel uncomfortable and could feel his resolve wavering. He excused himself and went off to find the gents toilet. When he returned to the table Clarence had left. Jeremy was relieved, but at the same time disappointed. He headed for the door, half expecting to bump into his new acquaintance on the way, but Clarence was nowhere to be seen. He had vanished into the night.

When Jeremy got home he poured himself a brandy, switched on the gas fire in the lounge and was about to settle down in his armchair when he remembered his grandma's mail. He went to the hall where his still sodden jacket hung and pulled the envelopes out of his pocket. He noticed that he had unopened mail of his own on the hall table so picked that up and returned to the lounge. He sat down and took a generous sip of his brandy.

He stared into the glowing fire, feeling its heat mixing with the brandy to chase away the chill from his bones. His spirits began to lift and he reached for the phone to call Molly, but changed his mind before he dialled her number, instead he picked up one of the envelopes, opened it and pulled out a letter printed on thick expensive paper. He smiled to himself when he saw the letter was from Nice Mr Wetly informing him that, as the last remaining heir and sole beneficiary to Mrs Patricia Brown's estate, Mr Jeremy Brown should visit his office to sign the papers needed to finalise the deceased's financial affairs.

The contents of the letter were hardly a surprise since Nice Mr Wetly had contacted Jeremy by phone just before Christmas to advise him that the letter was on its way and indeed had already booked Jeremy in for a meeting the following day.

However, the contents of the next envelope Jeremy opened most certainly were a surprise; it was a bank statement for Grandma Pat's savings account and the end balance stunned Jeremy. At the time of her death his grandma's account contained £100,324.26

Jeremy closed his eyes and shook his head. When he opened them again the balance figure had not changed. He lifted the brandy glass to his lips and drained the remaining gold liquid in one swallow. 'I need another drink,' he said out loud as he stood up and headed for the sideboard,

When he returned to his armchair he was carrying a half full glass of brandy. He sat down and picked up another envelope, still in shock from the realisation that his grandma had squirrelled away so much money. Where had it come from? He knew that she had dabbled in stocks and shares, but was it conceivable that she had been so successful?

Still in shock he tore open the envelope and pulled out a building society statement in the name of Mrs Patricia Brown. As Jeremy unfolded the statement to look at the balance figure at the bottom he half knew what he was going to find. He was right and he was wrong.

He expected to see a figure as large as the £100K in his grandma's bank account and he was right. Where he was wrong was that the figure was higher; much higher. Grandma Pat's building society account contained a figure in excess of £1 million.

Jeremy was past being shocked; he simply stared down at the statement trying to get to grips with the fact that he was about to inherit enough money to clear his debts, sort out his business problems and still have plenty enough money left to live comfortably for the rest of his life. But money isn't everything. Money would never bring Jane and the twins back. Money would not bring Grandma Pat back. He smiled gently as he decided what he had to do.

The following day Jeremy visited Nice Mr Wetly in his comfortable little office in Balham High Road, signed papers that showed that his total inheritance was close to £1.5 million and then gave his instructions about what should be done with the money, which debts should be paid first and into which accounts the balance should be paid.

When Jeremy left the office of Nice Mr Wetly he was whistling cheerfully to himself. Now that he had made up his mind about his future he felt happier than he had for months. He was still whistling as he entered Balham underground station and stepped in front of the Morden to Edgware train.

The garden was beautiful; the fragrance from the flowers was heavenly and the water in the stream that ran along the edge of the rolling lawns, before cascading into the valley below was clear and sweet.

At the edge of the garden was a picnic table round which sat a family. At the head of the table was a plump jolly woman with grey hair and ranged round the table was a young woman who was strikingly beautiful, two children who apart from their gender were identical and a man who seemed to have a permanent contented smile on his face. The man's smile widened as the woman passed him the dish of steaming vegetables.

'Thank you, Jane,' Jeremy said as he helped himself to vegetables, before spooning some onto the twins' plates. He paused as he glimpsed a movement from the corner of his eye. He glanced to his right and saw a man limping across the lawn with the aid of walking stick. He was dressed all in white and had a bald head that was surrounded by a halo of white hair.

'Hello, Clarence.'

'Hello, my friend. How are you settling in?'

'We are happy,' Jeremy said with a smile. 'Very happy.'

'Can I drag you away from your family for a few minutes?' Clarence asked, although the question didn't leave much room for discussion. Jeremy left the table and followed Clarence across the lawn towards the pond that lay at the head of the falls. 'There is something I think you might want to see,' Clarence said pointing towards the water.

As Jeremy stared down at the pond the surface of the water swirled into a kaleidoscope of colour before clearing to reveal a woman sitting in a sparsely furnished room.

Molly Martin sat at a table looking down at the letter that lay in front of her. The letter was from Wetly and Wetly Solicitors and it informed her she was the sole beneficiary of the estate of the late Mr Jeremy Brown.

Molly looked up towards the heavens with tears running down her face. 'Thank you, boss,' she said.

The Grotto

Brendan O'Keefe had to admit the Grotto was spooky. Not that he was worried; it would take more than an eerie atmosphere and a few masks to frighten him. Still, he could see what attraction the dark, damp cavern might hold for the steady stream of middle aged old biddies that edged nervously down the narrow stone steps with a hint of expectation flushing their cheeks. If they were looking to have their fear titillated by a brooding atmosphere that hinted of pagan rituals and the supernatural, then they had come to the right place.

Set in the grounds of an old castle, the origins of the grotto were unknown, although several ancient documents that were on display in the castle's museum showed that the cavern in which it was established had been in the castle grounds for several centuries.

One such document detailed the cavern's use by a 17th Century coven of witches and spoke of 'corrupt and blasphemous acts of perversion'. The parchment went on to explain how the witches were tried, found guilty and burnt at the stake, following which event the cavern was sealed up and abandoned.

Two hundred years later the cavern was opened up again and converted by the castle's then owner into a grotto, which became particularly popular in early Victorian times. Mysteriously, the grotto was sealed up and abandoned once again a few years later.

It had been only in recent years, following a decision by the estate's trustees to throw open the castle and its grounds to visitors, that the grotto had been excavated, renovated and extended to better cater for an ever increasing tourist trade. The walls were decorated with seashells and a line of single electric bulbs provided a dim light throughout the length of the narrow cave.

However, despite these newer, more artificial additions, there were still sufficient remnants of the original decor to provide evidence of the wicked deeds alleged to have been perpetrated in the dark underground chamber.

In the centre of the grotto the sharp points of a pentangle, faded but still distinguishable, were etched into the stone floor. Indecipherable mystic signs and symbols could just about be seen scratched on the smooth surfaces of flints that protruded from the damp walls of the original grotto.

The sinister tone of the grotto was heightened by several grotesque masks that were set into the walls and ceiling. Some were carved from stone; bizarre gargoyle faces, empty eye-sockets staring down menacingly at all who dared enter. Others, in some way more frightening, were simply knots cut from the bark of tree trunks. Twisted by nature into perverted and inhuman shapes, these wooden plaques resembled the anguished features of tortured lost souls.

And then there was the sacrifice chamber.

The grotto keeper had not mentioned the chamber to Brendan when he showed him round earlier that morning, but perhaps that was not surprising, after all, he was only temporarily employed to help whilst the old man's assistant took a holiday.

The old man had simply given the youngster a potted history of the castle and its grounds, including the grotto, and had then left him to his own devices.

Brendan spent the day wandering round looking for anything of value worth pilfering, a search that had been singularly unproductive until, by chance, he stumbled upon the secret chamber.

Brendan was six foot four inches tall and it was his height, and incurable curiosity, that led him to make his discovery. He was studying one of the stone masks positioned at the far end of the grotto when on impulse he stood on tip toes and peered through the eye sockets of the mask.

At first Brendan could see nothing, but as his eyes adjusted to the darkness behind the mask he made out one or two shapes that were even blacker than their surroundings. As his eyes became even more adjusted to the dark, he realised he was looking into a chamber of some kind. He took a lighter from his pocket and flicked it into life. He held the flickering light against one eye socket whilst he peered through the other one.

The chamber was tiny, little more than an alcove, with walls similar to those in the old, original part of the grotto, except they had not been decorated with shells. Positioned at one end of the chamber was a long flat ledge on which lay several white objects. With a start Brendan realised they were bones and he decided he was looking into a medieval sacrifice chamber and the ledge was the altar on which victims had been laid. Because of his restricted field of vision he could see neither how long the chamber was, nor, what lay at its far end.

Brendan saw that what light there was in the chamber, apart from the flickering flame of his lighter, came from a number of cracks in the ceiling. Several tiny rays found their way from the sunlit castle grounds above and filtered through the rock ceiling to shine weakly into the gloomy interior.

One such ray glinted on something metallic. Brendan's heart quickened as his imagination worked overtime. What could the object be? What treasures were hidden in the secret chamber? He immediately went looking for an entrance. But there was no sign of a door.

Shrugging off his disappointment Brendan made his way up a set of uneven steps into the castle grounds where he was able to investigate further. Perhaps there was a way through the roof into the chamber. He squinted in the bright sunshine and paused to get his bearings.

Behind him the castle rose tall and proud, the granite of its newly repaired battlements glared white as they reflected the sun's rays. To his left were several ornamental gardens and a massive expanse of lawn that rolled down towards a sparkling blue lake. To his right were more lawns and about a hundred yards or so away a large rockery.

Brendan smiled and walked over to the rockery. He noticed a black cat, resplendent in a pretty pink collar, stalking a plump starling in the flower bed that skirted the mound of boulders. Brendan stopped and for a few brief seconds, time stood still as he watched the cat watching the bird. Disturbed by Brendan's approach, the bird flapped up lazily from its stone perch and headed for the nearest tree. The black cat turned and stared malevolently at him before slinking off to disappear into a dark gap between two huge rocks.

There were several gaps in the rockery and Brendan realised that this was the means by which light was finding its way into the hidden chamber. However, whilst the gaps were large enough to provide sanctuary for a cat, not even a child could enter the cave by the same route. Unperturbed by this disappointment Brendan returned to the grotto and continued his search. This time he was more successful.

He found the door in a part of the grotto where the main cavern narrowed into what was little more than a passageway that led eventually to the smaller, darker area, which he now believed was a sacrificial chamber.

The door was hidden behind a curtain of hanging moss and he would have missed it completely if he had not slipped on the uneven floor. As he felt himself slide, he stuck out a hand to steady himself against the wall and felt the slight give of wood through the moss.

He pulled the moss aside and discovered an old door with heavy wrought iron fittings and a surface pitted with tiny colonies of mould. There were two huge bolts that Brendan half expected to be rusted up, but the top one slid open quietly and without difficulty, as did the bottom one.

Brendan tugged on the door but nothing happened. That's when he noticed a black metal padlock. He swore quietly. The padlock was not particularly heavy; however, any attempt to break it open would undoubtedly be heard by the old man in his ticket booth at the top of the grotto stairs. He decided to wait until nightfall before returning to investigate further.

To start with everything went well for Brendan; he broke open without much effort the small padlock used to secure the door at the entrance to the grotto and made his way down the stairs with the aid of a torch.

Now he pulled aside the curtain of moss and prepared to tackle the more substantial black padlock that was revealed; all that stood between him and whatever was within; riches, or, nothing? Who could tell?

Brendan grunted as he levered a jemmy against the lock. With a loud crack the lock snapped open. Easy! The young man pulled at the door but it was heavy and would not budge. He paused and felt the hair rise on the nape of his neck as a scratching sound reached his ears. He stepped away from the door.

'Don't be stupid!' He admonished himself out loud; his voice echoing eerily round the grotto. 'There is nothing there. It's all in your imagination, Brendan.' He shook his head in a determined effort to convince himself the noise from the chamber was all in his mind.

'There is nothing there. It's all in your imagination, Brendan.' The echo agreed with him; so did his ears. The scratching had stopped.

The young man laughed nervously to himself and pressed his ear against the door. It was cold and damp. He held his breath and listened hard. Total silence. He let out a deep sigh and pulled on the door again, harder this time. With a loud creak the door swung open and Brendan stepped into the end of the world.

As the beam of Brendan's torch probed the darkness he could see that the chamber was far larger than was apparent from his view through the mask. He turned and allowed the light to play on the wall opposite the ledge on which he had seen the bones.

Brendan gasped as he was confronted with the most hideous sight he had ever witnessed. Like the rest of the grotto the lower half of the wall was built from granite, however, at about six foot above ground level, limestone had been used to finish off construction of the wall.

At the spot at which the young man stared the smooth limestone gave way to two misshapen lumps, about eighteen inches apart and between these lumps was stuck a severed head. It was a woman's head with tufts of long straggly black hair and tight skin that was as yellow and dry as parchment. The ghastly head's eyes were wide open and upturned in a deathly stare and its mouth gaped in a twisted soundless scream.

Despite his horror, and the sick numbness that gripped his stomach, Brendan found he was unable to drag his eyes from the dreadful sight. The fascinated horror he felt deepened as he realised that the head was not in fact severed and the two lumps were the shoulders of the remains of some unfortunate who had been buried alive.

Plucking up courage Brendan let the torch beam probe deeper along the limestone wall and discovered another head and then another. There were seven heads in all, both male and female. Seven macabre testaments to the unspeakable horrors practised in the cavern so long ago.

Eventually Brendan dragged himself away from the grisly scene remembering the purpose of his visit. He turned towards the ledge, his eyes seeking out the metallic object for which he had broken into the chamber. He stepped closer and swore angrily when he discovered the object of his search was a soft drink can. Angrily he picked up one of bones and smashed it down on the can and watched in satisfaction as the bone shattered into a hundred pieces.

That's when Brendan heard the scratching sound again, but now it was accompanied by a quiet moaning. He froze as the scratching grew louder and more insistent. Suddenly, the wall behind Brendan exploded in a shower of limestone and with a banshee wail something sprang from the wall and launched itself at him. The last thing the young man remembered before he let out a primeval scream of fear was the feeling of talons sinking deep into the side of his neck.

The scream that reverberated round the grotto had a terrible finality about it. Fuelled by its accompanying echo, it raced through the cave, up the narrow stairs and out into the open where it pierced the tranquillity of the early summer night.

High in the castle, safe within the confines of the staff living quarters, the old grotto keeper awoke with a start. The scream filled him with dread. He crossed himself and then quickly pulled the bedclothes over his head.

The following morning when the old man discovered the forced entry into the grotto he suspected immediately who was responsible and when Brendan O'Keefe failed to turn up for work his suspicion was vindicated. The old man did not bother to go down to the secret chamber because he knew what he would find; instead he decided to wait until the police arrived.

'Ye gods!' Detective Sergeant Stan Hardin exclaimed. 'They wouldn't win any prizes in a beauty contest, would they, guv?' He grimaced, maintaining a healthy distance between himself and the row of heads that stuck out from the wall.

Detective Inspector Rupert Bridges was not so squeamish; he stood close to the wall and his tall stature allowed him to carry out a more detailed inspection of the mummified remains.

'Hmmm, very interesting,' the Inspector mused. He adjusted his half moon spectacles on the end of his long nose and stared in interest at a section of the wall in which one of the heads was mounted. 'See the way the top of the wall slopes back quite noticeably,' Bridges pointed out. 'Obviously at one time the poor wretches were totally buried,' he explained. 'However, over the years the limestone has crumbled away to expose the head and shoulders.'

He turned to the grotto keeper. 'Now, sir, you were telling me about this legend.'

The old man waited nervously by the door. He had never liked coming into the chamber and today was no exception. He certainly was not convinced by the policeman's theory.

'Aye, Inspector. Years ago this cave was used by witches and legend has it that after they were burnt at the stake their bones were dumped in this chamber. That's them over there.' The old man pointed towards the ledge at the end of the chamber. 'It's said that before she died, one of the witches cast a curse not only on those who persecuted her in life, but also anybody who denied her the peace in death to which she believed she was entitled.' He nodded towards the array of heads. 'The legend goes on to say that those appear when the bones of the witches have been disturbed.'

'But what's all that got to do with last night's break in?' Hardin asked. 'It all sounds like a load of mumbo jumbo to me,' he insisted, whilst at the same time edging away from the ledge on which the bones lay.

The grotto keeper did not reply at first, he simply stood staring up at the heads. 'Sergeant, yesterday there were seven heads on that wall,' he explained eventually. 'Today there are eight heads. I can't be sure, and of course it is in the shadows, but I believe that new head belongs to a chap named Brendan O'Keefe who...'

The old man was interrupted by D.I. Bridges who held up his hand in a request for silence. The policeman cocked his ear and then moved further into the shadows at the end of the chamber. For a while the silence was total and then Stan Hardin heard his superior officer's whispered voice, but could not work out what he was saying.

'What's that, guv?' Hardin asked, but received no reply. Then he heard Bridges chuckle. It was a sound Hardin had heard before and it told him the Inspector already had a pretty good idea what had happened in the chamber the previous night.

'I don't know to whom that head belongs,' Bridges said as he reappeared. In his arms he carried a cat. 'But it is not your Brendan O'Keefe, sir. Indeed, whoever he is, that poor fellow has not been in any fit state to break open a padlock for hundreds of years!' He chuckled again. 'Let me tell you what I think happened. Somebody broke in here last night with the intention of stealing something of value.'

'Valuables? In here, guv?' Hardin asked looking round the chamber.

'Greed can do strange things to one's logic, Stan.' Bridges replied. 'Who knows what goes on in the minds of our local villains? Anyway, what I think is that our little friend here got himself trapped somewhere near the roof of the chamber. If you look over there you will find a gap between wall and ceiling which probably leads to the grounds above. I suspect the cat eventually worked itself free by digging into the limestone, see the powder on its fur?' Bridges brushed the cat's side and white powder puffed up into the air. 'Eventually the wall crumbled away completely and the cat fell through, bringing a lot of the wall with it. There is a pile of limestone on the floor. That is how the head was exposed.'

The cat purred happily, as if agreeing with the detective. Bridges turned to the old man, who looked at the policeman with ill disguised admiration.

'I am impressed, Inspector,' he said.

'It was nothing,' Bridges replied with a modest smile as he handed the cat to the grotto keeper. 'If you would like to take this little fellow, we'll be on our way. It looks as if he needs a bath though.'

Hardin looked at his boss thoughtfully but said nothing until they were out of earshot of the old man. He didn't want to disillusion him. 'I've missed something haven't I, guv?' Stan Hardin said when they were walking back towards their car.

'I don't know what you mean, Sarge.'

'All that guff you gave the old man. Was it true?'

'Of course it was. Entirely true.'

'But?'

'There is a "but"?' Bridges asked as he opened the doors of the car.

'Yes, you're holding something back. I can tell by your face.' Hardin stared accusingly across the roof of the car at Bridges. 'Come on, what did I miss?'

'Well there was one small thing I didn't mention, Sarge.' Bridges smiled innocently. 'Remember that chappie who came into the station last night ranting and raving about being attacked by the devil?'

'Yeah, it took four plods to restrain him. Eventually they had to call in the quack to sedate him and he was carted away to the funny farm for his own protection.' Hardin paused, he began to understand. 'Don't tell me, you took note of the man's name.'

'Oh yes! I noticed his name alright.' Bridges allowed his smile to stretch into a grin as he interrupted his colleague. 'And yes, it was Brendan O'Keefe. I noticed also that he had some nasty scratch marks on the side of his neck.'

'The cat?'

'The cat,' Bridges agreed with another smile. 'The poor chap must have received one hell of a shock when it sprang out of the wall and landed on his shoulder!'

The Bogeyman

The couple lay in the darkened squat. The girl was young, little more than a child, but the man was much older; he had been around forever.

She was small and very pretty, but her smile was vacant and the pupils of her china blue eyes were dilated by the drugs that permanently polluted her blood.

He was tall, with the hard athletic body of a healthy young man, but his skin had the pallor and texture of death. He had a pale, thin face; made to look gaunter by the mass of black, wavy hair that framed his head and fell in long curls onto his shoulders.

The young man stared up at the mould encrusted ceiling and felt a numbing ache in his limbs. He swore quietly as his fingers and toes started to tingle. It had begun. Shrugging off the girl's embrace the man sprang to his feet and stumbled to the window where he pulled aside the filthy sacking curtain. Instantly the room was bathed in an unearthly white half-light.

The man stared into the cracked mirror that hung next to the window and soon found the first tell-tale sign of grey amongst the black curls. He felt age weigh heavily on his shoulders.

'A week and it will be over,' he said quietly to the lifeless eyes that stared back at him from the mirror. In a week's time it would be October 31st. Halloween: the night of rejuvenation. 'And by Satan's tail,' he sighed wearily, 'I need it.'

He always felt tired as he reached the end of his yearly cycle. The man had been on the move for as long as he could remember; travelling the length and breadth of the land, corrupting everything and everybody with whom he came in contact. Somewhere along the way he had picked up the girl. She was just another piece of the pathetic human flotsam to exploit and then throw aside.

Her name was Sandie Brodie, which sometimes the man remembered, but mostly he forgot. Sandie didn't seem to care; she was happy just as long as he continued to provide her with a steady supply of that fine, white powder.

His real name had been lost in the mists of time; identities came and went. For the past year he had been masquerading as Duncan Gallagher, but he had no idea what his name would be next week. Only time, and Halloween, would tell.

October 31st - Halloween

They stood in a shadowy alley that ran alongside the pub. The once upright figure of Duncan Gallagher was now bowed and he had the shuffling gait of an old man. The past week had seen a rapid deterioration in his condition and as the evening wore on the putrefaction process would accelerate until, by midnight, the flesh would be dropping in lumps from his stinking frame.

As always, it was Gallagher's hands that were the first to go, which was why he'd taken the precaution of wearing gloves to hide his ravaged fingers. Although his face had so far escaped the worst of the decay he still made sure the collar of his coat was turned up, and his wide brimmed hat was pulled down to hide features that might start to rot at any moment.

Gallagher would have preferred to send the girl into the pub, but only he could do what had to be done. He remembered many years before when he had been rash enough to allow one of his long line of companions to select the person who was destined to become his unsuspecting host. It had been a disastrous mistake; the host body simply had not been suitable and had rejected him. He shuddered as he recalled the agonies he had suffered, and the time he had wasted, when he found himself exiled in the wilderness of ethereal desert that is neither of this world nor the next.

'What's wrong?' Sandie asked.

Gallagher ignored the question. 'Do you remember what you have to do?' His voice, harsh and rasping, betrayed his irritation. Sandie was not very bright at the best of times, but when she was high she was downright stupid. He looked down at the girl thoughtfully, perhaps tomorrow he would get rid of her and find himself a new companion. But first he must complete the task in hand.

'Don't worry, darling,' Sandie smiled her vacant smile. 'I know where to go and what to do.'

'Go then!' Gallagher snarled. 'Now!'

He watched the girl slip out of the alley and scamper off in the direction of the cemetery then he stepped out onto the pavement, only to quickly melt back into the shadows of the alley as he heard the sound of approaching footsteps.

A woman came into view accompanied by a small boy, dressed in a witch's black cape and a red plastic mask, who walked several paces behind her.

'Stop dragging your feet, William,' the woman said as she paused at the mouth of the alley and looked back at the boy who either hadn't heard, or, more likely, was deliberately ignoring her. 'William!' she said sharply. 'If you insist on being naughty The Bogeyman will get you. Now come here this instant.'

The boy joined his mother and, after casting a nervous glance towards the alley, he willingly took her proffered hand, then they were on their way again and were soon out of sight.

'You couldn't be more wrong, my dear,' Gallagher whispered into the night and then chuckled mirthlessly. 'The Bogeyman has no use for naughty little boys.'

It was true; no matter how naughty the child, there was still far too much innocence and goodness in their bodies to ensure a successful transplant. What The Bogeyman needed was real badness; the more mean, vicious or nasty the host, the less likelihood there was of rejection. *Anyway,* Gallagher thought with grim humour, *I get claustrophobic in small bodies.*

The pub was warm, noisy and packed with Halloween revellers, many of whom wore fancy dress, and the air was full of smoke and boisterous banter. In one corner of the lounge bar a juke box blared out a disco beat and two witches performed a tight little boogie on an area of dance-floor barely worthy of the name.

Gallagher bought himself a brandy and limped to a corner table at which sat a group of youngsters in animated conversation. The group fell silent as Gallagher approached and smiled down at them. One by one the youngsters rose silently to their feet and moved quickly away from the table. None of them particularly wanted to give up the cosy corner table, and none could have told you why they did so, but, suddenly, each one felt a compelling urge to be as far away from the stranger as possible. One of the girls found she had to visit the toilet hurriedly. She didn't quite make it and was violently sick in the corridor.

Gallagher sat at the table and let his eyes roam hungrily over the people who were crammed into the bar. He examined every face in minute detail; studying, scrutinising and mentally sniffing out the one for whom he searched. Gallagher was not concerned about age, or, health, both were immaterial since, in human terms, from midnight onwards the host body would be clinically dead. It would be only his presence that would preserve the body in any semblance of working order; his power and energy would act as an internal life-support machine. He had perfected his technique over many centuries until now he was able to hold in check the inevitable decaying process until the very end of his yearly cycle.

In the early years his control was poor and within seven or eight months, usually with the onset of summer, the host body had already so badly decomposed that the thing that was now Gallagher had been forced to go into hiding until the following October. Now he was able to keep the thermal cauterisation treatment sustained right to the very end, ensuring the degradation, which started deep within the internal organs, did not affect the external surfaces of the body until those last few days before glorious Halloween.

Gallagher was also unconcerned about the physical appearance of his intended host. Of course, he preferred them young, handsome and virile - he had far more fun that way but he was in no position to be fussy. It was not the shape of the body that mattered; it was the level of badness within that body that was important. As long as somebody was wicked enough, Gallagher would accept him; warts and all. Now, as he looked from face to face, he discovered none of the tell-tale signs that he sought and he was just beginning to consider moving to another pub when a woman staggered through the crowd towards his table.

'Great costume!' The woman swayed slightly as she spoke. In one hand she carried a book of raffle tickets and in the other a plastic

sandwich box containing several coins and a couple of banknotes.
'Don't tell me,' she went on, sending a heavy whiff of alcohol his
way, 'you're The Bogeyman?'

Gallagher smiled to himself as he recognised in the woman
something of what he sought. She had peroxide blonde hair and wore
a leopard skin mini-dress that revealed too much of her plump
thighs. Gallagher had met her type before; she would sell her body
for a few pounds and her soul for less. In an emergency the woman
would provide a reasonable sanctuary for the next twelve months. It
was never his first choice and he would not use this woman unless
absolutely necessary. The problem was that, because of its biological
composition, it was less easy to control a woman's body and it
tended to decay quicker.

'Am I right?' The woman persisted.

Gallagher nodded.

'I thought so!' She squealed. 'Your make-up is great.' The
woman swayed again and then seemed to remember why she was
there. 'Want some raffle tickets, then?' She asked. 'The first prize,'
she went on, anticipating a question that he never intended asking, 'is
a night with me.' The woman winked. 'The second prize is...' she
paused theatrically, '...two nights with me!' She hooted with laughter.
'Two nights! Get it?'

Gallagher smiled and as his mouth tightened and stretched, he
felt his lips tear open, but the blonde woman did not seem to notice.
He pulled a bulging wallet from his pocket and deliberately thumbed
part of the thick wad of banknotes onto the table.

'How much?' He asked, his voice little more than a rasping
whisper.

'Pound a strip, darling,' the blonde replied, her eyes fixed firmly
on the pile of banknotes. Suddenly she looked slightly less drunk.

'I'll have ten,' Gallagher mumbled as he picked a ten pound
note from the table and passed it to the woman.

The blonde took the note, handed over the raffle tickets and then
scurried away. She was remarkably agile on her plump legs and was
soon lost in the milling crowd of revellers. Several seconds later
Gallagher saw her whispering in the ear of a man who stood at the
bar with his back towards him. The pair looked surreptitiously in

Gallagher's direction. He quickly lowered his eyes and stared down at the untouched glass of brandy, however, what Gallagher saw in the split second before he averted his gaze made his smile widen into a ghoulish grin.

The man was tall and broad shouldered with a strong, weather-beaten face that bore clear signs of a succession of brawls; his fleshy nose was broken and a thin scar ran from his right ear to the corner of his full upper lip. But it was the man's eyes that pleased Gallagher most; they were cold, dark and ruthless.

Terry Driscoll listened to what Freda whispered in his ear. He looked over at the old man who was dressed as The Bogeyman and stared hard at the wad of notes that still lay on the table.

'And that's only 'alf of what 'e's got in 'is wallet,' Freda told him.

Terry watched as The Bogeyman picked up his money, left his seat and hobbled slowly to the door. He unhurriedly took another long draft of his beer. There was no rush; he would soon catch up with the old boy. This would be a cinch. He downed the last of his drink with a final flourish then he sidled out of the pub.

He followed the old man down the brightly lit street; silent in his trainers. He kept far enough away; avoiding being seen by his quarry, yet he was close enough to take advantage of any opportunity that might arise to jump him.

The Bogeyman walked for well over a mile and a half, then, just when Terry thought he might have to make his move in the open glare of the street lights, the old man turned into the cemetery gates.

Terry swore silently as he entered the cemetery. The old man had simply disappeared; swallowed up by a night made darker by the brightness of the street on the other side of the high brick wall that surrounded the cemetery. Terry stood for a while and sniffed the air like a bloodhound and almost gagged as he smelt the repulsive stench of decaying meat close at hand. He looked down, fully expecting to discover the remains of some dead animal lying at his feet. There was nothing on the gravel pathway but brittle, brown leaves and an assortment of litter.

There was a movement away to Terry's left and he half glimpsed something white out of the corner of his eye, but when he turned there was nothing to be seen, just the wind rustling the bushes that bordered the path. Then, as his eyes became adjusted to the lack of light, the night dissolved into numerous shades and shapes. Where before there was simply blackness, now there were degrees of darkness; from pitch-black to grey. Where there had been a wide expanse of nothingness, now Terry could make out the crooked silhouettes of different shapes and sizes of tombstones.

In front of him loomed a particularly large vault; tall and wide, it rose like a ghostly monument. Standing in front of the sepulchre, solidly dark against its grey granite walls, the figure of an angel stood guard over a long, black, oblong stain that, even at thirty paces, Terry could see was the door to the tomb. Then he saw a second figure, smaller than the first, and this one was moving. Terry heard the click-click of the man's heels on the path and he set off after him at a run.

Terry quickly caught up with The Bogeyman and his nostrils were again assailed by the revolting smell of death. He closed his mind to the stomach churning stink and concentrated on how best to relieve his victim of the bulging wallet.

Suddenly the old man stopped and turned to face him, at the same time the moon shrugged off its shroud of cloud to make a brief appearance and momentarily Terry found himself staring at an obscene face on which moist lumps of flesh lay like swollen leeches and nostrils had flared into open wounds. He slipped his switch blade from his pocket.

'Give me your wallet,' he demanded, fighting back the nausea that threatened to choke him. He flicked open the knife and stabbed it in the general direction of the old man.

The old man shook his head and studied Terry's face with knowing eyes. The younger man stared back dispassionately at The Bogyman. Knowing immediately that his victim would be able to identify him, he decided he had no alternative but to finish the job properly. He stabbed the knife again, but this time he didn't hold back. The knife pierced the front of the old man's heavy overcoat as if through tissue paper and sank deep into his chest.

The Bogeyman crumpled to the ground. Terry crouched over the prone figure and deftly removed the old man's wallet from his overcoat pocket, but as he transferred the wallet to the pocket of his own jeans, the old man groaned and reached out a hand to grab his arm. Terry tugged his arm free and jumped to his feet. The Bogeyman levered himself upright and moved towards his assailant.

Terry snapped. The streak of viciousness, which was never far from the surface, took hold and he mounted a murderous attack on the defenceless old man. Again and again the knife slashed through the night air and plunged deep into The Bogeyman's body. The old man fell to the ground again and at last Terry stopped, then satisfied his victim was dead he walked quickly towards the cemetery gates.

'Trick or treat?'

Terry stopped in his tracks. The girl was sitting on a wall just inside the gate. She wore a white, flared mini-skirt and a jumper that was tight enough to leave nothing to the imagination.

'Trick or treat?' The girl repeated her question as she came over and stood in front of Terry. He stared down at her through narrowed eyes. His first thought was one of self preservation: had the girl seen or heard anything? He glanced down nervously at his legs and feet and saw with relief that it was far too dark for any blood stains to be detected.

Terry studied the girl carefully. She showed no signs of having witnessed the recent murder and he quickly regained his composure. He recognised the spaced out look on the girl's face; she was obviously into some pretty heavy drug taking. Despite the drugs, or perhaps because of them, the message was clear. This was not an opportunity to be wasted.

'Are you trying to turn a trick?' He asked with a grin. 'Or are you offering me a treat?'

'I'm offering,' the girl said simply.

'Why?' Terry asked, wary again.

'Why?' The girl repeated the question. 'Because it's Halloween; because I'm cold; because I'm high and because I feel horny. That's why!' She moved closer. 'Now, do you want that treat, or not?'

Still Terry hesitated. He wanted her, there was no question about that, but a voice deep inside told him to turn the girl away, walk out of the cemetery and get back to the safe arms of Freda as fast as his legs would carry him.

'This girl is dangerous,' the voice said. 'Don't do it.'

The girl reached up and touched his lip with her finger and his fate was sealed. All thoughts of caution were forgotten.

Terry reached down to kiss the girl, but she pulled away from him with a giggle. 'Not here,' she insisted, her eyes were unnaturally wide and feverish. Tugging at his hand she urged him to follow her. 'Come on. It's going to rain. Let's find shelter. I know somewhere. It's not far.'

She led him to the tomb that was guarded by the angel. She pushed against the door and it opened with a loud creak, but Terry paused when she invited him to follow her down the steps into the burial chamber.

'You're not afraid of The Bogeyman? Are you?' She mocked with a loud, almost hysterical laugh that echoed down the blackness of the stairwell. Terry thought of the crumpled old man who lay somewhere out there in the dark of the cemetery, and began to laugh himself.

'No,' he said as he followed her down the stairs, 'I'm not afraid. The Bogeyman is dead.'

At the bottom of the stairs Terry again tried to kiss the girl. 'Come on,' he urged, 'this will do.'

But the girl darted away again and Terry was forced to follow her deeper into the crypt; where the air was stuffy and heavy with the same stench of rotting meat that had turned Terry's stomach twice before.

'Over here,' the girl called.

At first Terry could not see her, then she was picked out by the light from a stray moonbeam that filtered through a crack in the roof of the vault and the whiteness of her clothes shone out like a beacon against the blackness that surrounded her.

And then...

They were on the floor and at last the smell of decay was overwhelmed by the sickly sweet smell of the girl's cheap perfume. He felt her hands on his body, groping and probing. Without protest he let the girl roll him onto his back and closed his eyes as she gently undid the buttons of his shirt and dragged her nails across his chest.

And then...

Terry felt her mouth on his face and then on his neck; her silky tongue flicked delicately across his skin. He gasped as he felt the girl's weight on his chest. She was surprisingly heavy for one so small.

And then...

The corrupt smell of death returned, so strong now that Terry was forced to open his eyes and what he saw froze his blood. The Bogeyman was upon him. That awful bloated, putrid face was grinning down at him. Torn, rotting lips were pulled tight across teeth on which rank, stinking pus seeped from mouldering gums to congeal in green globules. The monster's nose was half eaten away and there were maggots crawling from one eyeless socket. His other eye stared down coldly at him. Terry screamed and as he opened his mouth The Bogeyman kissed him.

And then...

Terry felt The Bogeyman's hot breath blow deep inside his body and the swirling mists of primeval nightmares slowly filled him, drifting into his brain, expanding and swelling, pushing out the walls of his cranium until the inside of his head was one huge cavern into which the endless horrors of the night could congregate.

First it was the mist itself; curling fingers slipped from the body of the swirling mass to solidify into wreathing, wriggling serpents that slipped away into the dark corners of the cavern to await the time when they could sink their fangs and inject their venom with the most effect.

And then...

There were the rats. Gnawing into the tendons that controlled Terry's stomach muscles, loosening the walls of his intestines, the better to gorge on the filth and waste that lay in the pit of his bowels.

And then...

There were the spiders. Crawling in through his ears and nose in their thousands; scuttling quickly along the minute channels that ran through the roof of the cavern, laying their silver trail and weaving their sticky webs.

And then...

There were the timeless creatures of the night that crawl from the graves of the dead to suck blood and innocence from their victims, leaving them their peculiar legacy of corruption.

And then...

There were the demons and the hobgoblins and the multitude of nameless monstrosities that sit at the feet of Beelzebub.

And then...

There was the spirit of evil in its human manifestation; the galloping Hordes of Ghengis Khan, the sadistic High Priests of the Inquisition, the columns of marching Nazi storm-troopers, the sycophants and fellow travellers who encouraged Stalin in his mad Pogrom, the terrorists and murderers and traitors and rapists and child molesters.

And then...

The Bogeyman was entering the cavern, but now he was younger and his back was straight and his hair was black and his name was Duncan Gallagher.

And then...

There was an air of expectancy in the crowded cavern inside Terry Driscoll's head and the assembled host dropped to its knees at the altar of the Anti-Christ. With heads bowed in submission they waited.

And then...

There was a huge roar as a mighty wind blew through the cavern and the flames of Hell engulfed the congregation.

And then...

Those that had been touched by the flames rejoiced. The fiery heat intensified and spread through Terry's body, scorching his insides, cauterising him, preserving him, sealing him.

And then...

There was nothing.

Terry Driscoll walked up the steps of the vault and out into the moonlight. The clouds had disappeared completely now and the threat of rain had lifted. He unbuttoned his shirt and took the old man's wallet from the pocket of his jeans. He took out the money and then carefully rubbed any finger prints from the wallet before throwing it into the darkness of the cemetery. He pocketed the money and smiled.

Terry stood for a while and felt the cool night air against his face. It felt good. He had a sudden longing for company and he glanced back towards the vault where the broken body of Sandie Brodie shared a shallow grave with the rotting remains of Duncan Gallagher. Terry momentarily regretted having got rid of the girl; perhaps he should have kept her for one more day. Then he shrugged his shoulders and his smile widened. There was always Freda. With this thought in his mind, and with a tuneless whistle on his lips, Terry strode purposefully out of the cemetery.

And then...

After he had finished with Freda he would find himself another, younger companion.

And then...

He had twelve months to enjoy himself before he had to find another host.

And then...

It would be Halloween again.

The Birthday

May 26th 1981. What a day; I remember it as if it were yesterday. It started as such an ordinary day; a normal, unexceptional, routine Tuesday. You know the kind of day I mean. You wake up, get out of bed, bathe, wash your hair, have breakfast and remember yet again the warmth of your love; sweet, endless love. No different to any other day in the past month. Yes, everything is normal. You feel good. The future? Who cares? Worries? None. Mood? Relaxed and complacent.

Such was my start to May 26th 1981. But what began as just another day turned into one of the most extraordinary days of my life. The change in my fortunes came like an unexpected car crash. One minute you are humming happily to yourself, concentrating on the road ahead, when suddenly another car hits you in the rear bumper and propels you into a state of shock. Tragedy took my complacent happiness, tore it apart and turned it into the bitter black ashes of misery.

The nightmare started with a knock on the front door. It was a South African Defence Force colonel with a sad face and sympathetic words; but first came the words of pain.

'Mrs Owen?'

'Yes.'

'My name is Colonel Van Vyk. May I have a word with you in private?'

The soldier tipped his head towards the next door garden where my neighbour was pruning her roses and pretending not to be listening to our conversation.

'Of course, please come in.'

I led the Colonel through to the lounge, my heart was pounding and I felt sick.

'I have some bad news,' he said without further preamble after they were both sitting down. 'Your husband's unit was ambushed on the border this morning whilst on active duty. I am afraid details of the engagement are sketchy, but...'

'Alan has been wounded?'

He shook his head. 'It could be worse than that I'm afraid, Mrs Owen.'

I went cold. 'Is he dead?'

'We're not sure. Not everybody has been accounted for yet, but it doesn't look as if there were any survivors.'

'But there is still hope?'

'I wish I could give you hope, mevrou, but sadly I think you must prepare yourself for the worst. The armoured vehicle in which Alan and his men were travelling was hit with a missile and - well it doesn't look good.'

I sat in shock, trying to comprehend the incomprehensible, as Colonel Van Vyk got to his feet.

'I am so terribly sorry, Mrs Owen. Alan was a good commander and a brave man. If there is anything the Defence Force can do to help, you must let us know. We want to be there for you in your hour of need.'

And then he was gone, taking his sad face and sympathetic words with him.

I did not cry at first, the tears just would not come; the deep shock that gripped me would allow no other emotion to surface. Stunned and full of disbelief, I could do nothing but sit and watch the door close behind Colonel Van Vyk as let himself out. The live Colonel Van Vyk. The Colonel who was off to perform his little ritual again. How many times? God! How many men were there in a unit? I did not know and in the depths of my despair I did not really care. As far as I was concerned there was only one man in a unit, Alan. My Alan. My man. My only man. *The* only man.

I was born plain, I grew up plain and I remained plain. Not ugly, just plain, with a capital P. Not that I have always accepted so easily what was patently obvious, indeed, I went through a phase, in my late teens, when I was very self conscious about my appearance. I tried to make myself more beautiful; cosmetics, treatments, hair colouring – the works. It was only as I grew older that I saw sense and came to understand that beauty really does come from within. Now of course I realise that there is beauty in everybody, but often it is other people who recognise beauty before we do.

Because of my youthful lack of confidence I never had boyfriends during my time at school; even at high school and university I deliberately kept myself to myself, believing that no man would want to be seen out with such a Plain Jane. I had a few female friendships, but these usually only lasted until those friends drifted into serious relationships.

Then I met Alan Owen.

Alan did not seem to care that I was plain, indeed, I am sure he did not even notice and so, for the first time in my life, my self-perceived lack of beauty was unimportant. We loved each other. It was a love I thought was impossible. It was all consuming. Alan was my life.

Within three months of meeting we were married. There were a few raised eyebrows and suggestively dug elbows, but did we care? Did we hell! Our love was so strong we were blind to all the insinuations, besides, we knew I was not pregnant.

We were blissfully happy and convinced it would last forever. We had everything we wanted; we were both working in jobs we enjoyed, we had a neat little house in Newlands, we had our books, our records, our health and, of course, our love.

Then Alan's call-up papers came and I lost him to the Defence Force for his two year's National Service. He wrote every day. Long chatty love letters that eased my aching heart, comforted my loneliness and warmed my empty bed at night. And now? Now there would be no more letters, no more comfort, no more love and no more Alan.

At last, with that realisation, I cried.

I cried for two solid hours, sobbing until I thought my chest would explode and then, when I could cry no more, I decided to kill myself. Kill myself? Was that possible? Was it not too late? Without Alan I was as good as dead already.

Why did I choose Table Mountain on which to end my misery? Well, in addition to the obvious practical reason that a jump from 1085 metres would lead to certain death, my choice was because Alan and I first met there, high up on the mountain's flat and rugged summit.

Alan was with a group of friends and I was alone, sitting on one of the benches outside the cable car station at the top of Table Mountain, reading a book and savouring the warmth of the sun and the crisp, clean air.

Something made me look up, the proverbial sixth sense I suppose, and suddenly I was looking into a pair of friendly brown eyes. There was one incredibly delicious spark that jumped between us, leaving my stomach fluttering with excitement. That was it; immediately I knew that we were meant for each other and Alan later told me that he felt the same way. What do you call that? Fate? Love at first sight? A little of both I guess.

During our time together we often went back to Table Mountain; using the occasions to relive and renew our first feelings of love. We came to consider it our special place and even when it was crawling with tourists we still, perhaps naively, looked upon it as 'our mountain'.

As I travelled up in the swaying cable car to my death, I remembered again our first meeting; Alan's nervous grin and my shy self-conscious smile. The avoidance of eye contact after that first electric interchange of looks, the covert glances and his flushed faced nervous greeting. He asked me if I would like a coffee and I accepted. He forgot his friends and I forgot my book. We had an instant understanding and after the coffee we exchanged telephone numbers. I remember the empty feeling when we parted company and the feeling of elation when the following day he phoned me. Would I meet him again? Yes! Yes! Yes!

Now Alan was gone forever and part of me was dead also. The tears were back, blinding me as I stumbled from the yellow cable car and walked determinedly towards the edge of mountain's rocky table top. For a moment I stared down at the Lilliputian city below me that was Cape Town.

I could see the City and Gardens area; the Foreshore with its towering skyscrapers; Duncan Dock lined with ships and boats; the wide sweep of Table Bay and Blouberg Strand in the far distance; the N9 National Road heading out of the city towards Paarl and then onwards all the way to Cairo; the mountains, Winterhoek, Du Toit's Kloof, Wemmershoek, Simonsberg and Frenschhoek. I could see all this and more.

It was early winter and above me the skies were leaden and grey, but in the distance the clouds were even lower, gathering darkly on the horizon, hiding amongst the peaks of the mountain range, waiting for the stiffening north-westerly wind to blow them and their rain into Cape Town.

Closer at hand, to my right, I could see Devil's Peak and the saddle of rock that connects it to Table Mountain. To my left I could see the more distinctive Lion's Head rock rising high above the suburbs of Muille Point, Sea Point and Bantry Bay.

I could see all this and yet I could see nothing. My mind was numb with grief and horror at what I was about to do. I balanced on a protruding piece of sandstone and prepared to step to my death.

'Don't do it!'

I heard the voice at the same time that I felt myself being tugged backwards. I spun round to be faced by a pleasant looking young man in trekking clothes and a baseball cap. On his back he carried a rucksack. He had sparkling eyes that enhanced his good natured face.

'What?' I stammered, suddenly feeling the hot flush of guilt on my face.

'I said, don't do it,' he repeated with a smile. 'You *were* going to jump, weren't you?'

I shrugged and looked over my shoulder at the drop behind me. I blinked away more tears. A little grey dassie poked its head out from a crack in the side of the sheer mountain face and looked up at me as if to say: 'What's all the fuss about?' I watched as it scampered effortless along a narrow ledge and disappeared into a clump of coarse grass. When I turned back to the young man he was sitting on a boulder.

'Is it really that bad?' He asked gently. He patted the boulder with the palm of his hand. 'Come sit with me and we'll talk about it.'

I shook my head and tasted the salt of my tears on my upper lip. I licked them away.

'Please!' He insisted. 'Talk to me and then jump, if you still want to.' He smiled again. 'Don't worry; if you do decide to jump I won't stop you. I promise.'

Without knowing why I walked over and sat at the stranger's

side.

'What's your name?' The man asked.

'Beth,' I mumbled through my tears.

'Please don't cry, Beth. Nothing is ever as bad as it seems.'

'What do you know?' I snapped as the man's words triggered an anger that had lain dormant in me since I learned of Alan's death. I jumped to my feet. What did this man, this stranger, know about anything? How could he know how I felt? How could he even begin to guess at the anguish I was suffering? Could anybody understand that feeling of utter emptiness?

'My name's Robin,' he said, brushing aside my angry outburst and ignoring my question. 'Don't be angry with me, Beth.' Again he smiled his gentle smile. 'I do understand how you feel, believe me. Please sit down again.' His voice was soothing and reassuring and my anger disappeared as quickly as it had flared up.

'I'm sorry,' I apologised. 'I didn't mean to shout at you.' I sat down next to him again and dabbed at my eyes with a tissue.

'That's okay. Now tell me, what's so bad that you want to kill yourself?'

So I told him; this total stranger who called himself Robin. I opened up my heart and told him everything; almost my life story. When I had finished he smiled knowingly and took my hand. His hands were cold, but somehow comforting.

'Listen to me, Beth, and trust me. However, bad it might appear, nothing is ever as black as it seems. I appreciate that right now you don't see any reason to live but, sies man, consider the possibility that your Defence Force visitor was wrong; perhaps there were survivors, after all he did say that not everyone had been accounted for. Suppose Alan is not dead? What if he did survive? How would Alan feel if he came home to discover you had thrown yourself from the top of Table Mountain? Wouldn't it be better to wait until his death was confirmed before doing something silly?'

I looked into the stranger's face and wanted to believe him. I wanted to hope there had been a mistake; an administrative error. I wanted Alan to be alive. I wanted to live.

'You've lost somebody you love and...'

'The only man I have ever loved,' I interrupted him, 'and the only man who ever loved me.'

'...and I know exactly how you feel, Beth,' he said quietly as if I had never interrupted him. 'You see, two weeks ago my wife and two children were killed in a car crash. Some drunken idiot hit them head on and wiped them off the face of the earth.'

I stared at him, shocked, and for a few minutes I could not speak because I simply did not know what to say, although I knew that somehow I must say something. 'Oh, Robin,' I said eventually, my own tragedy momentarily forgotten, 'how terrible! I'm so very sorry. But how can you still smile? When we first met you looked so happy.'

'It's easier now, Beth,' he explained with a resigned shrug. 'At first I was devastated, just like you. I couldn't think straight, all I knew was that I wanted to die. But now? Now I feel better. In the words of the Bob Dylan song; I have been released. I feel a new man, because today is my birthday. The twenty sixth of May.' He stood up and took my hand. 'Come with me a minute.'

Without protest I let Robin lead me to the south side of the mountain's flat top. My new friend said nothing, he simply pointed into the distance.

I followed his gaze just as a shaft of sunlight broke through the grey sky to bathe the surrounding area in glorious light. I could see the lush green of Constantia cutting its broad swathe into the heart of the Cape Peninsula's rocky spine. I could see the broad Cape Flats rolling away towards the township of Mitchell's Plain. I could see the blue waters of False Bay and the golden thread of beach that runs all the way from Muizenberg down through the series of small bays in which nestle the hamlets of St James, Kalk Bay, Clovelly and Fish Hoek, to Simons Town. I could see almost the whole length of the hooked finger of land that stretches from Table Mountain to where Cape Point marks where the cold waters of the Atlantic meet the warm waters of the Indian Ocean. I could see!

'The Cape of Good Hope,' Robin said quietly. 'Good *Hope*.' he emphasised, 'Isn't it beautiful, hope? Such a pity to turn your back on so much beauty. Heh? Listen to me, Beth, life is far too short as it is, don't sacrifice what you have. Just be glad to be alive.' He squeezed my hand as he spoke. 'Trust me, Beth. Everything will work out fine in the end, you'll see.' He smiled down at me, his brown eyes warm and soulful. 'My advice to you is to get into that cable-car, go home and be happy that you are still alive with your memories.'

I hesitated as conflicting emotions battled for ascendency, but eventually Hope won over Despondency and I realised that Robin was right. I nodded and let him take my arm and lead me towards the cable-car station.

'Goodbye, Beth.'

'You're not coming with me?'

He shook his head. 'No, I need to stay here on my own for a while.' He stared off into the distance, his eyes misty and full of sadness.

'But wouldn't you feel better if you had some company? I'll stay with you if you like. I really don't mind. It's your birthday, remember?' I suddenly felt immensely sorry for this stranger who had gone out of his way to rescue me from self destructive despair. I wanted to help him in the same way.

'No thanks, Beth.' He smiled. 'Yes, it's my birthday, but it's a pretty strange birthday. Don't worry about me. I'm over the worst of it now.' He gently ushered me towards the open door of the cable-car. 'Now, if you don't mind, I really would like to be on my own for a while.'

I looked again into his handsome, kindly face. There was so much more I wanted to say, so much appreciation to convey, so much - love? But I could not find the right words to express myself so I simply said: 'Goodbye, Robin.' I reached up and without hesitation kissed him gently on his lips as if I had known him all my life. 'Thank you.' I added with feeling.

He smiled again and tenderly touched my cheek with an icy cold finger. I shivered and for the first time felt the full effects of the north-westerly wind that whipped in from the Atlantic Ocean. I turned and quickly stepped into the shelter of the cable-car. When I looked back Robin had disappeared.

When I arrived home it was to discover a courier knocking on my front door. He carried an urgent registered letter for which he asked me to sign. Despite the envelope carrying the emblem of the South African Defence Force I was strangely calm as I took it from the postman, carried it indoors, sat down at the kitchen table and tore it open.

'Thank God!' I said out loud as I read the very short handwritten letter.

Dear Mrs Owen.

Having just returned from visiting you this morning I have discovered that your husband did indeed survive the ambush in which the rest of his unit was killed. I tried to telephone you but there was no response. I felt it important that you heard the news without delay so I decided to send this letter by courier. I hope it arrived in a timely fashion and finds you in good heart.

Unfortunately, Lieutenant Owen was injured in the attack and is currently being treated in Pretoria Military Hospital. However, I am delighted to say that although his injuries are serious they not life threatening.

As I told you earlier, the Defence Force will do whatever is needed to help you, including arranging for transport to Pretoria. Please do not hesitate to contact me on the direct telephone number shown at the head of this letter.

Yours sincerely
Colonel F.D. Van Vyk

'Thank you God,' I repeated. 'And thank you Robin.'

In that detached, zombie like state that is induced by deep relief, I walked through to the lounge. In passing I picked up the evening newspaper from the telephone table and a small headline in the bottom corner of the front page caught my eye. I read it in disbelief:

Cape Town Man In Suicide Horror.

LATE this morning a man was killed when he jumped from the top of Table Mountain. A policeman said that Mr Robin McCleary (37), who was a resident of Milnerton, apparently committed suicide.

Mr Frikkie Steyn, who was a business colleague of the dead man, explained that Mr McCleary had been deeply depressed since the tragic death of his wife and two children in a car accident.

The coroner's office said that it hoped an inquest would be held early next month.

At first my mind found it difficult to accept those few short sentences and then, as the truth sank in, I felt my stomach turn. I read the article again. So, after talking me out of jumping, my saviour had done exactly that. How awful!

I shook my head in despair. But why? Why today of all days? I remembered again his words: "At first I was devastated, just like you. I couldn't think straight, all I knew was that I wanted to die. But now? Now I feel better. In the words of the Bob Dylan song; I have been released. I feel a new man, because today is my birthday. The twenty sixth of May."

I remembered Robin pointing towards the Cape of Good Hope and what he said: "Good Hope. Isn't it beautiful, hope? Such a pity to turn your back on so much beauty. Heh? Listen to me, Beth, life is far too short as it is, don't sacrifice what you have. Just be glad to be alive."

I walked over to the apartment window and looked up to where Table Mountain stood brooding in the gathering gloom of a fast approaching storm. I sighed. *Today is my birthday.* Those words continued to haunt me. *Today is my birthday. The twenty sixth of May.*

Slowly the significance of that date filtered through the shock and sadness that had dulled my brain. Then I remembered Robin's icy cold touch and an eerie shiver raised the hairs on the nape of my neck. A quick glance at the top of the newspaper confirmed my suspicions.

That day's evening paper had not yet arrived, I had been reading yesterday's edition. It was dated Monday 25th May 1981.

The Mummy Angel

It was a magnificent Christmas tree; its thick trunk, deeply rooted in a brightly decorated tub, tapered over a dozen feet into the air until the needles on its uppermost shoots - fine and delicate and lime green in colour - brushed lightly against the wood-beamed ceiling. The tree filled the large bay-window of the lounge; wide and bushy branches sprawled out to cast inviting shadows across the deep pile carpet, forming a dark and fragrant grotto into which had been stashed an organised jumble of interesting looking packages, all beautifully wrapped in colourful paper and adorned with matching ribbons and bows. As soon as the presents were unwrapped the shadowy shelter would become a children's sanctuary, turned by young, uninhibited minds into a mysterious and magical cavern of make-believe.

The tree was laden with decorations; its branches sagged and groaned under the weight of the various baubles that dangled from them. There were glass balls of every type and size, some plain, others sprinkled with glittering white powder and still more with multi-faceted surfaces that mirrored surrounding images in a variety of distorted reflections.

There were also tiny musical instruments, gold plated and tied to the branches with golden thread; drums, trumpets, cymbals, harps and violins; the sounds of Heaven. Miniature toys poked out from deep within the dark green foliage; dolls, soldiers, trains and a variety of animals - wooden and stuffed cloth. There were other playthings too; novelties, blowers, streamers, puzzles, trinkets and small crackers which waited to be pulled to release their plastic charms and inane mottoes.

Little feather tailed robins were clipped alongside sparkling white snowflakes, glistening imitation icicles, tinkling bells, mouth watering sweets, candies, chocolates and other treats. Strings of polished beads and lustrous garlands were hung in golden drapes between branches over which had been looped gold lametta tinsel and on the tips of which were fastened crimson velvet bows and dainty glass candles.

And, of course, there were the fairy-lights; dotted among the branches, twinkling like distant constellations, their yellow flashing bulbs reflecting on the shiny metallic decorations against which they nestled, multiplying and spreading across the tree in a galaxy of miniature stars.

It was a beautiful sight, with only one thing missing; spoiling what otherwise would have been a perfect picture of Christmas: there was no Christmas Angel on top of the tree. But I am getting ahead of myself; the story really begins much earlier.

It was in August that their world fell apart.

The month started perfectly. For weeks the summer sun had beaten down from a clear blue sky and by the time David and Rebecca took their annual holiday the weather had settled into a pattern of long hot days and balmy nights. Their holiday was like a second honeymoon, although, as Rebecca pointed out, since they had been unable to afford a honeymoon first time round, they ought to consider their stay in the idyllic cottage deep in the Lake District as their official, if somewhat delayed, start of a new life together. Rebecca could not have been more wrong.

There were no problems with money now; those early years of struggle and sacrifice while David built up his practice had been worth it. He was now firmly established as one of the most sought after barristers in London and Rebecca, who was three years David's senior and who had supported them both for so long on her junior doctor's salary, now had a thriving General Practice in Hendon.

They could easily have afforded an expensive holiday abroad; indeed, they had talked about going on safari in Kenya. They decided against this idea primarily because they felt Sarie-Anne was not yet old enough for the African climate and the relative hardship that they would face on safari. In addition, if the truth be told, they both preferred the more homely comforts of Cumbria.

So they rented the cottage for a month and used the time to make up for the long enforced hours spent apart whilst they pursued their respective careers. The long days were full of swimming, walking, sun-bathing and reading. In the evenings they usually lit a barbeque and cooked themselves steaks, or chicken, or fresh caught fish, and, for Sarie-Anne, sausages and burgers. Whichever meat they chose it was invariably accompanied by large, pungent mushrooms, onion rings, corn on the cob and a fresh mixed salad, all washed down with a ready supply of mellow red claret.

Each evening, after they had eaten and Sarie-Anne was safely tucked up in bed, they would sit in companionable silence on the cottage's patio, sipping contentedly on generous glasses of cognac, savouring the last of the sun's heat and rejoicing in its beauty as it turned slowly from a pale yellow to a deep orange colour until, at last, it slipped silently into the dark, still waters of Lake Windermere. Every so often the silence would be broken as they chatted quietly about the day's events and made plans for the following day's activities.

Their nights were spent making wonderfully tender love; taking time to rediscover each other and delighting in finding again those special trigger points of passion. They both recognised their relationship had reached that dangerous stage where it becomes easy to slip into a comfortable state that borders on complacency and they were determined to continually rekindle the spark of excitement to prevent this happening. So far they had been successful.

And so the happy carefree days drifted on, with no clouds on the horizon to spoil what was a very special time in their lives. Then, in the third week of their holiday, Rebecca was taken ill. At first they thought it was a touch of food poisoning and Rebecca tried simply to shrug off the nausea and the headache, but by the fourth day, as her discomfort increased and the headache grew worse, she began to suspect her illness was more serious and they decided it was best to return home. That same night Rebecca collapsed and was rushed to hospital. She never regained consciousness and within twenty four hours she was dead.

'It was a rare and particularly virulent form of acute meningitis,' Dr Benjamin Wiseman explained, his eyes moist with the grief he shared with the man who sat opposite him. 'I'm sorry, David. There was nothing anybody could do.'

David did not reply, instead he sat and stared out of the window. His mind, recoiling from the suddenness of his loss and refusing to accept the shocking truth, sought refuge in the happiness of his memories of Rebecca.

He remembered the dark beauty of her face and how it would set in that look of concentration that was peculiar to her. He remembered fondly how her intense green eyes would mist over and she would become so distant, as if she had lowered a shutter on the outside world, including him. He remembered how that shutter would suddenly lift and how Rebecca would be back with him, her vibrancy restored and her eyes sparkling with intelligence.

He remembered Rebecca's gaiety and her impish sense of humour. He remembered the full bloodied laugh that would accompany earthy jokes that she took great delight in relating and how she would dissolve in giggles whenever she forgot the punchline, which she invariably did. He remembered her smile and the way her eyes would sometimes glint in an unspoken invitation, her mock protest when he tried to grab her and her squeal of delight when he succeeded. Most of all he remembered their loving.

'David?' Benjamin studied his friend miserably. He had known David Green since they were at school together. He was at university with Rebecca, treating her as the sister he had never had, and had gone on to marry her best friend, Lisa. The four of them remained close ever since, despite the pressure of pursuing individual careers; David as a barrister, Rebecca in general practice, Ben as a specialist in children's diseases and Lisa as an advertising executive.

'David?' He repeated gently.

At the sound of Ben's voice David snapped out of his semi-trance. He turned to face his friend. 'Yes, Ben,' he said quietly as he focused on the doctor's face. 'Sorry, I was...'

'Don't worry, old son, I know where you were,' Benjamin paused and the expression of anguish on his face deepened. He took a deep breath. 'David,' he went on quickly, not trusting himself to delay any longer in case his courage failed him completely. 'We need to talk. It's about Sarie-Anne...' The doctor's voice trailed off into silence. He and Lisa were Sarie-Anne's godparents and he felt sick as the cold hand of dread gripped his heart. He took another deep breath in an effort to control his emotions and keep up a semblance of professional detachment.

'What about Sarie-Anne?' David did not understand, or, rather he would not let the conscious part of his mind accept the possibilities being formulated by the sub-conscious, more instinctive side of his intellect.

'As a precaution we took some tests.' Ben explained eventually.

'Tests?' David repeated.

'Yes.' Ben's voice betrayed his distress. 'I am so sorry...' he began.

'Sarie-Anne has meningitis,' David interrupted his friend, at last accepting the inevitable.

Ben shook his head. 'I wish it were that simple. If Sarie-Anne had meningitis I'd be quite confident that we could cure her.'

David stared hard at the doctor. 'What are you trying to tell me, Ben?'

'The tests for meningitis proved negative, David.'

'But?'

'But the tests highlighted another problem. A worse problem. Sarie-Anne has leukaemia.'

David frowned and continued to stare at his friend in silence, trying to come to terms with what he had heard.

'David. What can I say? The odds on this happening must be millions to one.' Ben stood up and walked round the desk and placed a hand on his friend's shoulder. 'It's not one hundred percent certain,' he went on. 'We'll need to carry out further tests before we know for sure.'

'But you're fairly certain?' David asked, his voice flat and lifeless.

Ben nodded.

'Is it curable?' David persisted. 'I don't really know much about leukaemia. What exactly is it? All I know is that it is a type of cancer.'

David saw Ben hesitate.

'Be honest with me, Ben,' he pleaded.

'Leukaemia is a fatal, cancerous disorder of the leukote precursors of the white blood cells,' Ben intoned as if he was reading from a medical book. 'Until the advent of AIDS, leukaemia was considered one of the most malignant diseases to afflict children. As for whether it is curable; remission can be induced in most cases and can prolong a child's life for anything up to four years.' Ben paused and looked at David with sad eyes. 'However, I would be misleading you if I didn't tell you that only one percent of patients are ever completely cured.'

'So how long has Sarie-Anne got?'

Ben shook his head and looked uncomfortable. 'I can't say, David. Nobody knows. As I told you before, kids can live anything up to four years - perhaps even longer. All I can say is that we must make the most of Sarie-Anne while she is still with us.'

There was a long silence. David stared at his finger-nails, his eyes misty and his throat constricted, whilst Ben stood at his side, his hand still resting lightly on the seated man's shoulder. Eventually it was Ben who broke the silence.

'Will you tell Sarie-Anne?' he asked.

David shook his head. 'No,' he replied quickly, his voice empty and desolate. 'Not yet, anyway.' He paused and when he spoke again his mood was one of bitterness and cold anger. 'How the hell do you tell an eight year old child she is going to die?'

The weeks passed quickly. The hot summer made way for the autumn and the nights started to draw in, bringing with them the cool, damp mists that lay lightly on the ground, shrouding the land in a ghostly blanket that disappeared with the dawn and left behind a fine film of moist dew to lay like sparkling jewels across the intricate pattern of spider's webs that carpeted the lawns and hung from shrubs.

Then the autumn winds came, blowing in from the south and south-west, buffeting the trees and stripping them of leaves that were already turning the countryside into a patchwork quilt of browns, yellows, oranges and gold.

The wind carried in the rain from the Atlantic Ocean and the rain washed away the dust and dirt of the long summer months and softened earth that had grown dry, cracked and hard from lack of water.

Finally the winds turned to the north, the skies cleared, the temperature dropped and the first hoar frost dusted the trees and bushes and plants with a layer of crackling white powder.

Winter was upon the land.

But David did not notice the coming and going of the seasons, he was too wrapped up in the continuing nightmare that haunted his life.

Rebecca's death had hit him hard, she was the only woman whom he had truly loved and his sense of loss was total. His feeling of desolation was heightened by the knowledge that soon he would lose his last remaining link with his wife; Sarie-Anne.

Throughout this time his daughter was in and out of hospital; test followed test and treatment followed treatment, but all to no avail. Inexorably the leukaemia tightened its grip on the little girl, polluting her blood with its corrupting presence, weakening her resistance and draining her of life.

And David could do nothing to help. He was powerless. He would have spent all the money at his disposal, and more, if there had been the slightest chance of curing Sarie-Anne, but no amount of money could buy off the evil disease that was killing the most precious thing he had left in the world. He could only sit by and watch as his daughter wasted away before his eyes.

It was during December that David first heard Sarie-Anne talking to Rebecca. He awoke from his own restless slumber to hear his daughter's thin, reedy voice through the bedroom wall and his first thought was that she was talking in her sleep.

He was surprised to find her wide awake when he entered her bedroom and could see that she was hot and feverish. 'What is it, darling?' He asked as he gently mopped Sarie-Anne's forehead. 'Did you have a bad dream?'

He stared down at his daughter's tiny wasted body and his heart tightened in his chest as he saw the painful thinness of her arms, the bright red flush of fever that sat upon the otherwise deathly paleness of her cheeks, the sparse fluffy tufts of hair on her head that had once sported a mass of dark curls, and the glint as little droplets of tears welled out of her eyes.

'I want to see mummy,' Sarie-Anne whispered softly.

'Mummy's gone, darling,' David said gently as he brushed away the tears with a tissue.

'But she was here, daddy,' the little girl insisted. 'Mummy was talking to me. I could hear her, but I couldn't see her.'

'I know, Sarie,' David murmured. 'She is looking after you; looking after us both. You can't see her, but you can feel her and when you close your eyes you can hear her voice.'

'But I wasn't dreaming, daddy. I heard her when my eyes were open.'

'Of course you did, darling.' David caressed his daughter's forehead. She was burning up. 'Perhaps you will get to see mummy sometime...' he stopped himself as he realised what he was saying, but he was too late.

'When, daddy?' Sarie-Anne asked eagerly.

David did not reply for a while. He settled himself down on his daughter's bed and tucked her thin arms under the duvet, taking time to compose himself, struggling desperately for an answer. 'Perhaps at Christmas,' he said eventually.

'Christmas, daddy?'

David nodded. 'Yes, Sarie. But you probably won't recognise mummy,' he said, making it up as he went along.

'Why not?'

'Well, sometimes at Christmas, when God feels sorry for little girls who are sick, he sends an Angel down to earth to visit them and make them feel better,' suddenly the words were pouring out as if he was inspired. 'And when a little girl has lost her mummy, God tries to make sure that mummy is the Angel he sends. But, because God can't appear to have favourites, he insists that Mummy-Angels wear a disguise.'

David paused and felt a warm surge of love as he saw the total trust and innocent faith that shone out from his daughter's eyes. 'Of course,' he went on, 'only little girls who are good are visited and it is important that a nice home is prepared for the Mummy-Angel.'

'Where do Mummy-Angels live, daddy?'

'On top of the Christmas Tree, darling. Like the usual Christmas Angel.'

'But Mummy-Angels are special, aren't they, daddy?'

'That's right, Sarie, Mummy-Angels are very special and if we want one to visit us we will need a very special Christmas tree, in fact, we'll need the best tree you've ever seen. So, here's what we'll do. We'll go out and buy the biggest tree we can find and when we've brought the tree home you can help me decorate it and make it pretty and cosy, then, on Christmas Eve, whilst you're asleep, God might send mummy back to us as an Angel and when we get up on Christmas Day she will be there, in the lounge, sitting on top of the tree.'

Sarie-Anne did not speak for a while, she just lay there, her young face thoughtful and serious.

'Perhaps...' she mused finally, '...if I say an extra prayer, God will let mummy give me a cuddle before she goes to sit on the tree.'

David said nothing. There was nothing he could say.

That weekend David wrapped up Sarie-Anne in her warmest clothes and took her to the garden centre where they hummed and hawed over the vast selection of Christmas trees before finally settling for one that was tall and straight and bushy. Then, singing Christmas carols as they went, they triumphantly set off home with the tree strapped to the roof rack of their car.

Back home David set the Christmas tree in a tub of earth and positioned it in the bay window of the lounge. Next he retrieved the large box of decorations from the loft. These old treasures, each of which evoked a memory of one or other Christmas past, were supplemented by a supply of newly purchased decorations. David withdrew each of the new baubles from a brimming bag with a theatrical flourish that provoked an excited squeal from Sarie-Anne.

David decorated the tree whilst little Sarie-Anne sat propped up on the sofa directing the operation with a bossiness that verged on the dictatorial, but which, he was later forced to admit to Benjamin, showed a flair and an eye for balance that was far more creative than anything he could have achieved alone.

A lump came to David's throat when he discovered at the bottom of the box the old Angel with the white crepe paper dress that had belonged to Rebecca when she was a little girl and which had sat on top of their tree every year that she and David had been together. He looked at Sarie-Anne and raised an eyebrow. His daughter shook her head and pointed towards the mantelpiece. David nodded in agreement and positioned the Angel next to the large gilt frame that contained a photograph of his dead wife. The top of the Christmas tree remained bare.

The week before Christmas, David took Sarie-Anne to St Thomas' Hospital for yet another series of tests and when the tests had been completed he took her off shopping in the West End. They bought presents for his mother and father, Rebecca's widowed mother and for Sarie-Anne's Uncle Jacques and Aunt Sophie and their two children, Henry and Ruth.

They brought little presents for several of Sarie-Anne's friends and chocolates for the nurses at the hospital and, of course, they chose a special present for Ben and Lisa. In one particular department store, Sarie-Anne insisted on David looking the other way whilst she negotiated a sale on her own and he made a great show of putting his hands over his eyes and promising not to peek at the gift she brought for him.

As they left the store something caught Sarie-Anne's eye and she made David stop. It was a small hair-slide, inexpensive, but pretty, with diamantes set into a delicate ebony crescent. The hair-slide was just the type of stocking filler that Rebecca used to love. David bought it.

When they returned home they spent the evening wrapping the presents and storing them away under the tree, with the largest at the back and the smallest at the front. They wrapped the little hair-slide in gold-foil paper and, at Sarie-Anne's insistence David tucked the present high into the uppermost branches of the tree, just below where the Angel would eventually sit.

'That's so mummy will know exactly where to find it,' Sarie-Anne said with a wise nod of her head. David smiled and made a mental note to remember to remove the hair-slide and fix it to the hair of the Angel that he intended to buy.

The snow came on Christmas Eve.

It was perhaps not the best time for David to travel down to Kent, the roads were busy and the occasional fall of snow made driving conditions hazardous, however, the client he had to visit was of sufficient importance to make the journey necessary and of sufficient wealth to pay David well for the inconvenience.

The client lived in a country house just outside Faversham and when David's meeting finished he decided to pop down the A2 to Canterbury and finish his Christmas shopping. Sarie-Anne's presents were easy; an iPod, a huge teddy bear, a watch, books and a painting set. Buying the Angel proved more difficult. There were lots of the usual run-of-the-mill plastic Angels, but David wanted something different, something extra special. Then, just when David was beginning to give up hope and thought he would have to settle for one of the cheaper Angels, he found exactly what he was looking for.

David discovered the shop by chance. It was tucked away in one of the side streets that lay adjacent to Canterbury's main shopping area and was not so much a toyshop as an antique shop that happened to sell a number of traditional toys.

The Angel stared out at David from the shop window. She was about six inches tall and was dressed in a long, white satin robe. On her back was fastened a pair of large, gossamer thin wings and about her head floated a golden, filigree halo that was artfully positioned in such a way as to hide the pins that connected it to the Angel's head. Her hair was long and lustrous and a deep shade of auburn. She had a small, round, pretty face with eyes that were wide and green, and shining with love and laughter. However, the Angel's mouth was not laughing, indeed, it was not even smiling; her lips were set in a slight, enigmatic, almost disapproving pout that gave her whole face a look of deep concentration.

It was probably this, more than anything else that attracted David most. He found that if he hooded his eyes and squinted through the window, the glass of which carried the sheen of condensation on the inside and was starred with soft snowflakes on the outside; and if he used just a little imagination, the Angel was transformed into an exact, but miniature replica of Rebecca.

It had been gloomy all day, with the swirling showers of snow keeping the sky leaden grey, blanketing out what little light the short day offered. By the time David completed his purchase, and the shop assistant had wrapped the Angel and stored it carefully away in a brown cardboard package, and despite it being only three o'clock in the afternoon, the daylight had disappeared completely and the earlier showers had become one long continuous snowstorm.

The car journey back to London was a nightmare. The motorway was restricted to a single lane in either direction and as David crawled along in the slow moving traffic he resigned himself to a late arrival home. Luckily he had taken the precaution of arranging for Lisa to look after Sarie-Anne, however, he was still keen to get home as early as possible in order that he could wrap his daughter's presents and fix the Angel to the top of the tree before she woke up the following morning.

It took David almost three hours to get from Canterbury to the approach road to the Dartford Tunnel and another hour to get through the tunnel. By the time David finally made it onto the M25 it was just after seven o'clock. The weather was blowing up from the south-west and the covering of snow was, as yet, not so thick on the Essex side of the river and David's progress became easier, however, by the time he had reached the motorway exit to Barnet, the conditions were worsening by the minute.

Soon David was off the exposed motorway driving along more sheltered roads that were lined with bright street lights. The snow was falling much more heavily now, swirling down through the yellow glow of the lamps, forming a thick curtain through which the probing beams of David's headlights sliced, cutting out a brilliant tunnel in the whiteness. Large flakes settled on his windscreen in a brief, silent crust of glistening white before being compressed into hard wedges by the sweep of his wipers.

Despite the falling snow, wherever he looked David saw colourful lights. On either side of the street, fairy lights twinkled in the windows of houses. Christmas trees, bedecked with decorations and sparkling with their own little lights, beckoned from inside a hundred front rooms that glowed with red, inviting warmth. Some houses had lines of large coloured bulbs running along the facia, just underneath the guttering, lighting up the whole of the front wall and others had gardens that were transformed into winter wonderlands by the scores of lights that had been strung from trees and shrubs.

There were other lights, of course, a multitude of sizes and colours, all distorted in some degree by the persistent flurry of snow; traffic lights, blazing neon signs, car tail lights, brake lights and headlights.

The oncoming lorry slewed across the road in front of David the headlights filling his eyes and brain and his very being with a blinding white glare. Instinctively he twisted the steering wheel to the left and felt a dagger of fear jab into his guts as the careering lorry followed his car round. A collision was inevitable, even if there had been time to react differently; there was nothing David could do to avoid the crash.

The lorry hit him full on his offside wing and spun his car round on the slippery surface, its impetus pushing it towards a waste skip that stood by the side of the road. The lorry continued skidding and its back swung round and hammered into the side of David's car, crushing it against the skip, squeezing it as easily as a toothpaste tube, forcing the back to concertina forward towards the driver's seat. David was thrown with such force that, despite his seatbelt, he found himself hurtling towards the dashboard too quickly to take evasive action and, in the split second before his forehead smashed into the hard surface, he knew that he was going to die, then the blow came and David was tumbling into a black void of nothingness.

David stood on a platform of a railway station. The platform was crowded with people, mostly individuals, but there were some couples and one or two family groups. There was a long, sleek train standing at the platform, its pure white paintwork gleamed and its chrome fittings sparkled in the brilliant, unearthly glow of the roof lights.

The train doors were open and the folk on the platform were moving silently and purposefully towards the train where they were met by train attendants, all of whom were dressed in either white suits, or, dresses, who greeted each passenger with a smile of recognition and a helping hand aboard.

David joined the movement forward, but he felt his head swim and for a moment he thought he was going to pass out. He closed his eyes briefly and when he opened them again he saw Rebecca looking at him from one of the train doorways.

In that one moment everything fell into place and David understood. His whole vision became tunnelled and all his eyes could see was Rebecca's small face, her eyes wide and sparkling, her mouth set in a sad smile. She too was dressed all in white and the auburn hair that tumbled across her shoulders looked even darker against the brightness of her dress.

Vaguely David became aware that the platform was now almost deserted and the doors of the train were closed except for the one at which Rebecca stood. Fingers of mist snaked back from the black hole that was the station entrance, wreathing the gleaming train, spreading rapidly across the platform until finally they lapped at David's feet.

David started to run and soon he was standing at the train door looking up into the face of his beloved Rebecca. He reached up to catch hold of the handrail but it was too high for him. He cried out in frustration but the swirling mist filled his mouth and muffled the cry so that no sound escaped his mouth. He heard a whistle blow somewhere nearby and he sensed, rather than felt, the train vibrate.

David realised he was in danger of missing the train and that if he did he would lose Rebecca forever. Desperately he held out both arms and pleaded silently with her to help him climb aboard in the same way that the other passengers had been helped, but Rebecca shook her head and a tear trickled down one cheek. Then, through the mist that by now had penetrated his brain, David heard her voice.

'No, David. I'm sorry but I can't take you with me,' her sweet, precious voice said. 'Sarie needs you more.'

The train was moving now, ghostly silent, and David moved with it, quickening his pace until he was running down the platform with the mist thickening at his every stride.

'Sarie needs you more,' Rebecca's voice repeated.

Slowly the open train door drew further away and Rebecca's figure grew smaller. David could see the tears streaming down her face; they glistened and dribbled into her mouth as she repeated the same message over and over again. With one supreme effort David raced towards the train and hurled himself through the mist towards the door, he clutched desperately for the handrail, but the train had disappeared and all that remained was a black void into which he plunged with Rebecca's words ringing in his ears: 'Sarie needs you more.'

When David regained consciousness he remembered everything that had happened and when he found himself laying fully dressed on a bed in a curtained cubicle he knew immediately he was in hospital. He sat up and tried to determine the extent of his injuries. He had a headache and when he reached up to investigate he found there was a bandage wrapped round his forehead, but, apart from that, he seemed to have no other injuries.

The curtain slid open and a nurse appeared. 'Feeling better?' She asked brightly. David nodded and immediately wished that he hadn't. He winced and gingerly touched his forehead.

'It's just a bruise,' the nurse assured him. 'You are a very lucky man, Mister Green. I understand that your car is a write off.' She smiled and handed David a couple of tablets. 'Pain killers,' she told him, 'for the headache.' She poured some water into a plastic tumbler and passed it to him. 'Mind, you certainly gave the paramedics a bit of a scare. At one stage they thought you were dead.'

'Can I go home?' David asked after he had swallowed the tablets.

'Of course,' the nurse replied, 'but you'll have to come back in few days for a check up.'

Before David left the hospital he rang the police station. The duty officer was very helpful, which somewhat dented David's somewhat jaundiced view of the Metropolitan Police Force, a body of men with whom he came in regular contact. The officer explained that what was left of his car had been towed to a local breaker's yard. Then David asked if his daughter's presents, and the little Angel, had been recovered from the back seat of his car.

'Well, sir,' the policeman said, 'I don't know anything about no presents, or, the Angel, but if you like, I can get a squad car to pop round to the breaker's yard and check it out. If the lads find anything, I'll have them drop them round to you.'

The standing of the Police went up another couple of notches in David's eyes. What was the world coming to?

The snow had caused havoc with London's public transport system and by the time David managed to find a taxi, and it eventually battled its way across North London, it was gone midnight before he arrived home. He found Lisa in the kitchen.

'Where's Ben?' David asked after he had explained the bandage on his head and received Lisa's sympathetic expressions of concern.

'Working late,' Lisa replied. 'He told me he wanted to pop to the lab to collect some test results.' She looked at her watch and frowned. 'He should have been home by now.'

'I expect he's been delayed by the snow,' David reassured her. 'The traffic is almost at a standstill on some roads.' He smiled at her. 'How has Sarie-Anne been?'

'As good as gold,' Lisa replied. 'For some reason she wanted to sleep in the lounge so I tucked her up on the sofa. That's where she is now. The last time I looked in on her she was fast asleep.'

With Lisa following close behind him, David made his way on tip-toe through to the lounge. Sarie-Anne was indeed fast asleep and in the red glow of the gas-fire she looked healthier and more at peace than she had for many months. He leaned over to kiss his daughter and out of the corner of his eye saw the Angel on top of the tree. So, the policeman had been as good as his word. Well done Plod! David was even more impressed and resolved to write to the Commissioner of Police to praise his staff.

Then David realised there was something different about the Angel, but he couldn't put his finger on what that difference was. He smiled to himself and in the subdued light of the lounge the Angel's resemblance to Rebecca was even more pronounced. He saw something glinting in the Angel's hair and realised that Lisa had clipped the diamante hair-slide into place.

'Thanks for sorting out the little Angel, Lisa,' David whispered as he gently lifted Sarie-Anne and carried her through into the hall and up the stairs to her bedroom.

'That's okay, David,' Lisa called after him. 'She was no trouble.'

As David tucked Sarie-Anne into bed the little girl's eyes fluttered open and she smiled tiredly up at her father.

'Why have you got a funny head, daddy?' She asked.

'I'll tell you about it in the morning, darling,' David said softly. 'It's a long story.'

'Has Father Christmas been yet, daddy?'

'Not yet, sweetheart. Did you remember to leave a mince pie out for him?'

Sarie-Anne nodded before assuring him: 'And a glass of sherry and some milk for his reindeers.'

'That's a good girl.' David looked down at his daughter lovingly and was surprised to see that the colour in her cheeks was no longer that of a fever, but was the more natural flush of a child whose sleep has been disturbed.

'Mummy came,' Sarie-Anne said with a yawn.

'Yes, darling. I saw her on top of the Christmas tree.'

'She was ever so pleased with the hair-slide, daddy.' There was another yawn, longer this time. 'She said it was the loveliest present she had ever been given and that she would wear it forever.'

'I'm sure she will darling,' David said and silently thanked Lisa again for her initiative. He smiled as his daughter's eyes fluttered closed and he kissed her again.

'God bless you, my darling,' he whispered. As David straightened he heard Sarie-Anne mumble something. He bent over her again and held his ear close to her mouth.

'Mummy cuddled me, daddy,' Sarie-Anne mumbled, almost inaudibly. 'She cuddled me before she sat on the tree.'

'Thanks again, Lisa.' David said when he returned to the lounge. 'But how did you find out about the hair-slide?' He asked as he pecked her on the cheek.

'What hair-slide?' Lisa looked puzzled.

'The hair-slide...' but David was interrupted by the musical trill of the doorbell. He opened the front door and the lanky figure of Benjamin came bustling into the hallway, bow-tie awry and his face flushed red with excitement. Under one arm he carried several packages, whilst his other arm was held high above his head and was waving a thin buff coloured folder.

'It's a miracle!' Ben cried as he charged into the lounge and threw the packages onto an armchair. 'It's bloody marvellous, incredible, absolutely staggering mind boggling miracle!'

'What is it?' Lisa asked excitedly.

'It's Sarie-Anne!' Ben exclaimed. 'These are her latest test results.' He waved the folder at her, 'They are all negative; every single one. Not a sign of leukaemia anywhere.'

'But that's not possible!' David said.

'I know it's not possible,' Ben agreed. 'I told you it's a miracle!'

'Are you sure?' David held his friend's arm in a fierce grip. 'Are you absolutely sure?'

Ben nodded and a wide grip stretched itself across his face. 'I'm sure. I've checked, double checked and treble checked. I don't know how it happened, but Sarie-Anne is cured. Now, can I have my arm back?'

David released Ben's arm but grabbed him in an exuberant embrace, then Lisa joined them and they danced round the lounge in a mad, almost hysterical jig. Finally, exhausted and out of breath, they collapsed in a heap on the sofa.

'By the way,' Ben said once he had regained his breath. 'I have something for you, David.' He jumped to his feet and sorted through the pile of packages that still lay in the armchair. 'I met a policeman at the front gate and he gave me this for you.' Ben handed David a battered brown cardboard package. 'He said to tell you he was sorry but the toys were destroyed.' Ben paused and noticed for the first time the bandage round David's head. 'What the hell happened to you?'

David ignored the question; instead he staggered to his feet and tore open the package knowing what he would find.

The Angel was about six inches tall and was dressed in a long, white satin robe. On her back was fastened a pair of large, gossamer thin wings and about her head floated a golden, filigree halo that was artfully positioned in such a way as to hide the pins that connected it to the Angel's head. Her hair was long and lustrous and a deep shade of auburn. She had a small, pretty, round face with eyes that were wide and green and shining with love and laughter. However, the Angel's mouth was not laughing, indeed, it was not even smiling; her lips were set in a slight, enigmatic, almost disapproving pout that gave her whole face a look of deep concentration.

David spun round and stared up at the little figure that sat on the top of the Christmas tree. Now he realised what was different about it: the Mummy-Angel was smiling.

The Return of Anna Pavlova

Naomi looked out from the wings and smiled. The stage beckoned her; inviting the prima ballerina to leave the comforting shadows to make her long awaited appearance.

She smiled again. Today she would give her adoring fans a performance to remember. She would leave Naomi behind in the wings and give them something special: Anna Pavlova herself.

Naomi closed her eyes and breathed in deeply, savouring the atmosphere of the theatre. Oh, yes! This was definitely for her. This was just what she wanted. This was the world for which she had longed all her life.

Out beyond the curtain, rich purple drapes embroidered with shimmering gold thread, sat the orchestra. Individual musicians made last minute adjustments to their instruments until finally they were tuned to perfection. Good, she thought, there must be no discordant notes to mar what is going to be the dance of a lifetime.

Above the preparatory noise of the orchestra, Naomi could hear the late arrivals to the audience settling into their places. There were the smooth, barely discernible clunks as well oiled seats were lowered, the swish of silk and satin evening dresses brushing against plush padded upholstery, the rustling of glossy programmes and, of course, the inevitable coughs; some delicately feminine and others gruff and rasping.

Wrapped up in her thoughts, Naomi did some final loosening up exercises. Yes, today she would be Pavlova. She would give the audience Le Signe as only the greatest ballerina to grace the stage had performed it. Her performance would be magical, a milestone in the history of ballet. Her fans would be ecstatic and would applaud her as never before.

And the audience was becoming restless now, fidgeting impatiently in seats that cost a king's ransom on the black-market. Occasionally sporadic outbursts of slow hand clapping broke out in various parts of the auditorium.

Naomi could not see the audience, but she could imagine its composition. The cream of London society would be out there: lords, ladies, knights and dames; bishops, cabinet ministers, ambassadors and generals; industrialists, bankers and publishers; celebrities of stage, screen and the arts.

The men, immaculately dressed in tuxedos and bow ties, would be staring impatiently at the curtain; waiting for their "Angel" to appear. Their faces would be red from a combination of heat, excitement and the starched, garrotte-tight collared shirts they wore.

The women would be extravagantly dressed in expensive haute couture numbers imported from Paris especially for the occasion. Eyes that could detect a hair out of place at twenty paces would be casting surreptitious glances at neighbouring females in an attempt to evaluate the glamorous competition without appearing too interested in what they found.

And they had all come to see *her* perform.

Somewhere at the back of the auditorium a group of more boisterous men began an impatient chant: 'Mimi, Mimi, Mimi...'A few disapproving hisses wound their way up the aisle as some of the more staid members of the audience sitting in the expensive seats at the front attempted to quell the unseemly behaviour. But the chant persisted and grew in volume as more and more voices took up the chant: 'Mimi, Mimi, Mimi...'

Emotion welled inside Naomi as the incessant call filled her head and fed her lifelong need for recognition.

Finally there was a loud cheer and tumultuous applause as the conductor appeared on his rostrum. There was an expectant hush in the theatre as the he picked up his baton, raised it briefly above his head before leading the orchestra into the first bars of the overture.

Naomi closed her eyes and took a deep breath in an attempt to steady her pre-performance nerves. Somewhere inside her a voice spoke soothingly to her, calming her: 'Relax, Naomi, relax. They love you. Show them what you can do. Show them Anna Pavlova. Do it for him. Dance for your man.'

Slowly the curtains slid open and a low moan escaped from the multi headed monster that waited to both acclaim and devour her.

When Naomi eventually made her entrance she was greeted by wild applause and raucous cheering, followed by absolute silence. Her opening pas de bourée took her floating across the stage like thistledown in the wind; her wraith like body seemed weightless, as if it contained nothing but her soul and, perhaps, the spirit of her heroine, her inspiration, Anna Pavlova.

Her performance was masterly, she knew it immediately. This really was the special one; a performance to be spoken of in awe. A performance to rank with the greatest; no, his would be the greatest!

Naomi was truly inspired and she held the audience enraptured. They were as one; she belonged to them, and they to her. So superb was her interpretation of Le Signe, so graceful were her movements, so expressive were her port de bras, so exquisite the message of tragedy that played across her face, that at times, in the eyes of the adoring audience, the ballerina disappeared to be replaced by the swan she portrayed.

Yet, even as she danced, even as she cast her spell over the conquered audience, Naomi's eyes swept the darkened auditorium in search of a face. The face of the man she loved.

Rich and handsome, he attended every performance she gave. Whenever and wherever she danced he would be there. She would feel his eyes on her face and would know that he loved her as deeply as she loved him. After every performance there were a dozen blood red roses waiting in her dressing room; a gesture of his love.

Today Naomi decided she would reward that love. Her Pavlova inspired performance was just for him. Tonight he was taking her to the Savoy for supper and an inner instinct told her that he was going to propose. Today would be the start of endless bliss. But where was he? Her eyes scanned the stalls in vain. Panic rose in her breast. She faltered.

'Naomi? What on earth are you up to girl?'

Naomi stopped dancing and stared from the stage as a door opened at the back of the stalls and a man dressed in a blue overall similar to her own walked down the central aisle.

'Have you swept the stage yet?'

'Not yet, sir.'

'Well it's just not good enough. Stop this messing around and

169

get back to work. This isn't the first time I've had to speak to you, but let me tell you, girl, it will be the last.'

'I'm sorry, sir. It won't happen again.' Naomi said as she picked up her broom and started to sweep the stage. She sighed deeply as the brightness of her dream was extinguished once again by the reality of a life filled with endless drudgery.

Cross Lines

Ada covered the final few feet of her garden path in a panting, wobbling jog. She heard the telephone ringing as she opened the front gate and its insistent trill forced her legs to quicken their pace the closer she got to the house.

'Hold on,' Ada muttered to herself and then wheezed as she tried desperately to suck breath into her tortured lungs at the same time as she held in place her false teeth. 'Hold on!' She repeated, her voice rising in irritation. 'I'm coming.' Ada fumbled with the front door key as she spoke; her unaccustomed exertions making her fingers tremble even more than usual.

Finally, the key slipped into the lock and Ada pushed open the door and ungainly stumbled into the hallway. The sound of the telephone was much louder now, its shrill ring grated on Ada's nerve ends and not for the first time she regretted ever allowing her husband to persuade her to have a phone installed.

Despite her husband George's assurances, and his cajoling that it was nineteen eighty six and they were almost in the twenty first century. Although almost everybody she knew had a telephone, Ada had never really been at ease with what she still referred to as "that contraption".

She hurried to the hall table where the object of her displeasure lay crying out for a hand to hold. Red faced and seriously out of breath, Ada paused momentarily as she eyed the telephone with suspicion. She took a deep breath and warily lifted the receiver, but a fraction of a second before she lifted the phone from its cradle it stopped ringing.

'Hello. Who is there?' Ada asked anyway, but the dialling tone gave her no clue. For several seconds she stood granite like, with the receiver in her hand, staring at it with a look of deep disgust on her usually jovial plump face. Her mind searched for a suitably strong swearword with which to express her feelings.

'Bum!' She swore and immediately felt guilty, but then, deciding she might as well be hung for a sheep as a lamb, she repeated the word a couple of times before slamming down the receiver and walking through to the lounge. She lowered her ample frame into an armchair and kicked off her shoes.

Ada felt tense and agitated. She sighed deeply and then hauled herself upright again. *Perhaps a cup of tea will help*, she thought, heading for the kitchen. Five minutes later Ada was back in the armchair, a huge teapot and a milk jug on a tray before her, and already well into her first cup of steaming tea.

The mystery phone call worried her. As sure as eggs were eggs it was bad news. She had known that something else awful was going to happen today. First it had been Mrs Meridith's cat, Tiddles, which had somehow managed to get its tail caught in her rotary clothes line. Unfortunately, there was quite a wind today and it had given the poor wee thing quite a turn.

The second near disaster to disturb the tranquillity of Balaclava Road came about when one of the dustmen had slipped whilst throwing a black sack into the back of his dustcart and had almost been eaten by his own lorry. Luckily he was rescued by one of his workmates before he could be digested.

'You know what that means don't you, dearie?' Her friend Nellie had asked when Ada had recounted to her the morning's excitement. 'There's bound to be another mishap today.' Nellie answered her own question without waiting for Ada to reply. She folded her arms and nodded her head sagely. 'These things always come in threes.'

The phone call seemed to have proven Nellie right; obviously something dreadful had happened. But what could it be? Ada fidgeted nervously with her tea cup and tried to think who the mystery caller might have been.

Had it been someone from George's works? Perhaps he had been involved in an accident. Maybe at that very moment her husband was in a hospital bed, at death's door, or worse. At this thought, Ada lumbered to her feet, frantically trying to remember which of George's pyjamas were clean and in good repair. Should she ring the hospital, or the police station? She walked out to the hallway and stared at the telephone, but despite the worry that nagged at her brain, she could not bring herself to lift the receiver.

She made her way back to the lounge and stopped dead in her tracks as another possibility hit her. She flopped, weak kneed, back into the armchair. Suppose it had been George himself ringing? Suppose he had been made redundant? What would they do then? How would they cope?

Ada forced herself to remain calm. 'No,' she reasoned out loud to herself. 'It couldn't have been that. If George had been made redundant he would have waited until he got home to tell me and if he had been involved in an accident no doubt the police would have come round to tell me about it.' She let out a sigh of relief and poured herself another cup of tea as she tried to think of other alternatives.

Had the caller been her daughter? No, Deirdre phoned yesterday and she would not ring two days running, not all the way from Wales. Unless...? Unless there was something wrong! Deirdre had sounded a bit down in the dumps. What had she said? Dai had been out until late the night before. To a stag party! *Well, that's it then*, Ada thought. *He's having an affair and Deirdre wants to come home to her mum. Oh, my baby!*

She stared malevolently at the photograph that stood on the mantelpiece; it showed a large, middle aged woman dressed in a wedding dress, towering over a short man with a pencil moustache wearing a white carnation in the button hole of his wide lapelled suit jacket. Ada seethed as she thought of how her youngest daughter had wasted her life. *Deirdre you should never have married the short-ended Welshman*. She fumed to herself. *I've never trusted the weasel-eyed little squirt.*

Or, it could have been our Doris. Her Bert had been off work and dangerously ill for over ten years now. Doris said that some days Bert could hardly force himself to get out of bed and drag himself down to the betting office, or, the greyhound track, he was that poorly. Perhaps, Bert had finally given up the struggle and had gone off to join the great odds maker in the sky.

'Brrrr, brrrr, brrrr.' The telephone broke into her thoughts. 'Brrrr, brrrr, Brrrr.' It said in its tinny incessant voice.

Ada sat paralysed. *Oh, my!* She thought. *It's ringing.* Somehow she managed to raise her ample backside from the armchair and with dread filling her equally ample bosom she made her way once more through to the hall.

'Hello?'

'Hello,' said a deep male voice.

'Hello?'

'Hello!'

'Hello?'

'Good afternoon, madam,' the owner of the disembodied voice finally realised that the exhilarating conversation could go on all night if it was not terminated quickly. 'I've been ringing your number on and off all day. I am a telephone engineer. We had a complaint that your phone was out of order.'

'What?' Ada said weakly, 'But there's nothing wrong with our telephone.'

'Nothing wrong? Excuse me, madam, but what number are you?'

'Number? Er... six-one-five-one-six-five.'

'Oh, I'm terribly sorry, but I have the wrong number.'

The Vision

Oom Jannie de Groote tossed and turned restlessly in his bed. The old man was tired, but sleep had deserted him. The coarse sheets on his bed were wet with perspiration and they felt uncomfortable against his wrinkled skin and yet it was not his discomfort that disturbed his slumber.

With a sigh Oom Jannie rolled out of bed and struggled into a pair of baggy trousers and a crumpled linen shirt. As he dressed the moon came out from behind a cloud and he was able to look out of his bedroom window and see the rolling Transvaal veld stretching endlessly into the dark distance where Steinkop Koppie marked the boundary of his farm. Tears welled in his eyes. *My farm; my heritage; my land*, he thought, and in that instant the old man knew what he must do.

Oom Jannie was of the Old World. His ways were the old ways; the Afrikaan ways. His was an era in which white was white and black was non-white. In the Old World there had been no question who was the baas; the White Race was supreme. But times were changing; the New World was catching up on him and the old man found it difficult to deal with the changes that had been thrust upon his country.

In the New South Africa all men were equal. There were no longer kaffirs in his country. Black and white sat together side by side. They travelled together in the same buses and in the same carriages on trains. They slept in the same hotels, drank in the same bars and ate in the same restaurants. They married each other and prayed in the same churches. They made decisions together, they governed together, they legislated together and they ruled together. They ruled him together.

Oom Jannie had once sworn that he would rather die than accept a kaffir as an equal and as he trudged morosely across the veld towards the disused mine shaft he knew that the time had arrived to honour that pledge.

The old Afrikaaner stared down at the black gash in the veld that would soon swallow his body and he shuddered. He looked away quickly from what was soon to become his coffin. As he turned his head, the moon slid out of sight behind a cloud, plunging the veld into a darkness that was total, yet at the same time strangely reassuring. Oom Jannie had no fear of the dark. He knew every blade of grass on land that he had farmed for fifty years and more. He breathed in deeply, letting the warm sweet air of the African night flow into his lungs. It was the same air that had filled his gasping mouth as a new born baby so many years before. He bent over, took a handful of dry soil in his hands and let it trickle through his fingers. He felt a tear run down his cheek. *How I will miss this country*, he thought. *My beloved Suid-Afrika. The land of my birth.* Not only his birthplace, but the birthplace of his father, his grandfather and his grandfather's grandfather, who between them had carved out a farm from the wilderness of Africa with their bare hands.

The De Groote farm had seen the going of the lion and the coming of the gold mines; it had survived drought and plague and the deprivation of the Boer War. And the family had survived with it. *Ja, this is truly my country*. He thought sadly. It was the country in which his children had been born and their children. At the thought of his grandchildren he shed another tear. It was the little ones he would miss most of all.

The old man closed his eyes and prayed, begging his Maker to forgive him the heinous sin he was about to commit. But, as he closed his eyes he found himself haunted by the tiny innocent faces of his grandchildren and the thought of those he loved most made the old man realise he could not go through with it. With this decision came a sudden surge of relief.

And so Oom Jannie turned away from the gaping mouth of the mine shaft, but as he moved, so the ground on which he was standing collapsed beneath him and he fell into a black nothingness.

'Please God save me,' the old man prayed aloud as he fell, using The Taal; the old language – Afrikaans – used by fewer people these days, yet still the tongue that came naturally to him: 'Asseblief God help my.' He was praying even as he hit the ledge.

The old man lay still, the wind knocked from his body, his legs twisted awkwardly under him. It was so dark that he could not even see the hand he waved in front of his face and momentarily he was unsure where he was. Was he dead? Was this hell?

Then the pain came and with it the knowledge that he was alive, if not exactly kicking. Oom Jannie's legs throbbed with a pain that he had not thought possible and he knew immediately that they were broken. Yet, despite his predicament, he thanked God for saving him.

Then it dawned on the old man that his thanks were probably premature. With an increasing sense of foreboding he realised that he was no better off than if he had actually fallen to his death. He was stuck on a ledge in a disused mine shaft in the middle of the veld with two broken legs into the bargain. *Sies, I might just as well be dead,* he thought. *At least I wouldn't have this pain.*

And so he lay on the ledge for what seemed hours, praying and thinking. Praying he would survive and return to all that he held dear, and thinking about the very things he wanted to survive to enjoy; his farm, his wife, his children, his grandchildren and his country. Even a New Suid-Afrika was better than *no* Suid-Afrika.

Occasionally Oom Jannie cried out for help, but his unanswered cries echoed round his ears, mocking his helplessness and the periods of pain wracked silence between each desperate call became lengthier and more despondent. The old man did not hear the voice at first and when it did eventually filter through to his brain he ignored it, believing it to be a figment of his imagination. But the voice persisted.

'Hello!' It was distant, but definitely a male voice speaking in English. 'Hello, is there anybody down there?'

'Asseblief help my.' The old man shouted back in Afrikaans before repeating in English, 'Please save me.' His anxious pleading voice bounced against the black walls of the narrow shaft before echoing loudly about his head, filling his ears and making even more total the silence that followed. It was a silence that seemed to go on for hours.

'Hold on, meneer,' the far off voice called out at last. 'It won't be long now.'

Oom Jannie wondered who the man was. Was it one of his neighbours? 'Is dit jy, Johannes? Willie?' He shouted, then realised that neither Johannes nor Willie would be speaking in English. It must be a rooi nek then.

'Nie, meneer; just rest yourself.' The man said, although he spoke in Afrikaans - net rus jouself – reassuring Afrikaans. Whoever the man was he might not be a red neck Englishman after all, perhaps he was a broeder!

'Haastig, meneer. Hurry, man!' Oom Jannie urged. Again an endless pain filled wait and then he felt something hit his chest. A rope!

'Climb the rope,' the voice ordered, once again reverting to English.

Oom Jannie gripped the rope and pulled himself upright, gritting his teeth against the pain in his legs. It was no good, his disabled limbs would not hold him and he collapsed in a heap on the ledge. He let out a wail of pain and despair.

'Climb the rope,' the voice urged again.

The old man looked up in the direction of the voice and shook his head sadly in the darkness.

'Nie, man. It is no good. My legs are broken, my friend, and I cannot stand. It is impossible.'

There was another pause, longer this time; then the old man felt the rope move in his hand and heard a scraping sound above his head. Suddenly there was a clatter of noise above him and a shower of small stones hit him. The man was coming down the rope!

Oom Jannie felt, rather than saw, the hand approach him through the pitch black darkness. He grasped it tightly. It was a farmer's hand; large, hard, dry and calloused from years of honest toil; a strong and trustworthy hand. Slowly, and with some difficulty, the rescuer managed to manoeuvre Oom Jannie onto his wide and powerful back and they started their journey up the rope.

It was terrifying. The old man's unnatural weight on the stranger's back made balancing difficult and progress was painfully slow. Several times the man lost his footing and the only thing that stopped them sliding back down the rope was the rescuer's phenomenal strength that enabled him to cling desperately to the rope until he was able to find another foothold. Each time they slipped, the rope must have cut deep into the big man's hands, but no sound of pain or complaint escaped his lips.

Handhold by handhold, foothold by foothold, the rescuer battled his way up the rope, until finally Oom Jannie could see the sky above them and as he watched the moon slid behind a cloud. Then with a mighty heave the stranger shot them over the lip of the mine shaft and they lay on the cool earth of the veld.

The old man lay on his back listening to the gasps as his rescuer fought to pump oxygen into his tortured lungs. The moon was just beginning to creep back from where it had been hiding behind the cloud and Oom Jannie decided that it was the most beautiful sight he had ever seen and he thanked God for the second time that night. He rolled over on his side, wincing in agony as he moved his legs, and looked over at the stranger who had just saved his life. He put out a hand in a gesture of thanks and as he did so the moon escaped fully from its cloud cover. The veld was soon awash with moonlight and the old man drew back his hand in shock.

The stranger's face was as black as the pit from which they had just escaped. A frown of concern creased his shiny forehead. 'Are you in much pain?' The man asked. 'Do not worry. I will carry you to a doctor. Soon you will be safe.'

That's when the old man remembered. He remembered the emotions that had driven him to the edge of suicide. He remembered the threat that this black man represented to his world. He remembered the anger, the distrust and the hatred.

Then he looked again at the caring black face and at hands that had been ripped and bloodied by the rope with which the man had rescued him and he remembered his gratitude as the man had carried him away from a long, painful death. He remembered that in the blackness of the mine shaft the colour of the man's skin had been immaterial, and he remembered that they had something that linked them; they were both Africans.

Oom Jannie put out his hand again and this time he let it fall lightly on the man's shoulder. 'Dankie, meneer,' the old man said quietly. 'Thank you, my friend, you have truly saved me.'

Oom Jannie de Groote tossed and turned restlessly in his bed. The old man was tired, but sleep had deserted him. The coarse sheets on his bed were wet with perspiration and felt uncomfortable against his wrinkled skin and yet it was not his discomfort that disturbed his slumber, it was the nightmare he had just experienced, or, was it perhaps a vision?

The Windsorton Diamond Mystery

Detective Inspector Rupert Bridges poured boiling water onto the rooibos teabag in his mug and glanced at his watch. It was 10.20 am and the tea had to brew for four minutes so he would need to remove the bag at exactly 10.24 am; not a minute sooner nor later. He was very precise about time.

Bridges stood looking moodily out of the window through the half moon glasses that perched on the end of his long nose. He was bored. OK, so he had a few cases on the go, but they were all run of the mill minor crimes, none of which was stretching his intellect to the extent he wanted. He longed for a serious crime, perhaps another murder. The problem for him was that despite public perception serious crimes were relatively rare in shire counties such as Kent.

Not for the first time Bridges wondered whether he should apply for a transfer to the Metropolitan Police, but then he remembered all the good things about living and working in the Garden of England and decided to stick where he was. Something big would turn up, it always did.

He picked up his mug and fished the tea bag out with a spoon. With a well practised flick of his wrist he launched the teabag towards the waste bin in the far corner of the office just as the door opened and Detective Sergeant Stan Hardin walked in.

'Shot, Guv'nor!' Hardin said as the teabag landed with a splat in the basket.

'I've had plenty of practice, Stan,' Bridges said with a smile as he perched himself on the edge of his desk. 'Would you like a cup?'

'Not if it's that smelly muck you drink, thank you!'

'Rooibos tea is not smelly muck. It is wonderfully fragrant and good for you. It is tannin and caffeine free and contains antioxidants that help digestion. It also helps nervous tension. You ought to try it; you are always like a cat on a hot tin roof!'

Hardin grimaced.

'I take it that is a 'no'?' Bridges said with a chuckle before taking a sip of his tea.

'No, I mean yes, the answer is no. Thanks for the offer, but I'll get Rosie to make me a cup of my usual caffeine and tannin filled Tetley tea. If it was good enough for my old man, God rest his soul, then it's good enough for me!'

Bridges went to take another sip of his tea when his phone rang. He stood up as he put down his mug and picked up the phone.

'D.I. Bridges, here,' he said before listening quietly for a while without saying anything else and then: 'Okay, sir. I'll get onto it straight away.'

With that he returned the phone to its cradle.

Hardin stared at the tall gangling figure of D.I. Bridges, whose back had straightened imperceptibly during the telephone conversation.

'Well?' He asked eventually.

Bridges rubbed his bald domed head thoughtfully and then asked: 'Fancy a trip to Edenbridge, Stan?'

'Edenbridge? But that's not in our patch.'

'It is if the Chief Constable says it is.'

'Ye gods! The Chief? Is that who was on the blower?'

Bridges nodded and took a long swig of his rooibos tea.

'Yes, that was indeed the Chief and what he actually said was that he understood his was an unusual request, and appreciated Edenbridge was not in the North Division, but he wondered if I would agree to investigate the theft of the Windsorton Diamond.'

'The Windsorton Diamond? I saw something about that on the news this morning. Wasn't it nicked yesterday from Hever Castle?'

'Yes, it was part of a display of jewels being exhibited during an international gem brokers' conference that's taking place this week. It disappeared overnight.'

'I assume the diamond is worth a few bob?'

'The chief gave no indication of the gem's value.'

'So why's he so interested?'

'The exhibition was organised by the World Federation of Diamond Bourses, otherwise known as the WFDB, and is being sponsored by the British Department of Culture Media and Sport. The Windsorton Diamond is on permanent loan to the WFDB from the South African Government. Failure to find the diamond quickly could prove embarrassing for the British Government. In addition, it could prove embarrassing for the Force because security at Hever Castle was approved by Special Branch. The Home Secretary is not amused.'

'Ah!'

'Exactly. It is rumoured that the Chief has ambitions to become the next Metropolitan Police Commissioner and he will be doing his chances no harm if he digs the Government out of a hole.'

'But why you, Guv'nor?'

Bridges smiled, 'He wants somebody he can trust to get the job done quickly and efficiently. Why else? And, Stan, it is not me; it is *us.*'

'That's nice.'

'Let's hope his confidence is justified.'

'But what about our beloved Detective Chief Inspector?'

'The Chief Constable assures me that he has spoken to the boss and he is happy for us to take on the case.'

'That'll be the day!' Hardin said with a laugh. 'He'll hate the thought of us gallivanting off to West Kent for a few days. It will mean him having to do some real work for a change!'

'I'm afraid we do not have the luxury of a few days, Stanley. The Chief said that he wants the crime solved within the next 24 hours.'

'Bleedin' hell!'

'We probably will if we fail to deliver! Come on, let's get going.'

Hever Castle is located near Edenbridge, in the heart of Kent, and is where the second wife of King Henry VIII, Anne Boleyn grew up. The oldest part of the castle, the gatehouse and courtyard, dates back to the 13th Century, although much of it was built a couple of hundred years later.

'This is one of my favourite places in Kent,' Rupert Bridges said as he and Stan Hardin walked down the gravel path towards the castle. To their right the extensive lawns sparkled in the weak February afternoon sunshine, as they decided whether it was worth shedding their frosty coat, or, keep it on in preparation for the night that would fall in another couple of hours. 'It is so peaceful at this time of year when the castle and grounds are closed to the general public.'

'Peaceful, but blooming cold.' Hardin grumbled as he sank further into his heavy overcoat and trudged towards the castle's drawbridge.

'The conference centre is located in the Astor Wing, over there behind the castle,' Bridges said, pointing to his left. 'However, the jewel exhibition is taking place in the castle's dining hall.' He paused to add emphasis to the irony in his words: 'Special Branch thought holding the exhibition in the main body of the castle would be better for security!'

'Not one of their better calls.' Hardin grinned as they approached the entrance to the castle, which had been cordoned off with yellow and black tape. A uniformed policeman guarding the entrance viewed them with suspicious eyes as they approached. Bridges took his warrant card from the pocket of his expensively cut suit jacket and flashed it quickly in front of the policeman's face.

'D.I. Bridges,' he introduced himself, 'and this is D.S. Hardin.'

The bobby made no move to allow the two detectives to pass and for a moment Bridges thought he was going to be difficult and ask to see his warrant card again, but a tall, imposing woman with cropped dark hair appeared at his side as if from nowhere.

'You must be Inspector Bridges,' she said in a cultured voice as she artfully edged the bobby aside and extended a hand across the yellow tape. 'I was expecting you.'

Bridges smiled and shook the woman's hand.

'You must be Mrs Lambermont. The Chief Constable told me that you would be here to meet us. This is Detective Sergeant Hardin.'

The woman nodded briefly in Hardin's direction, but made no effort to shake his hand. '*Ms* Lambermont, Inspector. I am divorced. But, please call me Charlotte. I work for the World Federation of Diamond Bourses and I organised the exhibition.'

Hearing this conversation the uniformed policeman somewhat grudgingly moved aside the warning tape to allow the detectives to join the woman in the entrance to gatehouse, beyond which they could see an open courtyard.

'Does the portcullis work?' Hardin asked.

'Of course it works,' Charlotte Lambermont said, looking at the detective as if he were an imbecile. 'It is the oldest working portcullis in the country.'

Hardin, who at five seven was a good five inches shorter than the woman smiled genially at her. 'How absolutely super!' He said in a voice that affected to mirror the woman's own cut glass accent.

'Was the portcullis down last night, ma'am?' Bridges interjected quickly, before Hardin's attempt at sarcasm led to an unseemly confrontation. It had happened before.

The woman stared at Hardin with narrowed eyes, but then turned to face Bridges. 'Yes, Inspector, as were the inner gates.' She pointed towards the pair of heavy wooden gates that had been opened to sit flush against the wall.

'Are there any other entrances to the castle?'

'Yes, there are two. One is an internal door in the inner hall reception area that provides access to the Astor Wing. The second is an external door into the morning room.' Charlotte explained. 'Would you like me to show you?'

'Thank you, but would it be possible to see the exhibition first?' Bridges asked politely.

'Of course, Inspector, but as it happens we have to go through the reception area to get to the dining hall, so I will show you the inner hall door at the same time.'

'Has anybody been in the dining hall since the theft was discovered?' Bridges asked as they followed the woman across the courtyard and entered the entrance hall.

'No. I discovered the diamond was missing when the security guard unlocked the dining hall door for me first thing this morning,' Charlotte replied as she led them through into the inner hall reception area. 'I noticed the Windsorton had disappeared as soon as I turned on the exhibition display lights. Immediately I had the guard lock the door again and then I called the police and my head office.

'Head office notified the Home Office who in turn contacted the Chief Constable, who rang personally to tell me to expect a visit from you. A couple of policemen turned up to tape off the area and stop anybody from entering the castle, but I understand they were told not to enter the dining hall until you arrived.'

Bridges nodded in satisfaction. He was delighted that the Chief Constable had had the good sense to warn off the local plods. 'And you touched nothing when you entered the room?'

'Nothing except for the display light switches, which I left on when I left the room.'

Bridges looked around the inner hall. At one end there was a closed door cordoned off with yellow and black tape. A security guard was sitting behind the reception desk, but got to his feet when they entered the room and now sauntered towards the detectives.

'Is that door locked?' Bridges asked.

'No, sir.'

'Was it locked last night?'

'Yes; I unlocked it myself this morning when I came on duty.'

'And it leads through to the Astor Wing?'

'Yes.'

Bridges looked at the door thoughtfully before asking: 'And your colleague who was on duty last night would have sat behind the reception desk as you were when we arrived?'

'I assume so. He was certainly sitting there when I turned up for my shift this morning.'

'Thank you. Would you be so kind as to unlock the door to the dining hall?'

'I have to deactivate the alarm first,' Charlotte explained as she went to a small box affixed to the wall about four feet from the door. She took a small bunch of keys from her pocket and unlocked the box, before using a second key to deactivate the alarm.

'Who else can turn off the alarm?' Bridges asked. 'Do the security guards have access to the keys?'

'No. I am the only person who is able to set the alarm. We had it specially installed for the exhibition.'

'So to enter the room requires the presence of both you and a security guard?'

'Yes; neither one of us can enter the room without the other and of course, when viewings take place during the day, there is a guard present in the room at all times.'

With the alarm deactivated the security guard unlocked the door and pulled it open to allow Bridges to enter the room, closely followed by Hardin and the woman.

The last time that Bridges had visited Hever Castle was for a black tie dinner and on that evening the dining hall had been full of tables covered with starched white cloths, shining cutlery and sparkling glasses; now the tables had been replaced by several glass display cabinets containing a variety of precious stones.

They walked towards the far end of the dining room, where directly in front of the minstrel's gallery was positioned a particularly magnificent display case, at which the intricacy of whose construction Rupert Bridges stared in admiration.

The bottom part of the display case was a five foot high pure black stand in the middle of which was a stainless steel cradle about six inches high in which the Windsorton Diamond had no doubt rested until the previous evening.

Sitting on top of the stand, to enclose the cradle was, a four sided glass pyramid, the top point of which had been cut off squarely, that added another five foot to the structure. The base of the pyramid was about three feet square and the top about nine inches square. There were a number of small spotlights artfully positioned in the base of the pyramid and trained on the stainless steel cradle and several more attached to the top of the pyramid, pointing downwards.

Fixed to the front of the display case was a stainless steel holder in which a white card had been inserted. At the top of the card was a glossy colour photograph of a sparkling pink diamond, beneath which was printed in gold letters details of the missing exhibit. Stan Hardin began to read the card whilst Bridges examined the glass pyramid carefully.

The detective inspector tweaked gently on his spotted bow tie a couple of times, as was his habit when thinking, and then took an immaculate white handkerchief from his top pocket and rubbed it carefully against the glass. He frowned and then looked closely at the edge of the pyramid and its base where it joined the black stand. He nodded in satisfaction and turned to Charlotte Lambermont.

'The display stand comes apart, does it not?' He tapped gently on the glass pyramid with his finger nail.

'Yes, it is dismantled to make transport easier.'

'Would it be possible for you to arrange for it to be taken apart for me so that I can examine inside?'

'Certainly, Inspector, however, it might take a couple of hours; my exhibition fitters are currently in London and will have to be recalled. I will phone them as soon as you are finished with me.'

'Thank you.'

Suddenly Hardin let out a low whistle. 'Hey, Guv, listen to this: The Windsorton Diamond is classified as fancy intense pink,' he read, 'a high colour rating for pink diamonds... blah, blah, blah, it is 110 carats and is valued at, wait for it, forty five million pounds. Is that right?' he asked Charlotte Lambermont.

'Of course it is right. We would hardly have printed the information if it were not true, Sergeant.' The woman replied icily.

'No wonder the Chief's so excited, Guv.'

'Exactly so, Sarge,' Bridges replied, before turning once again to the woman. 'You mentioned an external door, ma'am?'

'Yes; in the morning room, but we have to go back to the entrance hall to reach it.'

They left the dining hall and waited in the reception area whilst the guard locked the door and Charlotte Lambermont reset the alarm. Bridges nodded to himself in satisfaction at this demonstration of tight security. Finished, the woman led them back to the entrance hall, followed by the guard who unlocked a door that opened into a much smaller room than the one in which the exhibition had been set up.

'The morning room, Inspector,' Charlotte said, 'and the external door is over there. Let me show you.' She led the detectives across the room and through a side door into a stairwell, on their left was a heavy wooden arched doorway.

Bridges knelt in front of the door; first he studied the lock carefully and then the door jamb. 'Is the door alarmed?' He asked.

'Yes,' the woman replied, 'it is connected to the same system as the dining hall door, although it can be deactivated with that box there.' She pointed to a box identical to the one in the inner hall. 'Isolating the alarm in that way enables this door and the morning room to be used without in any way compromising security of the exhibition itself.'

'How often has the alarm been deactivated since its installation?'

'I don't think it has ever been switched off, Inspector,' Charlotte said and turned to the guard for confirmation.

The man shook his head. 'Not as far as I am aware, ma'am. There has never been a need.'

'And who has access to the key to this door?'

'Only us,' the security guard explained. He held up the bunch of keys he carried. 'Would you like me to open it?'

'No, that won't be necessary; perhaps later,' Bridges replied as he got to his feet and headed towards the well worn granite spiral staircase. 'I would like to look upstairs now.'

He stood aside to allow Charlotte to climb the stairs first.

'I assume we can access the dining hall's minstrel's gallery somewhere on this floor?' Bridges asked when they reached the top of the stairs.

'Yes, this way.' Charlotte said, leading him down a narrow corridor to yet another locked door.

'Is this door alarmed?' Bridges asked.

'Not this one. It was decided the risk was low because you cannot reach the minstrel's gallery without going through a door that is alarmed. But it is kept locked at night. Could you open it?' Charlotte asked the security guard, who selected immediately the right key from his bunch and quickly opened the door.

The minstrel's gallery was very narrow, but offered a spectacular view of the exhibition. The gems in the display cases glittered and sparkled as each was highlighted by its own tiny spotlight. Directly in front of the gallery stood the case in which the missing Windsorton Diamond had been displayed. Looking down into the empty pyramid it became obvious that nobody could have got in from the top of the pyramid, the opening was far too small.

'D'you reckon it was fishing expedition?' Hardin asked.

'That was my initial thought, Sarge,' Bridges replied, 'but if you look at the cradle in which the diamond was displayed, it has a glass hood, which, although you can see from this angle, is invisible from floor level. It is a very ingenious construction that would have precluded any type of access from above.' He stared down intently into display case. 'Hmm,' he murmured.

'What is it, Guv?'

Bridges shook his head. 'Probably nothing, Sarge; let's have a look outside.'

The two policemen were escorted back to the entrance of the castle by Charlotte Lambermont, who having said her goodbyes went off to arrange for her exhibition fitters to come back from London and dismantle the display case.

'Who is the best lock man in Kent, Stan?' Bridges asked as they stood on the grass verge on the castle side of the moat.

'Larry the Lock,' Hardin replied without hesitation, 'but Larry is strictly small time and he was no expert in burglar alarm systems. He could never be able to manage a job like this. Anyway, he is supposed to have retired after his last stretch inside. I heard he is running a pet shop in Gravesend.'

'He might not have been involved in this particular crime himself,' Bridges acknowledged, 'but I will lay odds that he knows something about it. Retired or not, lags like him always keep their ear to the ground. Talking of which...' He pointed down at a single set of footprints that could be seen in the frost covered grass. They followed the footsteps round the side of the castle until they reached the outside of the small door that they now knew led into the morning room. The footprints disappeared to become a scuffle of disturbed frost. Bridges inspected the outside of the lock and grunted in satisfaction. 'Come on, Stan, I think it's time we looked up Mr Laurence Price.'

Price's Pet Products was located on a retail park on the outskirts of Gravesend. Rupert Bridges managed to find a space in the car park immediately outside the store, positioned between a furniture store and an electrical retailer. The automatic doors slid open silently and Bridges and Stan Hardin walked into the store side by side.

The store was huge and had a number of pets on show, with a variety of food and accessories for each of them. The two men managed to escape the clutches of the enthusiastic sales assistant who pounced on them and tried to interest them in a new formula dog food that was on offer that day at half price, despite neither of them having a dog, some top value wild bird food and a South American tarantula spider, that she assured them was not dangerous.

Eventually they managed to stop her in mid sales pitch and got her to tell them that Larry Price was at the rear of the store. They found Price soon after, feeding a monkey, dressed in a red tunic, which was sat on a table looking intently at the box of dates held by the pet-store owner. Bridges was immediately reminded of the Capuchin monkey in *Raiders of the Lost Ark* that saved Indiana Jones' life by eating a poisoned date. The monkey was holding a brightly coloured wooden money box.

'Hello, Larry,' Bridges said. 'I'm very impressed. When I heard you had a pet shop I imagined it to be some back street dive not a massive superstore. This must cost you a fortune in rent and rates.'

'Hello, Mr Bridges. Well, it's not cheap but I manage to survive. You know how it is.'

'Yeah; we know how it is, Larry.' Hardin chipped in. 'It's difficult earning an honest crust, but then you never had to worry about that, did you?'

'Naughty, naughty, Mr Hardin! I might have sailed close to the wind in the past, but these days I'm on the straight and narrow.'

'Of course you are, Larry,' Bridges said with a gentle smile. 'So, what do you know about the Windsorton Diamond theft?'

Price shook his head. 'No idea what you're talking about, Mr Bridges.'

'Not been keeping up to date with the news, Larry? The theft has been all over the television today.'

'No time for TV and most of the news they pump out is lies anyway.'

'Larry, let me be frank with you. I know that you know that I know you know something about the stolen diamond. You might not have been involved yourself...'

'Or he might have, Guv,' Hardin interjected and looked

menacingly at the pet store owner.

'Yes, Sergeant Hardin, I will concede that on his past record, Mr Price could well have been involved, but let us be charitable, if only for the sake of fairness, and assume that he is innocent. So, let me instead suggest that although he was not involved personally, Mr Price will have some idea who was involved.' He turned to the pet shop owner. 'Larry, it is inconceivable that you would not have heard about the theft of a forty five million pound diamond. You know everything that is happening on the Kent crime scene and it insults my intelligence to tell me anything other. So let me repeat my question, what do you know about the theft of the Windsorton Diamond?'

'OK, Mr Bridges. I might have heard something about the heist, but I didn't mention it because I don't want to get involved.'

'I respect your position, Larry. Quite obviously, you would not wish to risk going to prison now you have this fantastic store to manage. However, I am sure you understand that I will be forced to treat you as a suspect if you do not tell me everything that you know.'

'I swear I know little, Mr Bridges. But the whisper on the street is that the heist was pulled by a crew out of the Elephant and Castle.'

'So, who was the lock man, Larry? Somebody opened a couple of locks to gain access to the diamond and then closed them again. There are only a handful of people in the whole country who can do that and you are one of them. So if it was not you, Larry, who was it?'

Price said nothing for a while, instead he prised a date from the waxed box and handed it to the monkey who took it greedily. Finally he looked at the detective and shook his head. 'You know I can't tell you that, Mr Bridges. It's more than my life's worth.'

'We can make your life even more worthless, Larry,' Hardin threatened. 'For instance we could pick up Billy Wilde and accidentally let him know you had fingered him.'

Price looked alarmed. 'Come off it, Mr Hardin. Billy Wilde is nothing more than a mindless thug. He wouldn't know what a lock was, let alone be able to spring one.'

'True, but Billy would act first and work out afterwards that you were unlikely to finger him for a job he was incapable of doing.' Hardin grinned, 'He'd probably suss that out when you were already at the bottom of the River Thames with a railway sleeper tied to your ankles.'

'You can't do that!' Price wailed, before pleading: 'Mr Bridges, you're a gentleman. You wouldn't stitch me up like that, would you?'

Rupert Bridges shook his head sadly. 'Definitely not, Larry, such action would be both immoral and unethical. However, I fear that the good Sergeant here does not share with me the same scruples.'

'Too right, Guv'nor.'

Price looked from one detective to the other. 'Listen, Mr Bridges. I am telling you the truth. I know nothing more than that the heist was carried out by a crew from the Elephant and Castle.' He paused and looked over his shoulder as if he expected Billy Wilde to appear from behind the barley straw packs that were stacked at the end of the aisle and when he spoke again it was in a whisper: 'There is talk that they drafted in French Frankie.'

'Françoise de Toit? He is here in England?'

Price nodded.

Bridges looked at Hardin and raised an eyebrow.

'I'll get on to Interpol, Guv.'

Bridges turned back to Price. 'Thank you for that, Larry. It makes perfect sense. French Frankie is the best lock man in Europe. Better even than you.'

'Only since I retired, Mr Bridges.' Price insisted. 'In my prime Frankie wouldn't have come close to me.'

'It would have been certainly a close run thing,' Bridges acknowledged as he looked down at the monkey, who stared back at him before holding out the money box and waving it silently at the detective.

Price chuckled, 'He wants your dough, Mr Bridges. A quid will keep him happy!'

Bridges pulled a coin from his trouser pocket and popped it into the slot on the top of the box. He smiled as the monkey rattled the box to hear the pound rattle around and then pulled it close to its chest and bared its teeth in its own version of a smile.

'He likes you, Inspector.'

'No, Larry. He likes my money!' Bridges said before making his goodbyes.

'Is de Toit that good, Guv?' Hardin asked as they left the store and headed back to the car.

'The best lock man there is and more importantly he is a wizard with electronics.'

'Alarms as well as locks! What a combination, if you'll excuse the pun. Sounds just perfect for this job.'

'Oh, indeed it does, Stanley. The only problem is that French Frankie is currently residing in a Berlin prison courtesy of the German government, from whom he attempted to steal one hundred million Eurobonds.'

Hardin stopped and stared at Bridges, ''How do you know that? No, don't tell me, Guv. I don't want to know, because it will only make me feel even more inadequate! So, no call to Interpol then?'

'No call to Interpol, Stan,' Bridges agreed with a smile. 'However, you can ring the Divisional Commander and ask him to arrange for Larry Price to be placed under discreet surveillance. Meanwhile, I think it is back to Hever Castle we must go.'

By the time they arrived back at Hever Castle, and had made their way to the dining hall, two fitters were in the last stages of dismantling the display cabinet, moving the last of the four glass sides of the pyramid and standing it upright against the side wall. Bridges was pleased to see the two men were wearing white gloves. He quickly inspected the glass and then pointed to one panel and asked the men to turn it round so that it stood inside out, which they did without comment.

Charlotte Lambermont walked into the room and spoke to the fitters in a language that Hardin did not recognise. She tapped her watch impatiently. The two workmen shrugged and one of them answered in the same language.

'Ik leb geen idée,' then added in English, 'ask the cops.'

'Inspector, how long is this going to take?' The woman asked tetchily.

Bridges, who was on his knees staring intently through his half moon glasses at the glass panel he had asked the fitters to turn round, either did not hear the woman, or, chose to ignore her. Charlotte turned to Hardin.

'Well?' She asked.

'Well what?'

'How long are you going to take? I have been summoned to a meeting at head office and have to be at Gatwick by a quarter to five in time to catch a flight to Antwerp an hour later.'

Hardin smiled. 'It will take as long as it takes, love,' he said and was quietly pleased when he saw the woman bristle at his choice of words.

'Do not "love" me, Sergeant,' she said haughtily before flouncing out of the room, closely followed by her two fitters.

'Sorry, love,' Hardin called after her with a grin.

'Don't provoke her, Stan,' Bridges said as he puffed powder over the marks that he had found on the glass panel. 'Come and have a look at this.'

'Sorry, Guv'nor, but that posh bitch gets right up my nose. She ought to have stayed in Sloane Square, where she belongs.'

'I suspect not Sloane Square and probably not even Britain.'

'With an accent like that?'

'They speak very good English in Belgium.'

'Miss Smarty Pants is Belgian?'

'That is my conclusion; she was certainly speaking Flemish to the two workmen. However, ignore her. Let's get back to business.' Bridges pointed at the glass panel. 'What do you see?'

'Finger prints. So what's strange about that?'

'They are on the inside of the glass panel.'

'Perhaps it was the workmen?'

Bridges shook his head and said: 'They were wearing white cotton gloves.'

'But nobody could have got inside that case once it was put together because the opening at the top was far too small.'

'Exactly.'

'Perhaps the prints went on the glass before the case was put together.'

'That is certainly a possibility.' Bridges agreed, but his face showed his scepticism. He stood up and walked over to the black display stand. He took a pencil from his pocket and carefully eased something from a narrow groove on the stand's surface. 'Hold out your hand, Stan.' He said and laid what looked like a small almond in Hardin's palm.

'What is it, Guv? A nut?'

'No, I think it is a date stone.'

Hardin stared down at his hand and frowned. 'A date stone?' He mused, then suddenly his brain made the connection. 'Bleedin' hell, Guv! Am I thinking what you're thinking?'

Bridges smiled and took the stone back from Hardin and wrapped it carefully in his handkerchief. 'Stan, would you please check out if Larry has any external storage facilities, even a lock up garage, and while you're doing that I need to make a couple of phone calls.'

Larry Price's stockroom was in a row of ramshackle lock-up garages in a Gravesend backstreet in which most of the adjoining properties had been demolished in preparation for a long promised regeneration by the local authority that never seemed to arrive.

Bridges surveyed the desolate scene. 'Not the most salubrious area, Stanley,' he said as he opened the car door and headed towards a graffiti scarred windowless unit with double doors on which most of the paint had flaked away to leave exposed rotten wood. He knocked firmly on the door, which despite its appearance seemed sturdy enough. There was no answer, but that was hardly a surprise because the door was secured with a padlock fitted to a heavy duty hasp and staple.

''What do you reckon, Guv?'

'Shush, Stan,' Bridges put a finger to his lips and leaned closer to the door, 'can you hear that noise?'

Hardin could hear nothing but the pitter-patter of the rain that had just started to fall about their ears. 'Can't quite make it out, Guv.'

'Listen, there it is again. I think it is a cry for help from inside the unit,' Bridges said with a face that was inscrutable.

'I reckon somebody's had an accident.' Hardin said as he pulled at the padlock, testing its strength. Despite the poor condition of the door there was no give. He looked up at the sky.

'You're going to get wet, Guv. D'you want to get a coat?'

Bridges nodded without speaking and headed towards the car. No sooner had the Inspector turned his back than Hardin slipped a short jemmy from the pocket of his grubby raincoat, deftly levered the padlock hasp away from the door frame and returned the jemmy to his pocket all in one quick movement.

'Ooops!' Hardin said as Bridges reappeared at his side, still struggling into his coat. 'I appear to have broken the lock, Guv.'

'I am not surprised, Stan,' Bridges said with a shake of his head, 'the wood is rotten, look.'

He rapped the door with his knuckle to prove the point and immediately it swung open a couple of inches. He glanced quickly up and down the street and finding it still deserted he pushed open the door and slipped inside, closely followed by Hardin, who then closed the door behind them.

It was pitch black in the lockup, but Bridges found a light switch just inside the door and soon an ancient strip light flickered into life to reveal that the store was lined with shelving on which were stacked a range of goods no doubt destined for Price's Pet Products.

At one end of the store was a platform with steps leading to it, in front of which stood a tall object, covered with a tarpaulin canvas, that Hardin assumed was bulk storage of some sort. He tugged at the canvas, which slithered to the floor and left him stunned. He stared at Bridges in bemusement and saw that his boss had a smile of satisfaction on his face.

'Just as I thought!' The Inspector exclaimed.

'But it's...'

'Yes, Stan. It's a replica of the stand on which the Windsorton Diamond was displayed.'

'What the heck is it doing here?'

'For the same reason as that platform is here.'

'Which is?'

'To train a monkey,' Bridges replied as he took his mobile phone from his pocket and dialled a number. 'Is our friend still there?' He asked when the leader of the stakeout team answered.

'Yes, Guv, but I think he's just closing up now.'

'Thank you. I think you will find Mr Price intends to leave in a hurry. Please keep him under surveillance and follow him wherever he goes.'

'So let me get this straight,' Hardin said as he headed out of Gravesend's rain soaked streets towards the A2. 'Larry trained his monkey to jump into the top of the display case?'

'Not exactly; I think he lowered the monkey from the minstrel gallery and I suspect if we had taken longer to look round his storeroom we would have found stowed away the harness he used. I think also that Price trained the monkey to remove the diamond and bring it back to him by dropping a date into the glass pyramid as a reward.'

'That was the stone you found in the display case? Clever!'

'And the use of a monkey would account for the finger marks on the inside of the glass panel. Certainly no human, except perhaps a baby, could have squeezed inside the top of the pyramid.'

'So Larry's our man?'

'Of that there is little doubt, Stan. I am convinced that he broke into Hever Castle and stole the Windsorton Diamond. The problem will be proving it. Currently all we have against Price is circumstantial evidence that would be ripped to shreds by even the newest, wet-behind the ear lawyer.'

'So what now?'

Bridges didn't reply; instead he stared thoughtfully out of the car window. 'There are a couple of odd things about the theft,' he said eventually. 'The first is this; we know that Price is a master lock man.'

'Yeah, Larry could open and close any lock in the country.'

'Yes, but he has always worked as part of a team. Whenever he tried freelancing he came a cropper, mainly because he is no great shakes at disarming burglar alarms. That is why he spent so many years inside.'

'So?'

'So, how did he get into the castle without setting off the alarm?'

198

'Perhaps he was in cahoots with the security guard?'

'Unlikely, because we know the security guards do not have access to the burglar alarm code.'

Hardin saw out of the corner of his eye Bridges tugging at his bow tie.

'And the other thing is this...' Bridges paused and closed his eyes in concentration. 'What do we know about Price?'

Hardin shrugged.

'We know that although Larry is an excellent lock man,' Bridges went on, 'he has always been little more than a largely unsuccessful petty thief. Do you really think that he has the wherewithal to dispose of a 45 million pound diamond? More to the point, what fence do you know here, or, in London who could handle something that big?'

Now Hardin was looking very thoughtful. He shook his head, 'Nobody that I can think of, Guv'nor.'

'Disposing of a diamond that size, and that well known, can be done, but it takes specialist knowledge of the precious stone market.'

It began to dawn on Hardin what Bridges was getting at. 'Larry had an accomplice who is in the business?'

'Precisely. And who do we know who is in the diamond business and had access to the alarm code?'

'Miss Smarty Pants? Oh, Guv, I do hope you are right. I'd give my right arm to catch that stuck up bitch bang to rights, but surely the security guard would have noticed if she didn't set the alarm properly?'

'Not necessarily, Stan, if you recall the alarm for the rear external door can be disabled from a control box in the morning room. Lambermont could have easily disabled the alarm at any time during the day without being noticed and when she eventually set the main alarm in the evening the guard would not have known the external door was no longer covered.'

Hardin glanced at his watch as another thought struck him. It was half past four. 'Didn't madam say she is catching a plane at quarter to six? We're never going to get to Gatwick in time. The M25 will be chock-a-block with traffic at this time of day.'

'We are not going to Gatwick, Stan.'

'No? How so?'

'Because I rang the airport to find out if Lambermont was booked on a flight to Antwerp this afternoon and she is not.'

'Perhaps she booked under an alias.'

'That would be difficult, Stan, because there are no direct flights to Antwerp from Gatwick this evening.'

'Maybe she's going via Brussels.'

'She certainly is; but she is not travelling by plane. Lambermont is booked to catch the five-forty-five Eurostar train from Ebbsfleet International Station.'

As he spoke his mobile phone trilled. A glance at the display showed it was the surveillance team leader.

'Bridges,' he said then listened intently to the team leader, nodding his head slowly as he did so. 'OK, follow him, but from a discreet distance. I do not want him being spooked.' He cut short the conversation and turned to Hardin. 'Price has left his shop and has driven off in his car. Put your foot down, Stan. I want to get to Ebbsfleet before him.'

Although Ebbsfleet is only a couple of miles from the centre of Gravesend it took the two detectives almost twenty minutes to reach the station because of nose to tail traffic on the A2. By the time they turned into what looked to be a full car park Hardin was cursing loudly.

'Language, Stanley!' Bridges good naturedly admonished his sergeant after checking the whereabouts of Price with the surveillance team. 'Worry not; Price is still behind us somewhere, stuck in the same traffic jam that slowed us down.'

'He'll soon catch us up if we don't find somewhere to park, Guv'nor.'

'I'm sure something will turn up. Just get as close to the station as possible. Look! There is a space at the far end of that row.'

'Hell's Bells! That's a stroke of luck!' Hardin said as he manoeuvred his way into an empty parking space conveniently situated close to the short path leading to the station entrance. 'Or did you arrange for this space to be left for us?'

'It would be splendid to be able to claim credit for thinking ahead, but sadly on this occasion I must confess finding this space was simply down to luck. Still, it will give us a few extra minutes to get into position whilst Price finds somewhere to park.'

'How do you know where Larry will go once he gets here?' Hardin asked as they got out of the car and headed towards the station entrance.

'Ebbsfleet might be an international station, but it is not exactly St Pancras, or, Heathrow,' Bridges said as they entered the building. 'As you can see the concourse is not very large. Come on, I think I know exactly where Price will go.'

With that he headed towards the International Currency Exchange, where his charm and warrant card quickly saw them ensconced in a darkened office where they were able to peek discreetly through the slatted blinds that covered the window of a side door.

The window faced the Pumpkin coffee bar and shortly after the two policemen took up position a tall woman with cropped dark hair, carrying a smart leather attaché, approached the service counter and ordered a coffee that, once served, she took to one of the empty tables positioned alongside the coffee bar.

The woman sat down on a chair that faced towards the station entrance after carefully placing her attaché case on the table. She sat with one hand resting protectively on the case and blew gently on her coffee before sipping it whilst looking up the length of the concourse over the rim of her cup.

'It's Miss Smarty Pants,' Hardin whispered.

Bridges nodded but said nothing, instead he gently twisted the handle of the door and quietly eased it open a fraction of an inch. The exchange was only a few feet from the Pumpkin and Bridges was confident they could reach it in only a few strides. They did not have long to wait.

Charlotte Lambermont put down her coffee cup and dipped her head slightly, acknowledging Larry Price as he strolled up the concourse towards her table. He carried an identical attaché case to the one that already rested on the table and on his shoulder was perched the monkey, still wearing its red tunic and clutching the brightly coloured money box to his chest. He wore a red collar round his neck that was connected to Price's wrist by a lead.

Bridges tensed as Price sat down and put his attaché case on the table opposite its twin.

'Ready?' He whispered.

'Ready, Guv.'

'You grab Price's case and I'll get the girl's. Let's go!'

Seconds later Bridges and Hardin were standing either side of the table at which sat the man and woman; almost miraculously two other men appeared from nowhere at the same time and stood menacingly behind a stunned looking Charlotte Lambermont.

'Well done, gentlemen,' Bridges told the two man surveillance team as he snatched up the woman's attaché case. The case was heavy, so the Inspector balanced it on the table as he pushed the locks apart with a click. With a flourish he opened the case to reveal it was filled with stacks of tightly bound new fifty pound notes. 'How much is there?' Bridges asked the woman, but it was Price who replied.

'Half a million pounds.' He smiled.

'Open the other case, Sarge,' Bridges said.

Hardin snapped open the locks of Price's case and looked inside it. With a cry of alarm he dropped the case on the table with a crash that caused the lid to fly open and send the woman's cup and saucer crashing to the floor. The bottom part of the case was sealed with Perspex, under which crawled the largest tarantula spider that Bridges had ever seen.

'What the hell?' Charlotte Lambermont started to ask and then thought better of it.

Bridges looked at Price and raised an eyebrow.

'She bought it from me, Mr Bridges.'

'For a half a million pounds, Larry?'

'It's an expensive spider. Very rare in this country.'

'Don't make us laugh, Larry,' Hardin chipped in. 'No bleeding spider is worth that sort of money.'

'It's a seller's market, Mr Hardin.' Price smiled again.

Out of the corner of his eye Bridges could see that Charlotte Lambermont was watching this exchange with a mounting look of incredulity on her face. He chuckled and said: 'Do you know what, Sergeant Hardin, Mr Price's story is so unlikely that I am inclined to believe him.' He closed the lid of the attaché case and pushed the case towards the pet shop owner, whilst Hardin looked at him as if he had gone mad.

'This is ridiculous, Inspector!' The woman exclaimed, half rising to her feet, but one of the policemen pushed her back into her seat by her shoulders. 'You cannot really believe that I would pay so much money for a damned spider.'

Bridges shrugged. 'How do I know? There is no accounting for taste.'

'What have you done with it, you oik?' The woman shouted at Price. 'Where is the diamond?'

'Diamond, ma'am?' Bridges asked politely. 'Which diamond would that be?'

Charlotte Lambermont slumped back in her chair as she realised the game was up. 'The Windsorton Diamond.' She pointed at Price with a finger that shook with rage. 'He stole it from Hever Castle and now he's trying to steal it from me.'

'She's mad, Mr Bridges. I told you earlier, I don't know nothing about the diamond.'

Bridges took a coin from his pocket and rolled it deftly in his fingers as he looked thoughtfully from the woman to the man and back again.

Hardin watched this interplay with a frown on his face. *He's finally lost the plot,* he thought to himself.

The monkey, which was still perched on its master's shoulder, saw the coin in the detective's hand and held out the money box and rattled it. Still looking thoughtfully from one side of the table to the other, Bridges reached out distractedly to drop the coin into the money box, but just as he was about to release the coin he wrenched the money box from the monkey's paws. The monkey let out a squeal of outrage and leaped at Bridges, but the policeman stepped back quickly and the lead round the monkey's neck brought the animal to a jolting halt.

Bridges flicked open the top of the money box and tipped it upside down onto the table. Two objects clattered onto the table top; a single pound coin and a large brilliant pink stone that sparkled in the bright glow of the overhead strip lights. It was the Windsorton

Diamond.

'Take them away Bob,' Bridges said to the leader of surveillance team, 'and don't forget to read them their rights.'

'What about the monkey, Guv?' Bob asked.

'No need to read the monkey its rights; just him and her.'

'I meant, what should we do with the monkey?'

'I know, Bob. It was a joke. I suggest you contact the RSPCA and get them to collect it from the station.'

'How did you know Larry had the diamond with him, Guv?' Hardin asked as Lambermont and Price were led away.

'Price might be an old lag, but he is far from stupid. He was just being cautious bringing the spider along; in case something went wrong.'

'Which it did.'

'Yes, but it might not have gone wrong. I was pretty sure that Price would have the diamond with him somewhere. He would have wanted to do the switch.'

'But how did you know the diamond was in the money box and not his pocket?'

'How do you think, I knew?'

Hardin stared up at Bridges through narrowed eyes. He frowned and rubbed his chin thoughtfully. Suddenly he grinned and said: 'I know how you did it. It was the sound as the monkey rattled the money box. I remember that when you put the pound in the box earlier today it was empty, however, when the monkey rattled the box just now you realised there was more than one coin in it.'

'Bravo!' Bridges clapped his hands in admiration. 'We'll make a detective out of you yet!'

'Yeah, but I didn't suss it out at the time, Guv, you did. You must have phenomenal hearing.'

'Certainly my hearing is very good, but on this occasion it would be dishonest of me to claim I noticed a difference in the sound the box made when it was rattled, because I did not. How did I know the diamond was in the box?' Rupert Bridges said with a wry smile. 'It was nothing more scientific than an old fashioned hunch.'

Gordon Henderson

Gordon Henderson was born in Brompton Military Hospital in 1948 and is proud to be a true 'Man of Kent'. His early life was spent in the Medway Towns, where he grew up on a council estate in Chatham and went to Fort Luton Secondary Modern School.

Gordon left school at 16 to join Woolworths, where he worked his way up from being a 'stockroom boy' to senior store manager.

After spending some time in South Africa, where he had a restaurant, Gordon had a succession of jobs including being a political agent, a senior contracts officer in the Aerospace Industry and an operations manager for an international manufacturing company.

In 2010 he was elected as Member of Parliament for Sittingbourne and Sheppey.

Following this collection of short stories, many of which have been influenced by his own life, Gordon plans to release his first novel, the first of many.